XIMENA AT THE CROSSROADS

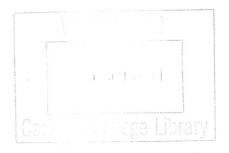

XIMENA
AT THE
CROSSROADS

———

LAURA RIESCO

TRANSLATED BY MARY G. BERG

WHITE PINE PRESS • FREDONIA, NEW YORK

WHITE PINE PRESS

10 Village Square, Fredonia, New York 14063

Copyright ©1998 by Laura Riesco

Translation copyright ©1998 by Mary G. Berg

This is a work of fiction. Names, characters, places,
and incidents are either the product of the author's imagination
or are used fictitiously, and any resemblance to actual persons,
living or dead, events, or locales is entirely coincidental.

Publication of this book was made possible, in part,
by grants from the National Endowment for the Arts
and the New York State Council on the Arts.

Book design: Elaine LaMattina

Printed and bound in the United States of America

1   3   5   7   9   10   8   6   4   2

Library of Congress Cataloging-in-Publication Data

Riesco, Laura, 1940–
[Ximena de dos caminos. English]
Ximena at the crossroads / Laura Riesco ; translated by Mary G. Berg.
p.   cm. — (Secret weavers series ; v. 12)
ISBN 1-877727-80-6 (alk. paper)
I. Berg, Mary G.   II. Title   III. Series.
PQ8498.28.I34X5613   1998
863—dc21   98–12694
                                        CIP

To my daughters,
Halina, Aída, and Ana María

CONTENTS

XIMENA AT THE CROSSROAD

I / THE TOYS

She has taken her father's encyclopedia to the dining room so she can look at the pictures. Kneeling on a cushion she has brought from the living room, Ximena turns the pages very carefully. The pages are of thin paper and stick to each other, but she has been told not to lick her index finger in order to separate them. She obeys because experience has taught her that the paper is bitter and that the taste and the guilt will stay in her mouth the whole rest of the day. She gazes in ecstasy at the colored illustration of poisonous mushrooms, repeating the color names she knows: white, yellow, red, orange. Her mother has told her that they are *amanitas* and she knows the big letters above the picture confirm the marvelous fact that they are truly called that and not something else.

She has already gazed without much interest at the black and white drawing on an earlier page of a solitary *almond* tree surrounded by rigid columns of words. Although she does not much care for it, she always looks at it for a while so that the tree will feel less bad about being so small and isolated. Farther along, she lingers on the picture of a jug that is more than a jug because it is called an *amphora*. She whispers that name slowly to herself so that no one will hear her. The soft sound of her own voice gives her immense pleasure. Not only because the word sounds so wonderful, but also because it makes her think of a jug in her bedroom at the ranch house in the valley. That jug is big and has deep blue edges; its middle is very light blue, almost white, the same shade that bluing gives her father's shirts and that she has seen in the eyes of a few melancholy children. The jug is just there for decoration since people never actually use it or the matching basin for washing their hands. Ximena remembers the time she carried water in, cup by cup, to fill the pitcher. She has never done it again; although they have not really convinced her that jugs do not feel thirsty even when they have been storing up emptiness for years, they did finally persuade her, despite her anxiety, that she should not touch it because it is very old and valuable.

A few pages farther and she comes to the illustration that makes her so uneasy. It is hard to avoid it because it is one of the colored inlays, printed on thicker and shinier paper than the regular pages. She hesitates before she can make up her mind to confront it, and at first she covers it with her hand. But gradually she pulls her fingers up, one at a time, and lifts her palm to see the outline of a man's profile. "What is this?" she worriedly asked her mother one day. Her mother was drying the crystal wineglasses, and she came over to see what Ximena was showing her. "Those are the main arteries," she said casually. Ximena stopped her, grabbing anxiously at her skirt. "Do you have arteries, too?" Her mother pulled her skirt away gently. "Of course, Ximena, all human beings have arteries." In a tiny voice she demanded, "Me, too?" And laughing, her mother answered, "Yes, you, too, or did you think your skin was stuffed with cotton?" Since then, Ximena has peered warily at the illustrations of the heart, the lungs, the bones, and the stomach. She feels so dizzy that her legs get weak when she thinks about how all those parts she cannot see are beating and working away inside of her. Ever since then, she imagines that under Ama Grande's clothes and under her brown skin, her heart, stomach and lungs, the ones that have been hers ever since she was born, trace out their rhythm along an invisible route and make her breathe, speak, walk, laugh, and see.

Distressed, she turns two pages quickly and stops at an illustration of an animal she just cannot believe exists. Her mother has already told her that, yes, somewhere in the world that beast with its rooster's feet and beak and its rat's body is hopping cheerfully through the fields. But Ximena knows that not everything grownups tell her is true, and, in any case, its name, *apteryx*, seems made up . Maybe even her mother does not know it is a trick, or maybe they made a mistake when they put it in the encyclopedia. She hasn't wanted to ask her father anything about this because he gets so nervous when she amuses herself looking at pictures in his books; he has been like this ever since that awful day she cut out a page so she could stick butterflies up on the wall of her room.

She comes to where the Arabic alphabet is, and gazes at it, marveling, as always. She runs her fingertip over the little squiggles, thinking that there are people who can read and sing in these mysterious characters. She looks at the other column, at the letters she is drilled on every day in her school book, and they look crude and dull in comparison. The Arabic letters have flourishes; they make her think of fish swimming through the water; they almost seem to move around by themselves on the page. They remind her—she doesn't know why—of the sea. She told this to her mother, who laughed and said it was curious because the alphabet was developed in sandy deserts far away, in places so distant she cannot even pronounce their names. Ximena sighs. Someday she will know how to read those other letters whose names she can already say. It astonishes her that they all have names and not even her father knows why or who first called them that.

Grownups read fast and without stopping. They hardly even see the letters that are all lined up, like platoons, in straight, even rows across the page and that turn into words, magically, as they are spoken. But not everyone reads the same way. When her mother has time and Ximena begs her and promises to be good, she pulls a book of stories off the shelf. Ximena hears her voice get high when the princesses or the little dwarves talk, and deep if the king is speaking, and sharp and scary if it is the witch. Her father reads all the voices in the same tone of voice, and sometimes he skips whole sections. She complains because she knows the sequence of what happens in the stories. Then he laughs and tells her it would be better to go over that day's reading assignment. Patiently he helps her, letter by letter and always in order, to spell out the words that are in big black print but that still don't give Ximena any echo of true things. The letters look solitary and shadowless, anchored to their sounds. Uncle Jorge, who lives on the ranch, has his own way of reading, too. Maybe it is just to annoy her, but he changes things, confuses them, puts in colonels and generals where there aren't any, and calls the witches "poor old things." He changes the endings of the *Aesop's' Fables*; very seriously, without taking his eyes off the book, he reads that the cricket lived happily ever after singing at village parties and that the ant died of ulcers brought on by the taxes levied by a socialist government. The grownups take care that Ximena does not spend much time with him. One day when she asked why, they looked at each other uneasily, reluctant to answer. Uncle Jorge both attracts and scares Ximena. His laugh makes the windows vibrate, his clothes are always rumpled, his face is unshaven, and the others say he is bowlegged from riding a horse so much. Sometimes she watches him when he isn't aware of it, and she sees his eyes cloud over in a sudden tide of anger and sadness. Other times she runs away in a hurry because his breath smells of liquor when he lifts her up to kiss her.

Her mother is humming in the bedroom that has the best light, where she has gone to sew. The door to the pantry and kitchen is open, and the smell of the stew reaches her along with the rattle of the silverware that Ama Grande is getting out to set the table. She has the radio on, and a tenor is singing the falsetto of a popular Mexican song. The old woman is crooning along. She is out of tune most of the time and gets the words mixed up. Although Ximena's mother keeps encouraging her, Ama Grande has never wanted to learn how to read. But even so, she likes to look at the pictures in storybooks. Ximena, full of self-importance, pretends to read the stories, and Ama Grande listens to her, smiling, also pretending that Ximena is reading. It is Ama Grande who tells her more stories than anybody: fantastic stories about snakes who wiggle through high weeds, who twine around tree trunks, who can tell the past and the future because the circles they make with their bodies encompass eternal time; stories about condors, the kings of space, who suffer and love, who draw silver maps in the sky to guide or confuse the steps of lost travelers and lonely shepherds; stories about pumas who lie in ambush in the branches and roar and hide precious stones behind the yellow light they look through; stories about holy mountains that punish anyone who harms the helpless plants and animals; stories about good and bad dwarves who live in sea foam, in dark caves, or in certain hollow trees; stories about mysterious sacred places that wait patiently to be discovered by kindred spirits; stories about trees, those wise grandfathers whose roots confer with each other about secrets that rumble through the bottomless depths of the earth. And there are the other stories, too—the ones that are all so similar to each other—about Saint Joseph, the Virgin, Saint Rose or the Holy Child. Although her father denies it vehemently, Ama Grande insists that these holy visitors sometimes come to earth disguised in various ways in order to test the fragile will of humans. Ama Grande's voice is as lulling as the sound of willow branches, and Ximena, snuggled up in her lap, would like to fall asleep in the middle of these stories, which have rocked her since before she can remember.

She hears the key turn in the living room door. Ximena lifts her eyes and her father stops halfway through the door, surprised to find her sitting at the dining room table. He has just put down a big paper bag on his left and carries another the same size in his right hand, but he does not come all the way in because there is another bag in his way, set down at his feet.

"Go to your room, Ximena." The tone is that of an order, not of a request. She would like to ask why, one of those whys that keep getting her into trouble, but she has the encyclopedia in front of her, so she decides to opt for docility. She obeys and gets down off the chair without touching the volume she has been looking at, in order not to draw attention to it. From her room she hears the rustle of the paper bags and then whispering and the muffled laughter of her parents in the other bedroom. A few seconds later her mother comes in and smiles at her.

"Close your eyes tight, and give me your hand. Your father has brought you a surprise because you've been sick and you've been very well behaved."

Her mother leads her by the hand, and she feels her mother's warmth and heartbeat in her palm. Without protesting, she squeezes her eyelids shut, and the same lights that always turn on behind her closed eyes before she falls asleep light up the path to the living room.

"Now open your eyes," her father says, sounding pleased.

On the red rug in the middle of the living room, in front of her father, who is looking at her eagerly, there are three stuffed animals.

They are huge; Ximena has never seen anything like them.

"Do you like them?" they both ask her at once.

Ximena nods politely because she doesn't want to ruin the happy moment. She looks at the brown dog, at its long silky ears, and its very red felt tongue hanging down comically. She looks at the cream-colored bear with its silly expression and at the yellow giraffe with brown markings on its back. Ximena notices that the giraffe's neck is out of proportion to the rest of the body and that detail irritates her. She is also irritated by how stupid the dog's expression is, but she tries to not let it show and stoops over to pick up the bear, which comes up to above her waist.

"And what do you say?" her mother reminds her

She thanks them with a barely audible voice and runs into her father's arms. He lifts and swings her. Ama Grande has come over to see what all the excitement is about. She laughs and makes a fuss over the new toys. She touches them, pets them, squeezes them, and laughs some more.

"They're so enormous!" she exclaims. "They are almost as big as she is! Just look at them! Amazing!"

Her mother runs her hand over the giraffe's neck and explains that the animals are American—that's why they are so well made. The three adults carry the toys to Ximena's bedroom. They tell her to put them wherever she wants, and they go off to see about lunch.

Ximena leaves them where they have been put, at the foot of her bed, and she looks around, trying to think where they will fit. They are so huge that all the spaces seem to have shrunk. She already has a lot of toys in her room: a wind-up carrousel that plays the notes of a Viennese waltz; a miniature porcelain tea set; an enameled brass top; a porcelain-faced doll inherited from her mother, very pale and dressed in taffeta yellowed by time, who opens and closes her blue glass eyes; another doll, Japanese, extremely elegant and stiff in her special glass case and the Raggedy Ann Mrs. Crane gave her for her last birthday. She never plays with these dolls. When other children come to visit, she shows them off, but she only looks at them when she is going to sleep and gazing at the shadowy room closing in around her.

She keeps her treasures under her bed in a shoe box: magic stones that she picked up out of a stream in the valley; colored buttons with secret properties, stolen one by one from her mother's sewing box because they were irresistible; foil she has unwrapped from chocolates with great care and smoothed out with her fingernail so the squares will be perfect and whole in their undulating chameleon sheen; images of beautiful people that she has patiently cut out of old magazines and with whom she converses when there is no one around; a handful of *boliches*, those round black seeds that remind her vividly of the Lima street where she picked them up long ago; luminous glass marbles of various sizes, some of them with bands of color that swirl out from their centers. She keeps one of Ama Grande's gifts there, too: a white rabbit's foot —miraculous bringer of good luck.

Where can she put those enormous things that are swallowing up all the warm air in the room? Finally she puts them—hides them— between the window wall and her bed. She arranges them so that all you can see when you come into the room is the bear with his frozen look of surprise.

When visitors come, right after they have told her that she has grown a lot, that perhaps she seems less skinny, that her eyes are just like her father's, right after they have found out from her mother that her lungs have been healthy and that she has been learning to spell out words, they ask her to show them her new toys. Ximena acquiesces and lugs them out one by one. She could drag out two at a time, but she enjoys the grownups' squeals, and each dramatic entrance increases the effect of the hugeness of the toys and of her own importance.

"How gigantic!"

"Only in the United States!"

"Where did you ever find such a sweet giraffe?"

"They must have cost a fortune!"

"They're as big as she is!"

When she is by herself, Ximena doesn't pay any attention to them and keeps them, half hidden, between her bed and the wall. But after a time, whenever someone comes to the house, she trots happily to her room without even being asked and brings them out because she likes to show them off.

"But Ximena! How are you going to go to market with the three of them? Don't you see that you can barely carry one?"

Ximena is obstinate. Going on a shopping trip to the market with Ama Grande is a long-standing tradition, a privilege to which she feels almost entitled; she spends happy hours in the din of the vendors' cries, the smell of vegetables and herbs, the squawking of the chickens, the sweet silence of petting rabbits and guinea pigs who don't run away even when she tries to reach in through the gaps in their cages. Best of all, there is the reward for good behavior: little clay pots, a pastel-colored balloon, or the strawberry-flavored shaved-ice cone absolutely forbidden by her parents. This time, for once, she wants to show off —as she walks along between the stalls of *ollucos* and ears of corn, lima beans, and *capulíes*—by carrying the three toys that attract so much attention. She wants the vendors to gaze admiringly at her monumental possessions. She begs tearfully, and finally Ama Grande gives in, insisting that it must be Ximena, all by herself and without any help, who will carry them the whole way.

Ximena carries the bear by his collar with one hand, and holds the dog in the other arm. She has not been able to manage the giraffe, so the old woman, complaining and grumbling, indifferent to the truck drivers' smiles and mocking comments, carries the giraffe—his neck sticking out over her shoulder and his head facing backward—now and then shifting him over so that he rests against her braided gray hair. When they turn onto the street that leads to the market entrance, Ximena sees a boy spot them, then leap over to station himself in the middle of the sidewalk so that he can see them better as they go by. His quickness, his split-second timing, remind her of something. Where has she seen him before? When? She thinks she recognizes him from someplace. Her heart begins to beat quickly; she puffs up with pride. She tries to walk calmly, straight ahead, without tripping over the dog's paw, which keeps slipping down to drag on the ground and get in her way. Alongside her, the old servant woman grumbles, "It is going to be your fault. Just to please you and because you're so spoiled and stubborn, we're going to be late."

Ximena pays no attention to her. Pretending to look past the boy, she watches as he plants himself right in the center of the sidewalk just a few steps away, and smiles openly. He is the same size she is. He is wearing a green felt hat like the ones Indian children wear and a brown sweater made of coarse wool. His black pants, baggy and too wide for his skinny legs, are torn. He is not wearing sandals, and Ximena sees that his feet are chapped and hardened by the dry cold of high altitudes. Ama Grande is so busy being grumpy that she probably has not seen him, has not even noticed his brown face, his rough, red cheeks, his almond-shaped eyes with their big black irises, shining with anticipation and joy. But Ximena has. Looking over the dog's head, Ximena sees the boy lift his hand to touch the bear's fur. Then she speeds up and quickly moves away from him, almost falling over.

"It's mine!" she hisses between her teeth.

The boy's hand just touches air, his fingers feel nothing except the two words that Ximena also feels as they nail themselves, fixed and hard, into space. She immediately wants to turn around and erase those syllables that echo in her ears, to shred them out of existence, turn back, and give him the toys. But she doesn't say anything. Holding her lips steady because she is afraid she will cry, trying to breathe carefully because she is afraid of choking, she walks straight ahead, holding on tight to the surprised bear and the silly dog. She walks alongside Ama Grande, who has not seen a thing and who tells her in Quechua, the way she does when she is annoyed, that today there will be no treats.

Ximena is sick. Her lungs have gotten worse, and Ama Grande, her mother and the pediatrician all pay a lot of attention to her. They bring her a gelatinous onion soup she loathes, they rub her with a sticky gel that burns her chest, and they boil eucalyptus leaves in her bedroom. Visitors tiptoe up to her bed to say hello, to console her, to offer all kinds of advice to her mother, who is very worried by Ximena's listlessness: she does not cry or kick when they rub the gel on, or when they stick the thermometer in her bottom, not even when they make her swallow a disgusting syrup. Without fighting back, she accepts everything. When she sleeps, she has dreams in which she sees someone is drowning and no one pays any attention to her cries for help. Her hands are paralyzed when she tries to lift them, so that she hopes the others around her, who seem indifferent, will save that unknown person, who sinks deeper and deeper until she wakes up with a cry that brings her mother racing to her room. Her mother hovers over her and touches her shoulder. She is shivering with fever chills, and the pages of the encyclopedia flutter like birds through her mind, brushing up against her eyes with the menace of knives.

She tries not to think about the boy because then her sobs choke her and the grownups ask "What's wrong, Ximena? Tell us, for God's sake, where does it hurt?" She quiets down then, turns over and says that she wants to sleep. She listens to the others speculating about what could be wrong with her. What happened to her that day at the market? What could she have eaten? Did she catch a chill? Who could be casting an evil spell on her? When her fever goes up and her temples hurt with throbbing, she imagines that, as punishment and without Ama Grande noticing, an *amanita* has fallen onto her plate, among the herbs and the garlic; that the almond tree has put a curse on her because she had looked at it just to be polite; that because she has dreamed so many times that she is caressing it, the amphora in her bedroom in the valley has shattered into bits and its emptiness roams the world, seeking out the guilty one; that the arteries are torturing her body to get even with her for never having liked them; that the Arabic alphabet mysteriously holds the key to the fate that has befallen her. She imagines, in her worst moments, that the boy in the market is really Jesus in disguise and that for her sins she is condemned to suffer until she dies.

One morning her fever goes down, her breathing is less labored, and Ama Grande proclaims, as she opens the blinds, that the color has returned to her face.

"Tell me, what would you like?" Ama Grande asks, giving Ximena a big hug.

Bravely, ready to confront the encyclopedia's bewitchments, Ximena asks her to bring her the first volume from the set in the bookcase.

The old woman comes right back with the book in her hands and lays it on her lap. Ximena, propped up by several cushions, is determined to exorcise the fearful images. Relieved when the pediatrician orders that the new toys be removed from the room because she may possibly be allergic to plush, and reassured by all the attention and the stories her mother and some of the attentive visitors read to her without her even having to plead, Ximena gradually convinces herself that the boy is only part of her fever dreams, an invention of her sickness, another of Ama Grande's stories, embedded in her mind like a thorn or splinter that, left to itself, is gradually absorbed and with time will be converted into a memory. But someone has switched the order of the volumes, and because Ama Grande does not know how to read, she has brought Ximena the wrong one. Smiling at her, she has gone on out to the patio to hang up the wash. Ximena sighs. She doesn't want to ruin Ama Grande's good mood by making another demand. She settles herself more comfortably to look at the illustrations and the pages open by themselves to one of the inlays.

These are not drawings; they are photographs of landscapes she has seen before along the road to Lima, scenes of the mountains near the valley, the chilly station in Ticllio, the Huancayo fair. Her face flushes because, without looking closely, she has realized that the boy at the extreme right of the page is the same one she saw that day at the market. There he is in color, standing there, his green hat pulled over his forehead, his almond-shaped eyes, unlike hers, hiding the line of his eyelids, his smile wide and happy, his wool sweater coarse, his pants ragged, and his feet bare. He gazes at her, waiting for her as he did that day, without shyness. She must have screamed, a little scream that, nevertheless, her father has heard all the way from the bathroom. Mistaking this cry of shock for a call, he comes into Ximena's room just after shaving, smelling of cologne and pleased because they have told him how much better she is feeling.

"Ah, Ximena, there you are again with the encyclopedia!" he says, kissing her hair and skipping his usual warnings about the proper treatment of his books. He stops for a moment to look over her shoulder at the book. "You have found Peru," he adds, and then looks at his watch, kisses her again, and leaves quickly because he is a few minutes late.

When he is gone, Ximena returns to her scrutiny of the boy, who, from the page, returns her stare. Though he is not Jesus, he isn't a made up story either. He is there, really and truly, in the encyclopedia, which in this case does not deceive; it simply retrieves him from her memory. She closes the volume, which weighs heavily on her legs, and, without even trying to stop herself, she tastes the salt of her tears and knows with certainty what it is she must do.

Because she has been so sick, they do not deny her anything. And she plays her part very well; she eats what they give her, she does not answer back, and, above all, she does not ask disturbing questions. The grownups are astonished: can this crisis have transformed her bad temper? She wants to go to market with Ama Grande and insists on taking along the new toys. Her excuse is that she is only allowed to play with them outdoors since the doctor still has them exiled from her room. And she promises that the old woman will not have to worry about them. Ximena will put them in her wagon, a gift from her father's boss, which is big enough to hold two children and which can easily transport the three animals, tied into place. Twice a week she goes out with Ama Grande, pulling the wagon, getting very tired but not complaining. Each morning it is the same story. She eagerly looks forward to reaching the place where they saw the boy, and each time she sees other children, who come out of different places and who run to meet them. They wear similar hats and they are just as ragged. They crowd around her to touch the dog, the giraffe and the bear. They laugh delightedly, saying "Look, how pretty!" The other one—the boy Ximena sometimes thinks she spots, with her heart in her mouth, and so filled with yearning that her eyes and feet are numb—never appears.

One afternoon, just as it is about to get dark, Ximena tells a lie. She says that she forgot her colored pencils and her eraser out in the patio. Her mother, surprised, lifts her eyes from the book in her hands. The lamplight and the poems she is reading have transformed her face, and Ximena sees her as beautiful, unreal, with the air of someone who has just arrived from afar and is completely separate from the daily scene.

"Let Ama go get them," she suggests. "The night is getting cold, and you could catch a chill."

Ximena, in an intentionally sweet tone of voice, points out that Ama Grande is busy and wouldn't find them right away, whereas it will only take her a few minutes. Not waiting for an answer, she slips out the kitchen door. On one side of the five cement steps that go down to the patio is the wagon with the toys in it. She runs and pulls it over to the gate, goes out, and drags it all the way over to the house next door. No one will see them there, she thinks; no one walks along here at this hour, and it is almost dark.

That night she hardly sleeps. She hears the train, which always whistles as it passes at the same hour every night. She prays, and, so that the time will seem shorter, she combines the lines of the four prayers she knows. She closes her eyes tight to see colored lights and concentrates on not falling asleep completely even when she feels very tired. Finally, dawn filters in, in horizontal threads through the closed blinds, and Ximena tries to relax her noisy breathing and not cough. She gets dressed as quietly as she can. Standing in the dining room she listens, astonished, to the silence of the house. She has never felt it this way, so close, its presence filling every corner and resting with such sweetness on the surfaces of the furniture. On tip-toes—she has not put her shoes on, just to be extra careful—she cross-es the kitchen and goes out into the yard, leaving the patio gate open. The air is cold, it is still not really light; the smoke from the copper smelter is everywhere, as usual. Surprised, she realizes that she can easily hear the rushing water of the Mantaro, flowing under the cliff on the other side of the house.

Ximena hurries along in the silence of this April dawn. She heads for the market, pulling the wagon and the plush animals, which bob around when the wheels bump on the stones. There is no one in the streets, which look desolate and gray when they are so empty. Not a single car goes by, nor even a truck on its way to the coast or the valley. Ximena is afraid that the light of day will come before she reaches the appointed place. She hears a rooster in the distance and a siren somewhere, signaling the end of night. She does not pray, she does not touch her holy medal, she does not cross herself in order to stave off the terror that makes her feel dizzy and tremble. She focuses her energy on her body, on her race through the cold and the smoke, on controlling the buzzing that tickles her chest. Finally she gets to the place that has obsessed her for days, weeks, an eternity. There she stops, and, after rubbing one foot against the other because they feel numb, she quickly unties the string around the toys, impatient at the stiffness of her fingers, then lifts the giraffe up by its neck and props it on the sidewalk, sets the dog on one side, and, on the other, arranges the cream-colored bear, which looks at her as always with raised eyebrows. She is about to retrace her route when she hears a motor start up noisily. She takes a deep breath, as deep as she can, to recover from the scare. The sound comes closer in bursts, then turns into a purr and trails off in the direction of the bridge.

In the morning they find her awake when they bring juice and carob syrup to her in bed. Her mother peers at her, feels her forehead, asks her if she is all right. Ximena tells her that she is fine and wants to get dressed all by herself. She closes her door and looks at the blackened and scratched soles of her feet. She sniffs her clothing, article by article. The odors of smoke, the sidewalks, and the dawn are blended together, blurred and distant as in a dream. Her eyelids are heavy; it is hard for her to keep them open, but she feels a current running through her from her legs to her temples that makes her vibrate with joyous electricity. She wants to shout, jump, and kick up her heels. She feels that, if she does not hold herself in, her body is going to burst right out of its skin. When she gets dressed for a second time, her anxiety of only a few hours earlier seems both remote and recent, fusing last night and today, yesterday and tomorrow. Everything eddies around her, singing to her and making her dance inside. She closes her eyes, imagining that the boy, smiling, picks up the toys one by one and pets them all he wants without being afraid. She does not want to think about the rest—about the moment when someone at home will notice their absence.

They have looked for them all over the house, in the patio, even in the outside shed where they keep tools and the wood cart. They have asked the neighbors. Ama Grande tries and tries to remember: when was it she saw them last? When? Where? At first they ask Ximena every little while, and even after a few days, the subject still comes up whenever they sit down at the dining table. Ximena shrugs her shoulders, lifts her eyebrows, does not remember, lowers her eyes, begins to pout, and then they say "That's enough! Poor thing! Anyway, they were bad for her." Anyone who comes by the house is sure to hear about the incident; yes, the three toys, yes, those very ones, the American ones, so expensive. They disappeared—someone took them. What a time we live in! Even in a neighborhood like this! Ah, but if they catch the thief, he'll go straight to prison! Ximena is taken aback. It has never occurred to her that children could be sent to prison.

She continues to go to market with Ama Grande. Maybe she will see him and can let him know he should hide the gifts. She looks for him here and there among the vendors' stalls, behind empty boxes, near the piles of garbage. She listens intently every time Ama Grande chats with the vendors about the incident. The women look at her sympathetically and Ximena feels uncomfortable, but she thanks them and is pleased by the consolation of a handful of *capulí*, a newspaper cone full of hot toasted maize, a red lollipop. The children who flocked to watch her when she pulled the wagon with the bear, the giraffe, and the dog, no longer come close to her. Now they smile at her from a distance, and some of them wave good-bye to her and go on with what they are doing. She never sees the one she seeks.

With time the grownups forget. Once in a long while, someone at home or a visitor will bring up the subject of the toys, but they move on quickly to other topics: the war, the Japanese whose houses and stores have been sacked by the police, the unavailability of certain products on the market. Little by little Ximena begins to forget her fear. She returns to her reading primer, to storybooks, to the photograph album, to her favorite illustrations in the encyclopedia. Only very rarely does she stop at the inlay that corresponds to the article on Peru. When she looks at that page, despite the slight uneasiness fluttering through her skin, she gives in to the smiling image of the boy's face and smiles back at him. She especially likes the smells of the market, and on the days when she accompanies Ama Grande on her shopping trips, she assigns a separate color to each smell, in order to block out the gray smoke that hangs heavily in the morning air. She has gone back to being demanding, and she wheedles and whines for a little clay pot, a marble, or a shaved-ice cone. Once they are back home, as she opens the gate so the old woman can come in with her baskets, she realizes that this time, once again, she has forgotten to look for the boy.

One morning at the beginning of August, a few days before they are to go down to the valley, she walks absentmindedly to market with Ama Grande. Suddenly, in the distance, she sees him. It is him, right there, in the same place as before and he is wearing the same green hat, the same sweater, the same faded pants, which are still too big. He is trying to drag a huge sack of potatoes from one side of the street to the other. Ximena's blood boils up in bubbles as she passes him. He is smaller than she remembers, but that must be because she has grown so much these last few months. She pauses alongside him for a few seconds and smiles at him in complicity over their great secret. The boy looks back at her impassively. He has not recognized her. He continues lugging the sack stubbornly, clenching his teeth in the huge effort he is making. Ximena would like to say a few words to him—something, anything—but Ama Grande hurries her along and the sullen adult expression on the boy's face locks her into silence. There is nothing to do but walk on, carrying within her the burden of a new weight as yet unnamed. The vacation in the valley, the games in the garden, and the servants' stories will gradually calm her distress and her bewilderment.

Weeks later, after their return, seated at the dining room table, she leafs through some volumes of the encyclopedia. Out of curiosity and a vague anxiety that rarely afflicts her anymore, she looks for the inlay on Peru. She decides ahead of time to look at the illustrations one by one, in order, as though she were reading them from left to right, until she comes to the last one, which has been such a worry to her. She closes her eyes for a few seconds and tells herself that she imagined everything in order to have one more story to add to the many stories she tells to vary the monotony of her daily routine. Nevertheless, when she opens the book, she has forgotten the intended sequence, and that unnamed weight, undiminished by the passage of time, implacably forces her to skip past the mountain landscapes and the Sunday fair and to halt at the last photo on the far right of the page. She can no longer deny or suppress the throbbing of her heart. There is the boy, very serious, without a smile, his expression adult; and his almond-shaped eyes hold her gaze sternly and interrogate her angrily, waiting for a reply.

II / THE GODDAUGHTER

Just as the cuckoo in the antique clock pops out to sound its ritual "one o'clock already and you've had a whole hour to finish your lunch," while Ximena tries to dawdle in order to keep hearing more details about the starving, weeping children who are dying in various parts of the world, someone starts to bang loudly on the front door. Her mother drops the fork she has been holding up to Ximena's mouth for a long time; Ama Grande hurries out of the kitchen as fast as she can, followed and almost shoved aside by her cousin The Blimp, who moves faster despite being fatter. Ximena's father, who was peacefully reading the newspaper, stands up so abruptly that his rocking chair tips forward. "It's the war," thinks Ximena, as she unobtrusively spits out a bite of by now unrecognizable steak. Frozen into their places, the three women crane their necks to the right to see who it is on the doorstep. Ximena takes advantage of the commotion to run to the living room so that she can see better.

It is Casilda, her mother's goddaughter, her cousin once removed. She is standing there, her face contorted, her expression oscillating between smiles and distress. Although it is not cold, she is wearing a scarf and gloves, and carries a worn-out rectangular suitcase that looks like a yellow cardboard box fastened with green straps. Her mother has also run to the door and has pulled Casilda inside, hugging her, asking her "Why aren't you in school?," then trying to disengage herself from the frantic arms that imprison her without letting her breathe, frowning, her eyes opening wide when Casilda, between hiccups that jerk her head up and down, cries "I want to die, Godmother, I want to die."

"The Germans have bombed Huancayo," thinks Ximena. But the images of a city in ruins, like the ones she has seen in the news shorts before the Sunday matinée movie, do not shock her nearly as much as the scene playing itself out in front of her in her own living room. She is not moved by Casilda's sobs, nor by those of her mother, who has also started to cry as she smooths her hair with one hand, while with the other she tries to unstick straggling locks of hair from her goddaughter's cheeks and to blot the tears that are melting her mascara into dark smudges.

"What has happened? What about your parents? Your brothers? What is going on? For God's sake, Casilda, tell me if there is bad news!"

Ximena is not moved, either, by the disconcerted reaction of Ama Grande and The Blimp who are watching the episode from the dining room and are hanging onto each other's hands as though they were old and fearful children. Her father is still standing by the door, very alone, forgotten by the others, without deciding to take a step toward the two women to console them, to assure them with his deep voice that no pain lasts forever, that they should calm down, that it will get better. Ximena can feel her heart throbbing, her breathing is labored and her ears burn. It makes her uneasy to witness the excessive emotion of two adults; it mortifies her that they take so long to get themselves under control and at the same time, she feels locked into place by irresistible curiosity. She wishes she had the courage to hold out her hand, which is still grasping her napkin, so that her mother can wipe off the ridiculous spot that Casilda's lipstick has left on her cheek. With her short curly hair in disorder and the red blotch on only one side of her pale face, she looks like a sad clown, escaped from some circus and out of place in the living room. Ximena is embarrassed for her mother and is even more embarrassed that she cannot share the grief that disfigures her.

Finally Ama Grande reacts and brings a glass of water and a wet towel that drips onto the rug. With gentle firmness, she pushes the two women over to the sofa, makes them sit down, wipes off their faces as though she were obeying Ximena's secret plea, and calming them down in Quechua, she goes back and forth between the two foreheads with the wet towel. The Blimp has busied herself in the kitchen. To Ximena's astonishment, her father is still paralyzed and only when he notices that she is staring at him does he pick the news-paper up off the floor and ask her sharply to leave the room. The Blimp must have heard him or maybe she guessed that he would give her that order because she comes out to meet her in the pantry and shuts the door of the dining room. Resentfully, Ximena settles herself in Ama Grande's wicker chair. The Blimp is being hateful and has also closed the door between the kitchen and the pantry, so no mat-ter how hard she tries she can't hear a thing. For a little while she is distracted from her frustration by the swaying of those immense hips that have always amazed her. Then, like the sudden assault of a slap, she feels the sharp noise of a door slamming on the other side of the house. It is her father who is going back to work and who is leaving without saying good-bye to her.

That afternoon Ama Grande and The Blimp bring a camp cot into Ximena's bedroom. They rearrange some toys, move out the little table on which she cuts out pictures from old magazines, and shove her bed over as far as it will go toward the windows so that the cot will fit and still let the door open and close without difficulty. While they are unfolding the starched sheets, spreading out a heavy wool blanket, and fluffing up the pillow with expert pats, the two servants shake their heads.

"Poor child, poor thing! Running away like that from school! Her poor mother! What are the nuns going to say, and how people are going to gossip!"

They tell Ximena that she must be good to Casilda and that she should let her borrow her things without complaining. But when she asks what it is that is happening to her cousin, and how long she will be staying there with them, and why she has not gone straight to her own house, they shrug their shoulders and act as though they do not know.

Casilda is resting on her parents' double bed. Ximena has been hovering around hiding behind the half-closed bathroom door while her mother has helped her to take off the white blouse with the Sacred Heart insignia on it, the gray pleated skirt, the black kneesocks. Half naked, the girl sits on the edge of the bed. Her breasts are conspicuous, bulging over the unmended lace of her slip; her white arms and legs are heavy like the rest of her body. She is not crying any longer, but every once in a while she shudders all over in a cutoff noisy wheeze that Ximena knows all too well from her own experience. Her mother has given her another cup of camomile tea with some drops of laudanum in it, only a few and measured very carefully because her father has strictly forbidden its use. After covering her up with the blankets, and stroking her head, she tiptoes out of the bedroom. Ximena takes advantage of the moment to slip in and have a close look at her cousin.

The goddaughter sleeps with her eyes half open and you can see her gray irises, like slivers of the moon, in the pupils of her tear-swollen eyes. A thread of saliva runs out of the corner of her mouth and pools into a perfect circle of dampness on the pillow. She has full lips, a turned up nose and round cheeks. Ximena gets the impression of a little girl who has grown up too fast and who is not yet accustomed to the idea of having breasts. She is still staring at her cousin when she hears her mother calling her from the living room.

"Come here," she says to her. "Give me a big, big hug."

She rocks her for a few seconds as though she were still a baby. Ximena is embarrassed by these effusive outbursts of affection, but she really likes the smell of her perfumed clothing and even more the fragrance of the skin of her neck, so warm, so much hers.

"Oh, Ximena," she says to her, hugging her even tighter against her, "if you could just stay little, or if you had been born a boy!"

Casilda does not eat with them that evening. Ama Grande and her mother have tried to wake her up, but it has been useless. She opens her eyes with great effort, mumbles a few unintelligible words and drops her head onto one shoulder to fall back asleep even when she is sitting up or on her feet, held up by the two women. They take her to Ximena's room and put her back to bed there so that she can slumber on in the oblivion of camomile and laudanum.

During supper her parents speak in hushed voices although Casilda is sound asleep and the door of her room is closed. One by one, in a row on her napkin, Ximena lines up the peas from her soup without her parents' noticing or scolding her. There are long silences, unusual at that hour. Ximena discovers with alarm that swallowing even sips of water makes a scandalous noise when it is so quiet. Every so often her mother repeats, sorrowfully,

"Poor girl! What is going to become of her? To get herself into this mess when she is barely more than a child!"

Her father forgets why they are being so careful and raises his voice. "Your aunt and uncle are the ones at fault," he points out. "Well developed the way she is, they ought to have taught her a few simple facts of life."

There is a long pause during which only kitchen noises are heard, and the voices of Ama Grande and The Blimp, who has still not gone back to the house where she works. Ximena decides that it is the perfect moment to ask what it is that Casilda has done. Her mother twists her napkin and says in a hard voice that it is none of her business and that it is a matter for grownups. Then her father turns to her joylessly and Ximena follows him with her eyes in order to not feel the injustice of the reprimand so deeply.

When they are finishing their coffee and she is happily eating a canned peach with lots of syrup, her father dares to break the silence. "How long has she been...?"

The question is broken off because her mother has stood up angrily. "She doesn't know if she is or not, and these are not things to discuss in front of Ximena."

Before her mother reaches her bedroom door they hear some long howls outside, and she stops abruptly in the middle of a complaint, covering her mouth with the back of her hand, and Ama Grande, who had come in to collect the dirty dishes, sets them back down on the table for a few more seconds so she can cross herself and ward off evil spirits.

Ximena is starting to detest Casilda. She hardly speaks to Ximena's father, who for his part does not seem very sure what attitude to adopt toward her. The girl only speaks to Ama Grande to give her orders in a gruff and bossy tone. She does look around for her godmother during the times when she is not stretched out on her cot gazing at the ceiling, or when she is not writing those very long letters that make her cry when she rereads them and that she always ends by tearing up. She closes herself up in the bathroom for long periods of time. Then Ximena pounds on the door repeatedly just in order to make her mad.

"What do you want?" Casilda asks after a long delay.

"I need to come in again," she answers curtly. On her way out, Casilda shoves her up against the wall with her body or gives her a barely disguised kick. Ximena has told on her, but to no avail. Her mother takes her goddaughter's side and the worst is that Casilda's parents have decided to let her stay on with them for a while. When her father protested, her mother said that family was family, which has seemed unanswerable.

Both of them displaced, he and Ximena tacitly join forces to get their own back. They play rowdy games in the living room and laugh excessively over any silly thing. Casilda, who at that hour does not converse with her mother and who tends to sit by the radio checking the stations for *boleros*, looks at them resentfully and slams the door when she goes to the bedroom. Then her mother comes and murmurs in exasperation, "Enrique, for heaven's sake, you're behaving like a child." But sometimes she forgets to scold them. She goes to bed early and uses those hours to read the poems or novels she likes so much, the ones she orders from Lima at regular intervals.

During the day Ximena spends more time than before with Ama Grande, but since she is jealous and resentment clouds her mind, she behaves badly toward her. She touches all the things that are off limits to her; she pesters her with questions, distracting her from her work, and she talks back to her naughtily, mocking the logic of the stories the old woman tells even though she actually adores them just as they are. Ama Grande finally gets impatient and punishes her by shutting her into the closet. Ever since Casilda came, Ximena has not even been able to yell at the top of her lungs to protest this exile among shoes, suits and dresses. Doubly isolated, she recalls the time when her cousin opened the door curiously and seeing her there crouched in the dark, burst into laughter. "So this is how they keep the spoiled brat in line!" she said in a teasing tone, doubling over in amusement.

Bored with entertaining herself by listening to the rising tones of her own yells, she has nothing better to do than comfort herself by planning how to get even; she imagines that God will punish Casilda for being conceited and will make her nose grow until it is just like her father's—Uncle Rogelio's—whose nose is big and fat with purple veins crisscrossing it; that she will forget how to read and write and will have to learn all over again, squished into a little school desk, big as she is, in a room crammed full of first graders; that if the Germans win, they will capture and torture her instead of going after ungrateful children who refuse to eat properly; that a witch will transform her into a hideous spider; and, worst of all, that Carlos, the one she cries about all the time and keeps talking about, will never come looking for her. Because despite the coded conversations Casilda has with her mother, sometimes they get careless, and Ximena, who listens avidly behind doors, has caught onto their stories about love affairs and tears like in the Mexican films that Ama Grande likes so much that are shown in town every once in a while.

Trying to puzzle out these mysteries of illicit love, little by little her anger fades and her attention focuses on herself. It would be better if she, Ximena, so sickly and an only child, simply died in that closet. It would be Casilda's fault that she had been locked in there and that the air got stuffy and poisoned her delicate bronchial system. When they finally opened the door, there she would be, poor thing, huddled in the same position she was in now but dead, really dead, and her soul would hover over their heads, invisible to the others but with two wings like a butterfly's, not so feathery as the angels in the engravings in her missal. Ximena, turned into a spirit, would listen to the frantic cries, her mother's sharp sobs, and observe her father's grieved face, Ama Grande's wordless sorrow, and then Casilda...how would Casilda react? Perhaps the goddaughter would keel over in a repentant fainting fit, or who knows, maybe she would only pretend to be sad in order not to offend out of politeness, when actually she was really glad. She would stay on to live there in her house, in her room, in her bed; she would become, finally, her parents' daughter. "No," Ximena rebels, "Not that." And as always, clenching her teeth and feeling as though the air is running out, she cries, "No, I don't want to die. Let her be the one to die!"

One morning Ximena wakes up and is surprised to see that Casilda is not sleeping. She is sitting on the floor, leaning back against the camp cot, reading a letter that is several pages long. She is so absorbed in her reading that she does not even notice that Ximena is staring at her from the edge of her bed, just a half step from her. Tears run down her cheeks and neck and soak into the high collar of her nightshirt. Her fingers are ink-stained and her nose is swollen. Ximena feels a slight twinge of anxiety, afraid that her nose really will turn into a copy of Uncle Rogelio's. She decides to wait a few more minutes like this and watch Casilda rip her letter into shreds and then cry desperately after that, breaking into noisy sobs so that her mother will rush in to see what is going on. But no. This time Casilda does not do any of that. She finishes reading the letter and folds it in three, lining up the edges carefully and smoothing the creases.

"You're spying on me," she says when she catches Ximena's eye. "Your face is going to break out all over from staring so much," she adds acidly. Ximena, startled out of her trance, snaps back an answer.

"Yours will be worse," she says. "Looking at yourself so much in the mirror, you're going to turn into the Devil's own image."

Casilda shrugs her shoulders and leaves the room without paying any attention to her. "Godmother, would you lend me an envelope? I want to go to the post office." Her sweet tone does not completely hide the demand in her voice when she asks a favor. Ximena's mother starts out by resisting the request.

"To whom have you been writing, may I ask?"

Casilda does not hesitate although she opens her eyes wide as if to fend off any possible suspicion.

"To Maritere, my best friend. Who else would I be writing to?"

Without inquiring any farther, her mother gives her permission to go out and tells her that Ximena will keep her company because it's a sunny day and the exercise will do them both good.

They walk alongside the river. Casilda strides along taking big steps and does not stop to look at anything, not the spindly bushes nor the fat cats stretched out on the cement steps of the gringos' porches, nor the rocks speckled with gold and bright colors that add sparkle to the dry earth, nor beyond the heavy steel barriers, the precipice and the rushing current of the Mantaro. Sometimes, absorbed in her thoughts, she'll squint her eyes and frown, making a horrible face, and then, a second later, she'll smile at her inner ghosts, nodding or shaking her head in an unspoken conversation with them.

"Wait for me, you're going too fast," pleads Ximena, running and skipping along to catch up to her. Casilda, unmoved, keeps right on going and when they reach the bridge, Ximena does not dare ask her if she can hold her hand and she has to deal all by herself with the fear that wells up in her every time she crosses. Over and over again they have told her that because she is so thin, any wind will just whip her away and drop her into the river, and despite her father's repeated assurances that this is not so, she is not too positive that they aren't right after all.

Downtown where there are people around them, Casilda stops making faces. The young men look at her out of the corners of their eyes and some of them greet her with a slight nod, or touch their hands to their hat brims. The women who do not know her scrutinize her openly and then comment among themselves because Casilda is pretty and new to the town. The women who have met her at her god-mother's house say hello to her and some expect that she will stop to chat for a moment. But Casilda pays no attention and is hardly aware of them.

Ximena notices that her cousin walks differently as she goes past different people. When she passes close by men, she does not stride along. She slows down, straightens up, throws her head back, and swings her hips. Watching her, Ximena fires up and then fades out inside, lights up and is burned. Baffled, she pretends she has smoke in her eyes and rubs them in order to not see and focus on that sparkling secret that makes her skin tingle.

The walks to the post office become a daily event. Ximena goes along happy to be outdoors, to see people, to stare at passersby and because it breaks the serene and familiar household routines. She goes along eager to overcome her timidity and build up defenses, outside, in the world. She has long ago lost all hope that Casilda will buy her a treat, a balloon or a little book, but it does not matter to her, she likes the post office's odor of rancid wood, of high altitude wool; she also likes its den-like darkness, the dim yellowish light shed by its single sad lightbulb, its dusty floor, crunching with footsteps. Besides, since they have been going to the post office, Casilda has not been monop-olizing her mother so much because she has been busy. As she explains, with a straight face, one day she writes to her mother, the next to a girl friend, and one after another to each of her cousins. She no longer weeps or stares mesmerized and unseeing at the cracks in the ceiling. Ximena's mother is relieved. Freed of worry over her god-daughter's problems, she has begun to sing again and sew things the Red Cross will send over to the Allies in the war. Once again she goes out visiting and even has time occasionally to amuse Ximena with a story.

One day, when they reach the window where she hands over her letters to the mail clerk, Casilda does not pull out her usual letter to be weighed so she can put the correct amount of postage on it. When that moment comes, her cousin always asks Ximena to hold her purse so that she can stick the stamps on in meticulously straight lines along the right-hand top edge of the envelope. Before she hands it over to the woman, with a quick gesture, so rapid you have to be watching carefully to see it, Casilda blows a kiss at the letter. This time she has nothing in her hands and demands in an authoritarian tone: "Look and see if there is any mail for Casilda Santa María."

The clerk, a very old woman who has white hair with bluish high-lights swept up in a huge bun, moves heavily over toward the pigeon-holes. She has to get close up to make out the S. Her eyeglasses have very thick lenses that pull them down to the end of her nose, and when she speaks, she looks out over them. If she needs to calculate the cost of the stamps, she tips her face back and her eyes look tiny. In that position and with her hooked nose and the three double chins that deform her neck, she looks like a bird giving thanks to God for the water she drinks.

"There's nothing here for Santa María."

"Look carefully," insists Casilda.

"I've looked carefully, Miss. There is one for Salas and another for Santisteban."

"Then look under M. Maybe they made a mistake when they were sorting."

Two men and a woman carrying a child on her back wait unmoving in line behind Casilda and Ximena. The clerk goes back over to the mailboxes wheezing and muttering in a low voice.

"There is no Santa María under M," she calls out from over by the pigeonholes.

The goddaughter does not say thank you or goodbye or anything. She gives Ximena a shove that makes her stumble and drags her toward the door. The other people have moved back and watch them curiously while Casilda strides along and Ximena has to run to catch up to her.

The same thing happens again the next day, only this time Casilda brings along a letter of her own. The following day and the one after that, the same exchange is repeated.

"Look and see if there is something for Casilda Santa María."

"No, nothing."

"Under C, but look under M, too."

"Nothing there either, Miss, I checked," the old woman replies triumphantly.

Her mother begins to worry. "This child is not well," she says anxiously, "she is losing weight." And it is true that Casilda hardly eats. She writes letters, tears them up, writes them again, walks aimlessly around the house, sits down, gets up again, sits down again, weeps and laughs without cause. At times she closes herself up in her room and they can hear her sob, or she lies down to rest after having drunk a cup of tea laced with the forbidden laudanum. At other times she is chatty and the mother rejoices. "Today you look much better," she encourages her. They talk about the farm, about uncles and aunts, about relatives, about the time when Casilda went to study in Lima and how she suffered at that school, of the worrisome lassitude induced by sea air, of the suffocating monotonous gray days, interminable in their opacity, of the drizzle that was a poor imitation of mountain thunderstorms.

She is clever at imitating how Lima women speak; she imitates their gestures and their exaggerated posturings. "Ah, yes," she exclaims pretending to be sipping tea with her little finger raised, "my four grandparents are Spanish and my name is listed in the sacred book of the *Conquistadores*," and then she adds, laughingly, "Black women starving to death, good-for-nothing idiots, posers, that's all they are."

When she does imitations, her mother and Ama Grande laugh, and Ximena, reluctantly, is amused along with them, infected by the women's contagious laughter. Then suddenly, without any warning, Casilda stops speaking, goes over to the rocking chair and tunes them all out or turns on the radio and any music makes her collapse into sobs. Ximena's father says this is a serious matter and he wants to send her home to the farm, but her mother argues that she will be worse off there, and comforted by signs that only she can perceive, she repeats, "These things happen at her age, they will fade, it is just a question of waiting it out..."

At night, as Ximena knows, the goddaughter does not always sleep. More than once she has been awakened by the light of the lamp on the night table between the two beds, and she has seen her writing furiously. One morning just before dawn, she does not see her lying in her bed. Casilda has brought in a mirror from the bathroom and she has propped it on the windowsill. She is brushing her hair slowly, very slowly. Ximena peers at her from close up without the girl even noticing the eager curiosity in those watching eyes.

It is the first time that she has seen an adult body completely naked; she has not seen even her mother like this. Shivering, Ximena is transfixed watching her although she feels that she is trespassing on forbidden territory. She would like to say a prayer and turn over on her other side, but somehow she cannot. Casilda looks so beautiful with her feverish eyes and her lips half open, surrounded by the hazy light that comes through the panes of glass and then becomes brighter and is warmed into transparent oranges as it blends with the lamp light. She is not the same as the person who ambles around the house during the daytime in her skirts, her clinging blouses, her short socks, and her movements constrained by the way the furniture is arranged in each room. She is not the same person as the one in clothes who strides along the road and crosses the bridge eagerly to reach the post office. This is someone else, free, unique, contained only by her skin and by the rounded curves of her breasts, her thighs, her white stomach.

"Casilda," she calls to her in a whisper of a voice, she is so afraid of being choked by emotion. "Casilda, you're going to catch cold, you'd better get to bed."

But Casilda does not hear her. Lost in her own image, perhaps conjuring up the devil, she remains frozen in the same position in front of the mirror and Ximena is finally rescued from the spell by a dream of gardens and statues.

One morning when the goddaughter is in a foul mood, the mail clerk parsimoniously hands her a letter.

"For Miss Santa María," she says, emphasizing the name.

Finally! Even Ximena, who is on bad terms with her cousin, rejoices. Casilda's hand trembles when she holds it out to take the letter. The clerk twists her thin lips and smiles in reverse under her eyeglasses. Her cousin's face, full of expectation, suddenly turns livid. They have hardly left the post office when she balls up the letter and throws it on the ground.

They walk back faster than they ever have before. Ximena is left behind, confused, feeling sorry for the crumpled wad that bobs along the road like an injured bird. When she tries to catch up to her cousin, who has reached the bridge, she trips on a shoelace that has come untied and falls flat. Her cousin does not wait. With the jacket borrowed from her godmother open and flapping like two brown wings at her sides, she keeps walking along. Furious and way behind her, Ximena asks what she has not dared to say before.

"Who were you expecting letters from? From him?"

"Yes," answers the goddaughter without turning around. "From him. Because he is the one I keep writing to all day and all night. From him. So that he will come and get me. So I can get away from your house."

Goaded, hurting, her skinned knee covered with dirt and little dots of blood starting to soak through, Ximena cannot restrain herself.

"Forget him, you know perfectly well he's married and that you can't marry him."

"What do I care!" answered Casilda striding along even faster. "What do I care that he's married! If I can't be his wife, I'll be his whore."

The word shoots through the air, sharp and penetrating, and echoes in Ximena's ears even though she tries to block it out. Mercilessly, the sound bores through her and beats rhythmically in her temples. "It is the ugliest word in the world," her mother said to her one night in Lima, when they both heard the word from a drunk, splashed with vomit, who kept yelling it as he came up to them menacingly. She was so terrified by that episode that not even in her moments of greatest rage had she been able to use the word in her mental insults. And now Casilda has flung it out and the sound of that word fills the gray air, taking it over, and invades her, too, reverberating in her every step.

Casilda is in bed prostrated by cramps that make her moan. Ximena goes into the bathroom through the door that opens into her parents' bedroom and surprises Ama Grande and her mother peering at the bloodstains on a pair of pink lace panties. When they realize Ximena is there, they give a startled jump just as she does, and hide the panties from view as best they can, telling her to go along, that she shouldn't stick her nose into adult matters. So Ximena goes around through the living and dining rooms, and goes into her room and listens through the crack of the other door which leads into the bathroom.

"According to her, it wasn't due now, but as you can see, here it is. What good luck!"

"Yes, well," answers the old woman, "the anxiety made her skip two periods. Poor lamb! She doesn't know anything."

"Not a thing!" repeats her mother, her voice shrilling. "She's such a child she doesn't even know if she is intact or not."

Ximena cannot figure out what they are saying and the murmuring of the two women makes her curious. Trying to puzzle it out, she goes over to Casilda and asks her, "Are you hurt?" and Casilda's angry voice rises up out of the cocoon of blankets. "No, I'm fucked." Looking for an escape from her appalled confusion, Ximena goes over to the back door and glumly gazes out into the yard for a long while.

For the rest of the day, her mother is happy and, in her own way, so is Ama Grande. Only Casilda, huddled on her cot, keeps complaining. Whatever it is that has put the two women into such a good mood does not seem to have affected her. Finally she gets up, wanders into the house in her robe with the expression of a sleepwalker, and then shuts herself up in her room again. Her mother has loaned her novels that she has gotten from several friends because her own do not interest her goddaughter. She encourages her to read to pass the time, but after turning a few pages, she tosses them down on the night table and complains unhappily.

"It's worse, godmother, it makes it worse. When I read, everything makes me remember. I don't want to look at any more words."

Even so, the next morning, feverish and with circles under her eyes, there she is writing again with more determination than ever. Fascinated, Ximena discovers that Casilda does not just change with her mood or her clothes. She counts on her fingers the different people her cousin can be: one is the Casilda with clothes on, two, the naked Casilda, and now, most vividly, three, the Casilda who writes. How come she did not notice this before? Maybe because it wasn't the same, maybe because before there was not such purposefulness to her effort and now there is, now Ximena can accurately predict which Casilda she is going to see.

At first it is harder to spy on her because when she starts to write, Casilda is completely there in front of her sitting at the dining room table. She sets her new lined pad on the table and begins to fill up one or two pages without stopping. She is completely there when she begins to pause every so often, thinking for a moment and then reading what she has written in her big even handwriting in very dark ink. She is completely there when she pulls out her address book, distractedly looks up a listing, and quickly writes it on the envelope. And she is still completely there when suddenly she notices Ximena's presence and brusquely warns her, "Don't you go giving me the evil eye. Go pester Ama!" This is invariably the first phase of Casilda-who-writes. She finishes one or two letters quickly and shoves them to one side, indifferently, as though she had fulfilled an obligation.

It is when she begins to write the third letter that the miracle happens and only happens to Casilda, because neither her mother nor her father is transformed this way when writing. She leaves the dining room and refuses to use the little desk in the living room. Over and over again her godmother has said to her "Sit over here, Casilda, you don't have to write in the bedroom where it is so uncomfortable and where there isn't good light." Sitting on the floor, leaning her back against her cot, the pad on her knees, forgetting to turn on the lamp that is just a step away, Casilda writes in the semidarkness of the room. She writes and crosses out, reads and corrects, tears it up and begins over again. Absorbed in what she is doing, she withdraws from her surroundings. Everything ceases to exist for her: the beds, the dresser, the toys, the windows, Ximena herself who little by little creeps up to her until she is right next to her, until she feels like everything else, invisible. Where has Casilda really gone? Ah, that game of absences and presences, those scrawled marks that erase things and then make them reappear: Ximena can see them coming. How she contemplates them, curious and fearful, her heart pounding with throbs that deafen her, spying on their mystery, as she yearns for but dreads the coming of that day when she too will be transformed and will transform with the terrifying magic of the pen!

When she has finished, so much later that Ximena is on the point of falling asleep, hypnotized, Casilda reads the sheaf of pages, distances herself, begins to recover her earlier face and by the time she folds the pages carefully to put them into the envelope, the magic spell is entirely broken.

One night, after supper, while her parents are listening anxiously to war news on the radio, the goddaughter interrupts them. "Godmother, can I give my correspondence to the errand boy who comes to get the parcels?"

Her father, impatient, replies that he is not an "errand boy" but a Company employee.

"Ah, I forgot that here you speak gringo language," answers Casilda turning her back on them without waiting for an answer.

He has stood up and seems about to go after her. Ximena's heart gives a leap. How do big girls get punished for answering back? But her mother catches hold of his arm and stops him. "Leave her alone, Enrique; it's not worth the effort. You're never going to win on some issues, you know that perfectly well. Casilda comes from a world you have never managed to understand. But I do," she adds thoughtfully, "I do."

Casilda settles herself in the kitchen to wait for the Company van which makes a stop at the house before going down to the coast. The young man who travels with the driver usually comes to the door with his felt hat in his hand to ask if there are any packages for him to pick up. They have him come in and if the packages or the letters are not ready yet, Ama Grande sends for the driver so they can both come in and have coffee while they wait. The young man is new at the job. He does not speak Spanish well and he is very timid. Ximena always notices how well shined his shoes are and how much brilliantine he uses to keep his bristly hair slicked flat. When he notices that Ximena is looking him over, he turns and faces her for an instant, as though questioning her, without making up his mind to smile, without managing to say anything and immediately, he lowers his eyes and turns his face another direction without moving away. Ximena thinks that it is funny that he is so big and yet so childlike, but she likes to see him get flustered and so she stares insistently at him every chance she gets. The driver is different. He is from the jungle, from far away, from a place Ximena has never been, but which she has heard about because the name is woven into the marvelous landscapes of Ama Grande's stories. The driver is shorter than Ama Grande and has a flutey happy voice. He jokes with the old woman.

"You're looking really pretty, Mama Cristina. You've gotten younger since last Tuesday. If you keep on like this, I'll end up falling in love with you."

Laughing, she responds that he should stop being such a fibber, that he shouldn't tease her, because the moon will punish him by tangling up his routes.

Time and time again, Casilda has gone near the kitchen to listen to the laughter. Then the two men get to their feet, they greet her with a respectful nod, silent, forgetting their coffee, Ama Grande and Ximena. They are both full of admiration. Casilda pays no attention to them and since they stop talking the moment she appears and nothing interesting is going on, she turns away and leaves, even though even Ximena can see the swing of her hips as she goes off. It takes the men a little while to recover; they drink their black aromatic coffee in big sips, and after a few moments, the driver starts making jokes again.

That morning Casilda waits, but the van does not appear at the usual hour. Every once in a while the girl goes out to check the time on the antique clock in the dining room. A minute later she comes back to her post and stands next to the door, one hand on the doorknob and in the other hand a paper bag in which she has put her three letters. She keeps swinging the bag up against her thigh impatiently. Suddenly, as though hypnotized, she turns her head toward Ama Grande, without seeing her, but the old woman feels summoned and gets annoyed.

"Go on inside, *niña*," she recommends. "I'll call you the minute they come. They aren't going to arrive any sooner just because you're here wearing yourself out. Go on in, Miss Casilda; I'll be sure to let you know."

Casilda mutters something with her teeth clenched and doesn't budge. Ximena, who has just been making a heroic effort to finish an egg and that last little bit of bread, dares to ask her a question. "And why don't you want to put your letters in the mail?"

"Because I don't want to. Because the nitwit who works there is jealous of me and I don't trust her."

"Ah," sighs Ximena while she remembers all their long treks to the post office and feels nostalgic.

When they hear the roar of the van motor, inexplicably Casilda leaves the kitchen. Ama Grande shrugs her shoulders over the dishes she is washing. While the young man is knocking gently on the door, Ximena runs off to look for her cousin. "They're here," she announces what Casilda knows perfectly well already.

The goddaughter walks around holding her breath, with the paper bag that is shaking because her hands are trembling. "Hey," she says to the helper, "How far is the van going?"

Cornered, twisting the brim of his hat, the young man answers her, "To Lima, Miss."

"Does it make stops before that?"

"Yes, Miss, three or four at least."

"Well then, at the first place you stop that has a post office, mail these letters for me."

Before handing them over, Casilda double checks that all three are still in the sack. "Who gets out to do the errands?"

"I do, Miss. The driver waits for me in the car or in the place where we stop to eat."

"All right, here is the money for the stamps. You can keep the change. Hey," she asks as she give him some coins, "do you know how to read?"

The young man lowers his eyes even farther. He shrinks down so far, his clothes start looking too big. Without raising his head, he shakes his head no. Ximena is amazed at Casilda's obvious satisfaction.

"It doesn't matter," she adds. "But don't you take them out of the sack until you get into the post office itself. I don't want them to get dirty, so make sure you leave them right where they are without touching them."

"Yes, Miss," mumbles the helper.

The two girls stand in the doorway until the van is out of sight around the bend.

Several times in a row, twice a week, the goddaughter sends her correspondence with the driver's helper in the van. Each time he has come to collect the letters, before Casilda has come into the kitchen, he has furtively left the change from the previous mailing on the table where Ama Grande eats and works. Later, Ama Grande picks up the coins, gives them to the goddaughter or puts them on her night table, but Casilda keeps saying to the young man "Keep the change," and he always keeps his eyes lowered and doesn't answer.

One morning Casilda announces that she is going to the post office and Ximena is pleased to have a chance to go out. The weather is fine even though the sky is always the opaque sky of the smelter and the air smells of copper. They let her go out without a sweater and Ximena swings her arms as she walks along, sweeping them around like windmills in that hard air, feeling the metallic breeze against her skin. Casilda walks silently up ahead. Not even once does she turn around to see how far behind Ximena is.

Ximena is getting along better with her cousin these days. Her moods are not so extreme, she is less brusque with her and she has even been teaching her a song in French. In a beautifully melodic voice she sings the words of "A la claire fontaine..." and with unexpected patience she corrects Ximena's accent and intonation. Sometimes she tries to get her godmother to practice with her in that strange guttural language the nuns teach them in their schools, but Ximena's mother laughs at her own mistakes.

"Over the years," she says resignedly, "I've even forgotten how to breathe the way I used to as an unmarried girl."

Her father has commented dryly one afternoon that Casilda would be better off learning English, and without replying, she frowned and kept on cutting out a dress pattern.

In the morning, the old woman at the post office greets them with the same malevolent expression as before. This time, at least, Casilda does not have to insist and exultantly receives a thick envelope, redeeming herself from all past humiliations. In the fraction of a second when it is whisked past her, Ximena has recognized an envelope from home, with the address written in Casilda's unmistakable handwriting and ink. Her cousin quickly stuffs the letter in her purse without thanking the old woman and when they are on their way out the door, Ximena turns and sees her, standing there stiffly, hating them from behind her eyeglasses and petrified in her own ugliness.

"He wrote to me; as you can see, he wrote to me," Casilda says to her as they near the bridge. "But if you tell my aunt and uncle, I will accuse you of stealing the chocolates your mother keeps in her wardrobe, because I've seen you standing on a chair, on top of two volumes of the encyclopedia, in order to reach the candy with both hands and take it. In any case," she adds, trying to smile in a way that looks natural, "this will be our secret, yours and mine, and no one else's."

That day Ximena does not have to run in order to catch up with her. Casilda walks more slowly and for the first time, when a space opens up between the two of them, she pauses for a moment to wait for her. Ximena has never seen her so radiant as that morning and reassured that her thefts are not going to be revealed, cheered by her cousin's happy face, she doesn't hurry to stay by her side; she has a good time jumping along on one foot and then the other, and she wanders off picking up pieces of flint on the road or black and yellow feathers that birds have dropped in their escape from such a barren and unfriendly town.

Her mother is talking on the phone when they get home and waves her hand at them, scrutinizing her goddaughter's face for the results of the expedition. Casilda closes herself up to read her own letter and then her mother asks Ximena if her cousin received something.

"Yes," answers Ximena, and without remorse, allying herself with her cousin's strange behavior, she adds, "She received a letter from Maritere."

Every once in a while they go out to the post office and Casilda always receives a fat envelope that Ximena recognizes immediately, and occasionally she gets another, in a thinner and more ordinary envelope, a letter she reads noncommittally as they go along the road. She always whisks the fat envelope into her purse and just as soon as they get home, she closes herself up alone in her bedroom to read its pages. Several times during the day, as though unable to resist an attraction that is more urgent than anything else in her life, she interrupts any conversation even when there are visitors there, gets up from the table without finishing her meal, or leaves Ximena in the middle of a story and goes into the bedroom where she flops down on her bed and immerses herself in the pages, later stuffing them back into the envelope and hiding them under her pillow. Ximena has been spying on her through the half open bathroom door and knows that if someone interrupts her while she is reading, Casilda hides the letter in a flash and pretends to be resting. More than curious, Ximena is intrigued. It had never occurred to her that grownups could write to themselves. She does not understand it at all, but her experience tells her not to ask questions about it. Any question about it could enrage her cousin and break the tacit peace treaty now in force between them.

Casilda's temperament has changed radically since she started receiving letters. Little by little she begins to confide in Ximena.

"He is tall, very handsome, and he says he really misses me," she tells her one time.

"He just had some good luck in a business deal and he is going to buy a new car so he can come and get me," she croons another time.

"A few days ago he felt very sad because he heard our song at a band concert," she confides to her with nostalgic eyes. "His birthday is day after tomorrow and he is going to get out of the city using any pretext he can find, because he can't bear to be celebrating without me," she exclaims happily.

Ximena asks her what color his eyes are, if he knows how to ride a horse, if he speaks English. She would like to know something about his wife and especially whether he has children, if they go to school, if they know how to read already. But her horror of hearing the unbearable *wh...* word again makes her keep silent.

One morning the unforeseen happens. At the post office, the old woman comes back from the pigeonholes with empty hands. Casilda makes a gesture of impatience, rolls her eyes upwards, and clicks her tongue all at the same time. Their previous exchange is repeated in exact detail.

"Look carefully."

"I've already looked carefully, there's nothing there, Miss."

But this time Casilda does not give up even after the clerk has checked again under M and under C. "There has to be a letter there," she hisses in a low, menacing voice. "There has to be!"

They get home in no time because rage drives the girl's furious strides. "Godmother, how do I make out a complaint against the head of the post office?" she asks her mother. "That old doddering idiot they keep like a monkey behind the counter is stealing my letters."

Her mother tries to convince her that that is not possible, that it would be against the law.

"Who cares about the law!" sobs the girl. "I need to speak to the postmaster. Since when have you had so much faith in half-starved government employees?"

That night her father promises to find out what is happening, and the next afternoon, a short bald man with greenish skin waits on Casilda. When the clerk sees Casilda and Ximena arrive, she stands to one side so that he can step into her place. Both postal employees are deathly pale.

"Are you the postmaster?" asks Casilda looking him up and down with scorn.

"Yes, Miss, I am the postmaster and I assure you that no one has intercepted your letters. This lady here," he indicates the old woman with his head, "has worked in this establishment since it opened and there have never been any complaints."

He speaks mechanically and his public functionary's glacial and courteous expression scares Ximena much more than it would have if he had started yelling.

"Well, a letter should have reached me yesterday," insists Casilda without backing off.

"Sometimes letters are delayed and sometimes they are even lost, but if it had arrived yesterday you would have received it, Miss. Let there be no doubt about that."

They leave the post office without resolving anything. The post-master has said good-bye ceremoniously in the midst of Casilda's angry complaints about the inefficiency of the mail system. On their way home, Casilda suggests, her voice hoarse with anger, "Unless the boy is the one to blame, or maybe even the driver, too, and the two of them are having a high old time with my letters."

"Maybe he is sick and that is why he hasn't answered you," replies Ximena, trying to console her, surprised by her own words.

"He had to answer me, I know for sure that no matter what, he had to answer me," her cousin insists doggedly.

The young man who accompanies the driver, more nervous than ever, and with his eyes on the floor, twists the brim of his hat and reiterates that no, that he has never disobeyed her order. Casilda accuses him of being a thief, of pocketing the money she gave him for the stamps, of keeping the letters. The poor young man has no alternative but to defend himself pathetically. "No, Miss, no, I really did exactly what you said! Ask the driver, please, just ask him and he will tell you, I always put them right into the mail."

Without intervening, the driver and Ama Grande are present during this conversation, their expressions grave and distressed. Ximena starts hating her cousin again and unable to contain herself, explodes. "Leave him be, Casilda! He hasn't done anything!"

Her eyes wild, it takes Casilda a moment to even recognize her and by the time she has registered who is speaking to her, the driver has grabbed hold of his young helper and with their heads down, they have made a beeline for the door. The two go off, leaving Casilda frozen into position in the middle of the kitchen.

The next time they come, and three or four more times after that, Casilda entrusts her letters to the young man, urging him to take great care with them. She speaks to him without arrogance, with an awkward affected sweetness. Ximena is aware of how disgusting Casilda's efforts at cordiality seem. However, the answers do not arrive even though Casilda keeps on writing regularly.

She is in such bad shape by then that only when she is writing does she seem to recover some energy and a little interest in life brightens her changed face. Her cheeks are less round than they were. Her cheekbones stand out like a grownup's, the circles under her eyes make her eyelids seem sunken in, and her lips have thinned out, making her look more and more like her mother. Ximena's mother is upset, but draws strength from thinking that within a few days Casilda's parents will come and get her.

When they go to the post office, Ximena no longer has to run to keep up with her. She has even dared to take hold of her hand as they cross the bridge without her cousin protesting or shaking her hand loose. Casilda's hand, fuller than her mother's, softer than Ama Grande's, does not pull away from the touch of the little fingers that seek hers. Feeling her hand, Ximena senses that she is touching something bland, cold and swollen. When they get to the other side of the bridge, she takes her hand back even though Casilda doesn't seem to care, and she rubs it on her clothes to clean off the viscous feeling that has stuck to her palm.

Downtown, Casilda walks as though she were at home, distant from everything. Ximena observes that people look at her, raise their eyebrows and whisper to each other when she goes by. Even though she is not very fond of her cousin, she does not like the idea that people are sorry for Casilda and that they might include her, too, in their outsiders' pity. When they get to the post office, the goddaughter waits her turn with hunched shoulders and mutters her name as though the old woman did not have it already tattooed on her memory. Given a negative answer, she no longer insists and defeated, she starts along the route home.

There are nights when Casilda, with the pretext of a headache, goes to bed before she does. While her mother makes her say her prayers in a hushed voice so as not to bother her, Casilda does not move and one would think her asleep. But a little later Ximena hears her sobbing and it is then that she asks God not to pay any attention to all the bad things she has wished for her cousin and that now all she is asking is that whoever is coming to get her should hurry up.

Two days before her aunt and uncle come from the farm, at suppertime they cannot find Casilda anywhere. They call the neighbors but they have not seen her go by. They call her father at his office and he asks around and calls back saying that no one has seen her walking toward the post office. Her mother goes out to the front doorstep, and as though it were sunny, shades her forehead with her hand, learns forward and squints her eyes to see if she can spot her along the highway. But there is no one anywhere along the straight unpaved roadbed, no one in the distance from where the darkness advances dense and heavy with its coppery cold. In the silence of the house, the cuckoo announces that it is late. Ama Grande makes an effort to remain calm.

"A young girl's whims," she offers without much conviction, "she'll turn up when she's hungry."

Ximena looks for her as though they were playing hide-and-seek. Under the beds, behind the armchair, back of the living room curtains, in the wardrobes. She opens forbidden cupboards where her cousin could not possibly fit, and stimulated by the excitement of the game, she runs from one place to another calling out.

"Casilda, are you here?"

She is about to open a cupboard in the pantry when through the window she sees the shed in the courtyard where they keep tools, the cart for firewood, and discarded old things that are piled up under the spiderwebs and years of dust.

"She must be hiding there," Ximena shivers with the anticipation of having guessed right. "She isn't afraid of the bugs, and she must have gone in there."

She runs out to the courtyard without the two women noticing her absence and she opens the door which is ajar and never closes completely. The wood creaks and the rusty hinges squeal. It is very dark inside and she has to wait a few seconds for her eyes to adjust to the creepy dimness that has always made her uneasy. She raises her arms so that the spiderwebs will not get tangled in her hair and she keeps her eye cautiously on the rickety floor because she is afraid of falling and even worse, because she imagines that a mouse might run between her legs.

And that is how, before she sees Casilda, she discovers the oozy spot under her feet. She looks up and on one side, almost brushing her with her foot, she sees her cousin half reclined between two boxes, her eyes closed, her head tipped over onto one shoulder, From her two wrists, the blood flows in uniform ribbons, across her palms and through her fingers, and drips down on the sides until it joins into a single stream and forms a thick puddle that extends right up to Ximena's feet.

Immobile, feeling that her knees are weak and are going to buckle any minute, Ximena wants to escape to the courtyard, but instead of turning around, involuntarily she takes two steps forward. Her shoes bump into Casilda's leg. To her left, on top of some old boards, Ximena sees, incomprehendingly, some pages of writing paper, the pen the goddaughter uses to write, and on top of the little bottle of laudanum that she recognizes right away, a razor. She wants to run, but she cannot; her legs are too heavy and weigh down every step and when she turns her head to see if they are chasing her, she realizes in horror that her footprints have left bloodstains on the dry earth of the courtyard.

She hears the voice of her mother who is coming toward her, and she sees the outline of Ama Grande who waits for her with open arms in the kitchen doorway. Her mother lifts her up just as Ximena, weak and faltering, in the moment before panic makes her faint, tells her that they must flee quickly, very quickly, because the Germans are surrounding the house right that minute and they have drained out Casilda's blood.

III / THE COUSINS

The house is turned upside down. The servants run back and forth, coming in one door, going out another. Her mother, a red kerchief tied over her hair, orders, pleads, and argues. Two barefoot field workers heave bucketfuls of water over the patio paving stones even though they gleamed that morning after last night's rain. Every time Ximena thinks they are finally finished, because she hears the servants stop to chat in some dark corner of the passageway, her mother's voice rings out clearly from some nearby room, calling them, telling them urgently that it would be better if they took this one off and please hurry and put this one on. When there is nothing left to clean, polish or dust, she asks them to go pick flowers in the garden, and then, seated in the huge dining room, which makes her seem smaller because of Grandfather's massive dark furniture, faded by the light that streams in through the high windows, she selects vases of various sizes, looks at them over and over again, considering, imagining, biting her lips in the effort to choose between silver, ceramic or crystal containers. Ximena already knows that her mother will take forever to get the flowers arranged in a way that pleases her and that, then, for a few seconds, reassured, she will pace up and down, sighing with contentment. Then, thoughtfully, she will straighten this painting or that one, but before she admits that she is done, that the tasks of the last few days have finally been completed, she will remember some detail and frantically summon the servants again until some force outside herself makes her stop at last.

"That's enough!" yells Ximena without noticing that she has raised her voice. The tornado in which her mother spins is suffocating her. But her mother looks at her without seeing her, as though Ximena were one more table or chair, already dusted and set back in its proper place. She blows her a kiss and says that no, there is a lot left to do yet, please don't complain like her father does, and would she go ask Ama Grande or any one of the servants to comb her hair and exchange her overalls for a cleaner pair because the cousins from Lima will be arriving any minute now.

The cousins from Lima! No one has talked about anything else for days. After resolving the mystery of which shoe and which sleeve goes on the right or the left, and after putting up with Paulina's rough hands yanking at her hair, Ximena carries the photo album over to the new bench that has just been put out in the summerhouse in the garden in order to please her. All that is left of the summerhouse is its outer shell, broken and rough boards that have lost most of their white paint and now just function as a trellis for a tangle of blue morning glories. Ximena looks first for the photo of her mother, the one where she is wearing a strange dress from the olden days, very short, with the waist way down at her hipline. Her only jewelry is a chain wrapped around her forehead, and in her hands she is holding a book and a crimson rose, a dark blotch against the light sepia of the rest of the photo. She is sitting there, on the solid white steps of that very same summerhouse. Ximena loses herself for a few moments in that borrowed memory and then she turns the pages looking for pictures of the Lima cousins.

There they are in one of the photos, though not in the garden, but rather in the doorway of Grandfather's house, the same house her mother has been bustling around in all day. Ximena is with her cousins, all three of them looking unwillingly at the camera, small, dwarfed by the massive doorway that frames them. She can't remember that day and the photo does not bring her a clear mental picture of those children. She does not remember them, does not recognize them. Even though she is very little in that photo, she knows it is her because she has learned how to recognize herself in pictures through her mother's or Ama Grande's words, when they point her out with their index fingers and proclaim "here you are." Edmundo is in the middle, and she and Cintia are on either side. Ximena shivers: she will have to make a big effort and not call them Elmundo or Cinta, or she will suffer the huge embarrassment of their thinking she is dimwitted. How skinny and feeble she looks when she compares herself to her cousin! Cintia has light hair, rounded legs and a gauzy dress. Edmundo, on the other hand, is dark haired and much taller than either of them.

Ximena closes the album. Her palms are sweating because she knows they will be coming soon and she does not remember them. She doesn't know them and there are two of them coming, brother and sister. And the grownups will make her kiss them one at a time while the other one, over to one side, will watch them and especially watch her. The cousins will have secrets, who knows how many secrets, how many games, how many photos in common.

A passing bee brushes against her hair. She holds her breath and then follows it with her eyes, very quietly, without moving, while the bee flutters within the yellow and white center of a blue flower and then goes flying off, vibrantly alive and golden, tracing ever wider circles, farther and farther until it is lost to sight among the broom flowers over at the edge of the garden.

Before she even greets her Aunt Constanza, before she focuses on Edmundo, Ximena is paralyzed by Cintia's corkscrew curls. They are golden rolls that hang down below her shoulders, and to one side of her forehead a cluster of curls are held by a blue bow that matches her dress. She has made the long journey from the coast in a party dress and without overalls. They have both changed a lot; they don't look at all like the two children in the photo. Ximena is surprised that Edmundo is almost as slender as she is, and that he is hardly any taller than his sister. Only Cintia still has the soft-curved doll-like arms, legs and cheeks. When she kisses her, she realizes with amazement that Cintia is wearing perfume like a grownup woman. All three feel uncomfortable; they dart furtive looks at each other while her aunt and her mother exchange updates about them. Aunt Constanza, laughing ostentatiously, pretends to protest her mother's compliments as she admires Cintia. Ximena, embarrassed, listens to the descriptions of herself; yes, she is still having bronchial problems; yes, there seems to be no way to fatten her up; yes, she has her father's eyes; yes, she is still an only child. She has never before been aware of such lack of brothers and sisters, or felt so ridiculous in these baggy everyday overalls she usually wears when they are staying in the valley.

Ximena's mother's daily routines, and the plans she has made for her cousins' visit, are abandoned one after another. Aunt Constanza gets up late, spends hours getting dressed and fixing Cintia's hair. Edmundo gets up early to go out with Grandfather and Uncle Jorge on their rounds of the hacienda, but the other two appear for breakfast when it is almost lunchtime. Aunt Constanza drinks cup after cup of black coffee and smokes lots of cigarettes while she talks. Cintia accepts everything she is offered. She even eats the nasty badly-fried eggs without gagging. When she finally finishes, she wipes her lips carefully with her napkin and crosses her silverware on her plate, waiting for instructions. It is then that her mother says "Go on and walk around a bit in order to help you digest, and then go practice the piano."

The two go off together to the garden to look at the rabbits, the guinea pigs, the hens and the ducks by the pond. The servants and the field workers always stop what they are doing and stare every time they see her go by with her elaborately bejeweled hair and her fancy dresses. Intimidated at first, Ximena stops feeling so shy after the first two days. She assumes the role of guide and introduces her to the wonders of the valley. Since Cintia listens to her open-mouthed and asks unconnected questions every once in a while, Ximena is easily sidetracked from fact and says whatever comes into her head. This way she forgets to envy the rendition of "Für Elise" that her cousin plays on the old out-of-tune piano. And this way she can also manage to forget about those pastel dresses Cintia never dirties and that good appetite that so surprises her mother and Ama Grande. But above all, at those times she forgets to envy her her blond curls, those thirty six golden curls, even without counting the others that are tied back by the hair ribbon. Ximena would like to smell them, touch them, feel their texture with her fingertips, pull their tips down in order to see them spring back up as though they were alive. But just like flies that are adapted for flight, with their thousand eyes that see in all directions, when Ximena sneaks a trembling hand up behind Cintia's back, Cintia, who is usually so passive, reacts violently:

"Don't touch me! You're going to muss up my hair!" she protests angrily. Ximena's hand only manages to brush up against a face that, in anger, bears a startling resemblance to her brother's sharp features.

They are bored together. Under her mother's strict supervision,

Cintia spends a lot of time at the piano, whimpering that it is not her fault if the notes sound flat, insisting that the piano is no good even though it looks fine. She does not like having stories read to her nor is she interested in looking at the beautiful illustrations in Grandfather's books nor at the photo albums. Nothing will lure her into the kitchen to hear the wonderful stories Paulina or Raimunda tell while they make blancmange or skillfully chop up vegetables.

"It's filthy!" she complains when Ximena tries to coax her into that dark corner where fantasy blends with the kettle's steam. She is afraid to brush up against the soot that darkens the walls, or go near the garbage pile over which flies hover happily, and she does not know how to appreciate the half spicy half sweet odors of curing meat nor those of the immense oven from which their sesame seed rolls emerge as well as the servants' flat bread. And she is a scaredy-cat besides. She is scared of Uncle Jorge because his hugs are rough and he has such a loud laugh. She is scared of Grandfather because he is the tallest man in the world and because he has thick gray eyebrows all across his forehead over his hard lead-colored eyes. She is scared of the field workers because they smile and speak to her in Quechua, and of the servants who, like Ximena, sometimes want to touch her hair. Ximena has disappointed her cousin, too. She has never learned how to play jacks, and dolls bore her.

Frustrated, they hang around their mothers and interrupt their lively chatter. They lean up against them, they pull at their hands and dresses.

"Oh, for heaven's sake, go out and play! Find something to do!" they tell them. And since they don't move, the grownups are forced to speak in code and without using people's names, until the girls finally go off.

One morning when they are petting the baby rabbits, Ximena suggests that they should hide and eavesdrop on the grownups' secret conversations. Cintia refuses flat out. "No, we can't do that, because God will see us and punish us," she whispers into Ximena's ear.

Ximena tries to convince her that nothing will happen to them, but to no avail. She gives up because her cousin threatens to tell on her to her mother. "Tell me about the ocean," she says then, to change the subject.

"The ocean is huge and scarey because you can't see the shore on the other side."

"Tell me something more," begs Ximena.

"If you aren't careful, the waves will knock you down and pull you under."

"And what else?" she asks her.

"The sand is nasty because it sticks to your skin and makes you itch."

"And what about the sirens and water spirits and magic fish?"

Cintia puts her face right up close to her cousin's, and Ximena breathes the fragrance of her perfume. "No, there is nothing like that in Lima, but on every beach in the world, children who tell lies are drowned."

Ximena knows her cousin is referring to her. "Someday I'm going to lock you up in Crazy Grandmother's room," she threatens, pointing to the rooms you can only get to by going up the forbidden stairs without any guard rail, on the left hand side of the garden.

"Nobody lives there, and anyway, Edmundo would tear you to shreds," answers Cintia scornfully and she smiles triumphantly, thinking that it is fear that suddenly darkens Ximena's eyes.

The men have gone off on a trip, and Edmundo spends more time with the girls. He teaches them how to play dodgeball but Cintia always loses or cries when the ball hits her hard on the legs. Then they play hide-and-seek, but the cousins give up quickly. Ximena knows every inch of the house and all the best hiding places in the garden. She knows which tree trunks are hollowed out by age, and she knows where the discarded barrels are, covered with moss, hidden in the bushes. She goes right to the darkest corners of the henhouse and without being afraid of being scratched by branches, she knows how to make herself invisible in the thorny underbrush. Edmundo, humiliated, vents his anger on her and insults her. "Skinny little snot, disgusting snob, dwarf skeleton!" he yells at her and lowering his voice menacingly, he growls, "You're going to die soon because you've got TB."

Ximena holds up under these attacks with a show of apparent serenity. She can't remember a time when her breathing didn't sound raspy, and she is so accustomed to asthma that it feels like her own skin. The jibes at her skinniness do hurt her feelings but not seriously. She realizes that she feels as indifferent as she has pretended to be. What she resents the most is being called a snot. Not because of what it might mean—someone has explained it to her, laughingly, vaguely—but because the sound of the word disgusts her to the point of making the hairs on her arms bristle up straight in goosebumps. On these occasions, she turns around and leaves Cintia looking startled and Edmundo, still furious, spluttering nonsense.

During the times when Cintia is practicing the piano or when she insists on staying next to Aunt Constanza, Edmundo goes out into the garden alone. From the dining room or from her room, Ximena spies on him through the window. She sees how he tries to hit birds with his slingshot; she watches him hunt for birds' nests, torture bugs and scare the hens with a stick. Sometimes, climbing up in a tree, he smashes the weakest and smallest branches as though he were discharging stored up rage. Then afterward he comes into the house sweating and shivering, and asks for water. They see him come in dirty and scratched up, with threads of blood streaking down from his skinned knees and always with a new rip in his pants. Without a fuss, Aunt Constanza wipes the sweat and dirt from his face and hair. Ximena has given up hoping that they will scold him.

One afternoon, they are sitting on the bench in the summerhouse peacefully eating lumps of brown sugar. Edmundo holds a piece of a thick branch he has turned into an official-looking staff by polishing it, with the help of the *pongo*. He has even put on a layer of varnish, and he does not let it out of his sight for a moment. "I am the Mayor of the garden," he proclaims. Ever since he saw the pictures of a southern village council meeting, on Grandfather's desk, he has been imitating the gestures and poses of the town elders. At first he went around asking them to take him to see an Indian village council meeting, and he was only now beginning to be convinced that around here there is no *varayok* gathering like the one in the photos. That afternoon, as soon as they have finished their brown sugar, they run to the cistern to rinse off their hands. Leaning on his staff, Edmundo twists his lips into an authoritative grimace. "I've thought of a game, but you," he says turning to Ximena, "have to promise not to tell."

She agrees eagerly.

"Is there someplace in the garden that is out of view of the workmen and of the house?" he asks with a commanding expression.

Ximena leads them to the very back of the garden. On the left there is an adobe and stone wall that separates Grandfather's property from the road that winds up past the neighboring fields. There is dense myrtle growing all along the wall, on the garden side. Where the wall ends, at the edge of the garden, there are lots of eucalyptus trees and woven among them, straggling climbing roses that no one fertilizes or tends. Ximena goes to this clearing to eat the candy she steals and to quietly think over the servants' stories. It is there that she dreams up her adventures, there that she lets herself be floated up to the clouds by condors who will turn into princes, there that she makes pacts with both benign and malign elves who live in brooks and caves, there that she allies herself with the spirit of trees in order to fortify herself against grownup injustices. She likes to stretch out on her stomach on the ground and breathe in the smell of decaying leaves on the warm and slightly humid earth; she likes to feel the little snowy eucalyptus nuts trapped under the weight of her body, poking her gently. She shivers, absorbing through her pores the wind which carries the joyfulness of the valley and which smells of the greenness of the country and of cattle manure.

Edmundo peers around him with a satisfied look. "This is fine. It will do," he says, leaning on his staff. After a pause, he adds pompously, "I am the Mayor. You are my wives and you have to obey me. Take off your underpants."

Ximena is on the brink of refusing and arguing that in the photos of town council meetings there are no women, but at that instant, she realizes that Cintia, after looking around cautiously, is beginning to pull hers down, unperturbed. When they are down to her knees, she shakes her body until they slip down onto her shoes. "I can't do it," protests Ximena, "I'm wearing overalls!"

"Yes, you can," orders Edmundo. With the tip of his staff he points to her shoulder straps. "Unbutton them."

Ximena is reluctant.

"If you don't, " he threatens, coming up close and brandishing his staff over his cousin's head. "If you don't, I'll make mincemeat of you. And it won't do any good to tell on me because the two of us will say that you are lying again."

The overalls come down right away. Cintia tilts her head to one side and waits.

"Now pull down your underpants," he orders, pointing again at her underwear with his staff.

"What about her?" asks Ximena in alarm. "You can't see a thing."

"It doesn't matter. When you pull down your pants, she'll lift up her dress."

Lifting her dress by the hem as if she were going to make a curtsy, Cintia pulls it up above her navel. For the first time, Ximena feels the open air caress her thighs and legs. The two look at each other curiously. In that instant, Ximena thinks that she has never consciously looked at her sexual parts, not even in the tub when they bathe her. Often at night, pulling her knees up to her chest, she puts her hands between her thighs to feel the heat between her legs, and in the cold darkness of the room, curled under the blankets, the odor that emanates from her own body consoles her.

"You're the same," he pronounces, disappointed. "Now get dressed."

"And you?" asks his sister in surprise. "What about you? Now it's your turn."

"Not now. Next time," he promises. Then he tells them that now they will do the Redskin Dance. Without difficulty, he plants the staff upright in the center of the clearing and begins to jump rhythmically, bending over, leaping up, slapping his mouth with his hand at intervals to make loud war cries. Behind him, Cintia and Ximena imitate him. Cintia follows him along, making shorter hops, but without losing the beat. Ximena keeps getting it wrong because she gets too close to Cintia, attracted by the curls bobbing up and down with the dance movement. When they brush against Ximena's forehead, it makes her lose track of the game and feel dizzy and distracted. Without laughing or speaking, they hop around for a long time, hypnotized by the small circle they follow. When the staff wobbles and seems about to fall, Edmundo catches it in time and gives the order to stop. Panting, they head back to the house.

Edmundo halts under the peach tree that grows right close to the patio. He looks directly at Ximena, fixing his little caramel eyes on her. "You already know. Not a word to anybody."

That night, before going to bed, Ximena corners Cintia against the wall in the hall that leads to the bedrooms. "Aren't you afraid that God will punish us?"

"No," replies Cintia calmly. "Don't be stupid. Edmundo says that God doesn't mind about these things because we're all related."

The next time they go to the secret place, they do the same thing again. The two of them take off their underpants and wait for him to examine them attentively. Then he plants the staff in the dirt on his left, and begins to pull down first his pants and then his little white underpants. Ximena looks at his penis appalled. "How ugly!" she thinks, without being able to take her eyes off it. Suddenly she feels her whole body fill with a crazy desire to laugh out loud, but Edmundo is too close, with his mayor's scowl, and his staff right beside him. They remain like that, half naked, gazing at each other without breathing. A finch's song pulls them out of their trance, and as though it were a signal, the three of them dress in silence.

As they are heading for home, Ximena, alert again, thinks about her cousin's body, about his thin, hard legs, and about that small lumpy thing knotted between his thighs. In sudden horror, she realizes that they must all be like that, that her father, her uncle, her grandfather, the field workers, all of them, every one of them, must walk around all day long with that uncomfortable dangling thing attached to their bodies. A smothered cry pulls her brusquely out of her reverie. They are near the summerhouse and a bee is hovering over Cintia's hair. Edmundo quickly steps off to one side. "Edmundo! Help me!" pleads Cintia, terrified.

"Don't move," advises Ximena. "It has gotten tangled in your hair. Let me get it off you."

The bee dances for a few moments on the yellow ribbon and eventually flies on. Cintia has closed her eyes. "Get it away from me!" she implores.

Ximena takes advantage of the moment and gently puts her fingers into the golden curls. She pulls them just a little, lets them go, strokes the insides of the rolls, and lets them wrap around her hand. Edmundo, almost to the patio, turns around toward them. Only then does Ximena withdraw her hands, reluctantly. "Now you can walk," she murmurs.

They go back together and Ximena feels lighthearted, happy.

Uncle Jorge is sitting on the old tree trunk that serves as a bench under the peach tree. He moves over and gestures to Ximena to come sit next to him. Before she dares, she looks all about to see if her mother is anywhere around. It is late afternoon and a cool, fragrant breeze has begun to blow. The hens are quiet at that hour, and the voices of people coming up the coast road do not reach them, nor does the sad sound of old truck motors chugging up the steep grade. Even the birds are silent. Ximena listens more carefully, then, comforted, she breathes in the smell of the eucalyptus and of the nearby flocks of sheep, and with pleasure that seems ever fresh to her, she listens to the noisy chorus of the crickets.

She sits down on her uncle's firm thigh. He is smoking, blowing out great puffs. "Niece," he says to her, "why don't you keep me company—I have to go to a First Haircut."

Ximena sighs without answering. They both know that she will not be allowed to go with him. Ximena does not understand why a First Haircut for an Indian boy is such a ritual, and she is surprised that she has never thought to ask him before. Uncle Jorge, who has been watching her through the cloud of smoke, roars with laughter. "It is an important occasion, niece. Kind of like a Christening or a First

Communion. A boy stops being a baby. Some of his childhood gets cut off along with his hair. From that moment on, he will take his responsibilities more seriously, he will be stronger, he will learn what it means to be a man."

"What about Samson?" she remembers to ask.

"Ah, niece! They have told you that story backward! Delilah loved Samson and knew that his hair weighed a thousand years. That's why she cut it off and the two of them ran away jumping over the stones of the brooks; they escaped from their enemies singing a song about lovers, pretending to chase a frightened little fawn among the mountains and rivers until they got to a great bed of flowers where they became man and wife. That story about how Samson tore down the temple columns with his own hands is something shoemakers made up."

Ximena thinks this over without deciding whether to accept this new version. Her uncle's laugh rings out over the garden; even the branches shake, it is so loud. He gets to his feet, picking her up with one arm. "You don't weigh a thing," he says to her, kissing her awkwardly on the cheek. With his free hand, he pulls out a small well-worn chamois bag, and without setting Ximena down, he opens it and spills out some tiny gold coins into his huge palm. "A coin for every shorn lock," he calculates. "Choose one for yourself and let's hope it brings you luck."

Ximena looks at them, gleaming against his rough and hardened skin. She has never seen a palm with such a deep network of lines. The coins are almost orange-colored and when he moves them they jingle like little deaf bells.

"Give me two," she asks. "That way I can give one to Cintia."

"To Cintia?" he starts laughing again, jiggling her and making the coins jingle even more. "What would Cintia want them for? She's already got all the gold in the world on her own head."

Ximena feels confused. "They are calling me," she lies, and she frees herself from the rough embrace to go running toward the house with her hands empty.

That morning, before they go in to have breakfast, Aunt Constanza washes Cintia's hair. They close themselves into the bathroom for a very long time, an eternity chopped up by the sounds of her cousin's complaints. "Don't put on any more of that!" she pleads, whimpering. "It makes me feel sick."

Ximena and her mother, tired of waiting, have had to use the servants' toilet, back of the henhouse. When Cintia emerges from the bathroom, she is wearing a pink bathrobe and plush slippers, with a towel wrapped around her head like a turban. Her eyes are swollen and she is pale. To Ximena she looks like a grownup woman shrunk down in size.

"Have breakfast quickly and let's go to the garden," she suggests to her.

"I can't; I have to wait until the camomile and lemon rinse has a chance to work. And then, when my hair is still damp, my mother will take a long time to roll up my curls. You go on ahead," she says resignedly.

Edmundo is walking through the garden as if he had lost something.

"What are you looking for?"

"I'm looking for a special place because this afternoon we are going to do something important. Very important," he says, puffing out his chest and making the words emphatic.

What else can there be to do? Recently Edmundo has been ordering them to touch him. He doesn't have to insist. The two of them, barely suppressing the nervous laughter that shakes them, reach out their hands to caress that miniscule protuberance that reacts to touch. The Redskin Dance has gotten more complicated. With black-berries, cherries, and the pollen of certain flowers, they paint their faces and sometimes their sexual parts. When Edmundo signals, they march in Indian file to the cistern and there, without speaking, they wash off before they go back to the house. Grateful for the chance, Ximena gathers Cintia's curls with her two hands to make it easier for her to wash. Later on the two of them go into the bathroom and unit-ed in complicity and rattled by fear and the need to hurry, they clean off the rest of their bodies.

"This afternoon I am going to die," proclaims Edmundo. Ximena is startled.

"Don't worry about it. I am the Mayor and I will come to life again. In the meantime I have to find the place where I will be buried."

While the grownups take their afternoon naps, as Edmundo digs determinedly in the earth behind the shrubs that shed aromatic pink flowers, the girls strip branches, gather leaves, alfalfa, and handfuls of coarse highland grass. It is very hot. All three of them are sweating and they are flushed. Cintia's just-washed hair looks very blond and gleams against the light like an aureole. Exhausted, Edmundo stops shoveling. "That's enough," he decides. "Stay on guard to let me know if anyone is coming."

He starts undressing slowly while each one of them watches over a section of the garden, which is usually empty at this time of day. When he is completely naked, he takes a small folded paper out of one of his pants pockets and buries it in the place where he has dug just enough so that he can fit his body into the space. Rigid, his eyes in a trance, he has one hand resting on his staff and with the other, palm side down, he points to the sky. "May your will be done," he exclaims and suddenly falls on his knees as though he had been invis-ibly wounded in the back. He rolls on the ground, contracting himself, making horrible faces, relaxing little by little, and straightening his limbs until he is stretched out at full length, immobile, his arms crossed over his chest, which is covered with earth.

The two of them moan and tear their hair the way he told them to, before the game began. They howl hoarsely so as not to make too much noise, and those smothered cries are so strange that it scares them and they start to cry for real.

They cover him up with all the things they have gathered. On their knees next to the burial mound, Cintia and Ximena crouch and wait fearfully for a long time that buzzes in their ears.

"We'd better dig him up," suggests Ximena. "He's going to smother."

But Cintia has her head tipped to one side, in a gesture that is characteristic of her, and her eyelids are lowered as though she were not listening. She is kneeling beside Ximena, her white embroidered piqué dress still spotless, without a single trace of green or of dust. Ximena thinks that any minute now Cintia is going to fall asleep by her brother's tomb. Suddenly, who knows from where, Paulina appears in front of them. "What are you doing? Praying?" she laughs. In her hands she is holding a white colander full of garbage for the garden compost. "Are you playing bonfire? Or making a roasting pit for a picnic? Do you need some matches?"

"No!" they both yell in unison and look over to see if the burial mound has moved. Everything is still immobile, even Paulina herself who for a few instants has been frozen like a bucolic statue with the colander now resting against one hip. Intrigued, she looks at the low mound at her feet.

"Go throw the peels in the garbage. What are you waiting for?" Ximena orders her imperiously. "We want to play by ourselves."

Rather than stepping back, Paulina stoops down to examine the tomb more closely.

"Didn't you hear me? Go away!"

The maid finally goes off, humming a cheerful song. Only when she has disappeared among the trees behind the henhouse do the two turn their attention again to Edmundo.

"Do you think he's died for real?"

With Paulina's unexpected appearance, Ximena has forgotten the signal they had agreed upon which would indicate the lifting off of the coverings of grass and branches.

Just after Cintia murmurs that they had better wait, a slight movement shakes the top layer of leaves. They lean over worriedly and suddenly the wind begins to blow hard, the leaves are caught up in a whirlwind that knocks the two of them backwards. Getting over their fright, they come close, pull the branches apart, and Edmundo rises up. The layer of earth on his skin makes his ribs stand out, and parts of his body are shadowed with dust, giving him a ghost-like appearance. His face is splotched greeney-yellow and some plants cling to his forehead, like a withered crown. For the time being, he does not spit out the bits of clay stuck between his lips that deform his mouth into a grotesque smile. The two come up to him and clean him off, praise him, and clap their hands in joy, just as they had agreed. On his feet, stiffly erect, he holds onto his staff. The dirt has left his hands a terra cotta color and his knuckles gleam white because he is clenching the staff so tight. Without looking at them, he begins to get dressed.

Cintia and Ximena dig down to recover the little buried packet. They open up the paper and with the greatest of care they remove dry kernels of corn. They place them on the spot where the corpse had pressed the earth down in its shape, and they arrange the kernels there, laying them down in a figure eight pattern. Then they cover them up with the fine dust that they have made by crumbling clods of clay, and with the palms of their hands they smooth out the soft surface.

During the next three days, Edmundo again goes out from morning until night with Grandfather and Uncle Jorge. The magical adventures of the clandestine games stops, and Cintia and Ximena are bored. Ximena assures her that the two of them could invent interesting situations, too, but Cintia misses her brother a lot. Sometimes Ximena suggests climbing the forbidden stairway and listening at that door which has a brass door knocker on it, in the shape of a woman's hand. Cintia is scared. Aunt Constanza has said something to them about Grandmother's ghost that has made even Edmundo, who pretends not to be interested, refuse to go near there. Then Ximena falls back into her usual behavior during her family's stays in the valley. She curls up in a corner of the kitchen and chewing on toasted corn, she regales the servants with the true history of Samson. In order to hear it all, sometimes the women stop their work and ask her to tell it to them again. Pleased with herself, she adorns her version of the story with elaborate details and mixes in episodes from other tales. When it is their turn, the servants tell her again about the true adventure of the condor, who fell in love with a very beautiful girl and carried her off to his cold haunts on the moon, and the story of the unpredictable and playful water elf who lived in a stream and demanded small or big offerings, depending on his whim, as payment for his miracles. While one is speaking, the other servant, whenever there is a suspenseful pause, acts as a chorus, repeating the last words and crying out in sad laments or in joyous exclamations.

When they do not want her in the kitchen any longer, she goes to gaze at the pen and ink drawings and the illustrations in Grandfather's old books. She sees exotic women wearing extraordinary costumes, set in the midst of unreal landscapes. They all look quite similar to each other, except that they have different hair styles, but not one of them has hair as beautiful as Cintia's. She goes through the family photographs again looking to see if among all of those relatives, most of whom are dead by now, she can find some aunt with curls like her cousin's. Crazy Grandmother, when she was young, is the prettiest. She must have had light hair, too, although in the photo she is wearing it austerely piled on her head despite her mocking eyes and her dimpled smile. Before she goes to sleep at night, Ximena tries to imagine how she herself would look in Cintia's curls. She can daydream about a lot of things, but no matter how hard she squeezes her eyelids tight in order to concentrate, she cannot manage to see herself with her cousin's blond curly hair. And if for one fleeting second she succeeds in capturing the desired fantasy, she has to admit that she looks ridiculous. Her concentration breaks as she drifts into sleep, and she is left with scattered images of Cintia's warm corkscrew curls that wrap around her as the haze claims her.

On the third day, Edmundo does not go off with the men. The night before, in the passageway that leads to the bedrooms, he has let them know that he has a great idea for tomorrow's game. Lunchtime seems to last forever because they are so eager to get out into the garden. Edmundo, with his usual gruffness, tells them to wait for him over by the wall, that he won't be long. Pretty soon they see him approaching with his slow self-important walk. As always, he holds his staff in one hand and with the other he is carrying something under his sweater. Solemnly he undoes two buttons and pulls out a yellow duckling, very quiet, with its eyes open and unblinking. It is a ball of golden fluff and so small it looks miniscule in Edmundo's nervous hand. The two girls gaze at it eagerly.

"You shouldn't have separated it from its mother. Now she will reject it," Ximena scolds.

"It doesn't matter. She won't see it again anyway because we're going to sacrifice it."

Neither Cintia nor Ximena understands what that word means.

"Can I carry it, too?" asks Cintia.

Edmundo shakes his head negatively. "It is sacred from now on," he answers. "Only I can touch it."

He takes a few steps and stops in the very center of the clearing. He plants his staff next to him. With his free hand he makes some mysterious gestures and his face takes on the distant quality it sometimes does. "Kneel down!" Edmundo commands. His voice is so imposing that they do not dare to contradict him and they obey immediately. "You have to look, otherwise the sacrifice doesn't count." He looks hard at each of them in turn. His eyes are feverish and something cruel and fanatic is concentrated in his enlarged pupils. Ximena wonders whether through some sort of secret magic her cousin is turning into a cat or a bird of prey. Skillfully, Edmundo pulls out a penknife and clenches it in his fist after he has managed one-handedly to open out the blade.

She has understood and has to try with all her might to not let a growing suffocation cut off her breathing. She tries to inhale deeply without coughing. "Don't do it!" she thinks she manages to say. But no sound comes out, and she is, like Cintia beside her, frozen into paralyzed silence. Edmundo has turned pale and both of them feel the same chill sweep through them when they see that suddenly he has gone from being himself to becoming that other, who, as on other occasions, is a total stranger to them. He loosens his grip and the duckling opens its wings a little in a feeble attempt at flight. Recovering a bit, it moves its head, and for a few instants its invisible eyelids seem to close, very briefly. Edmundo, at the mercy of unknown powers, obeys the dictate of his hands. With the point of his knife he finds the center point of the blond chest that has fluffed up just then as the duckling, fully conscious again, frantically tries to escape. But it is easier to cut earthworms, pull off butterflies' wings, amputate bumblebees' legs, or finish off the dying birds wounded by his slingshot.

The point of the blade is not sharp enough, and goes in with difficulty. A slight sound, barely a crunch, can be heard in a silence so pure that not even the eucalyptus branches soften it to keep it from filling the air. Edmundo's hands tremble from the effort. For a few seconds that seem interminable, the animal still moves, beats its wings rhythmically and keeps its head erect. Her cousin yanks out the stained blade. It is only after a few more equally painful seconds that blood begins to run over his hand. Stupefied, Ximena and Cintia's eyes move back and forth between that bloody hand and the boy's aged, weary face. He does look like a mayor now, and they do not know which of his two selves frightens them more and they do not have time to escape in order to stop seeing because this whole eternity only lasts as long as the cry that fills their lungs and is held in suspension there because Edmundo is advancing upon them, leaning on his staff, and he leads them to the place where a few days before he had died and been resurrected alive from under the leaves.

Without exchanging a word, they bury the duckling. Once again, Edmundo asks them to swear to keep the secret, and the three of them start to walk back. The sacrifice has tired him out, but even with his head hanging and his shoulders stooped, he only has to crook a finger to indicate that they should follow him. Neither of the two moves, and he starts off alone, putting his weight on his staff as he walks along. When he is out of sight, Ximena looks for a stone the size of her open hand. She places it in the center of the burial mound.

"What if it comes back to life?" asks Cintia.

"It will never come back to life. You put a stone there, too, so the place will be truly sacred."

When night falls, Aunt Constanza finds the two of them weeping under the peach tree. "What is wrong?" she asks, looking at Cintia. "Who has made you cry?"

Their only response is to cry harder. Aunt Constanza wipes their noses and their faces with a handkerchief printed with faded violets. "Tell me. Who has caused this?"

They do not answer, and then she drags them toward the house by the arms.

"Stupid, nasty Indians! They have scared you with those demonic stories that have twisted Ximena's mind!"

They no longer play in the secret place. When Edmundo does not go out with the men, he goes back to his earlier amusements and keeps busy alone in the garden. Since the afternoon of the sacrifice, his rituals hold neither the interest nor the intensity they had before. They have managed to return to the clearing, but even in the wild Redskin Dance, the two girls step through the paces mechanically, lifelessly. Ximena and Cintia, without consulting Edmundo, have continued to venerate the place and have been piling up stones into a pyramid. He has not asked questions, but when he is with them, he is noticeably taciturn. He is surly with Ximena; he watches her and listens to her suspiciously, and when they play games he tries to stir up discord between the two girls. Cintia, docile with him, lets herself be trapped by his ploys, and she is willing to turn against Ximena, in order to follow him. But something about her attitude has changed. Over and over again Edmundo has been left perplexed or furious because his sister has given him a terse and definite "No"—seriously, but without any intent to hurt him.

The days follow one another, colorless, long, and insipid. It is hard for Ximena to take refuge in her own familiar world because Cintia's presence, and her very indifference, break into it and rip open that world which inexplicably yearns to turn itself into a place that includes Cintia, or at least expand itself so that she can inhabit it, too, with her yellow corkscrew curls and her party dresses, with the stubborn opacity that covers her and seals her deep within her hazel irises.

One Sunday morning the three are given an unexpected allowance bonus so they can go to town and buy treats. In all those days they have never gone out by themselves to walk around the little plaza in front of the church. Where a few years ago there was an arcade with restaurants and little shops, recently a new hotel has taken over. Ximena still has some memories of the old pillars, the small round tables made of dark wood, the chairs carved with high backs where gentlemen with hats and canes sat and conversed while they drank apérififs and ate olives that were brought in jars all the way from the coast. The new hotel is a simple construction with two floors, windows with wrought iron bars, and a red tile roof. It is empty most of the time because there is nothing to attract tourists. Those who stay over there, stop for just one night, on their way to join tours of the jungle. They arrive with altitude sickness, with cameras hanging around their necks. They stroll around the little plaza, they take photos of the Indian women in the market, and sleepily they return to the hotel to gaze at the pool which is covered with leaves and stagnant in its immobile gray green.

Since the cousins have come down to the valley, they have only gone into town to go to mass. That Sunday afternoon they encourage them to go out so that Cintia won't cry because her mother is going to go horseback riding with her aunt. The three of them go skipping along, hopping down the dirt path that crosses through the town and then goes down the hill. All along the path there is an irrigation ditch or canal that begins someplace way up the mountainside, maybe behind the Spanish ladies' mansion. The channel is fairly wide and its water is a muddy light brown color. Sometimes it has a bad odor, but sometimes after a heavy rainfall, it smells the same as the wells and the earth. On the other side, paralleling the course of the ditch, and less than a meter from its edge, there is a wall with a cheap straw roof and some very narrow doors set in it at intervals. There are no windows and if it were not for the doors no one would guess that it is lived in by the field workers who come seasonally from other places to look for work here. Gangplanks of thick boards connect the door-ways to the road.

The three of them are walking alongside the ditch. Edmundo, as usual, goes first. He has changed into a new pair of short pants because it is hot and of course he has brought his staff along on this jaunt. Ximena follows him breathing in the smell of the water, paus-ing for a few seconds to see how it runs smoothly along for stretches and suddenly makes little waves. Cintia is quite far behind, com-plaining because her shoes pinch and because it is hard for her to catch up to them. Edmundo throws rocks and dry branches, and he kicks at the dirt along the sides of the ditch so it will fall in, making circles in the water. He finds an empty cigarette pack and throws it in to see it float.

"You shouldn't throw that in," Ximena warns him. "The Indians use this water to water their fields down there, on the other side of town."

"How disgusting!" he answers with a grimace. "Don't you see this isn't clear water?"

"But it isn't dirty," replies Ximena, refusing to accept that it might be a sewage ditch. "The channel starts way up there, up high."

With her finger, she points to the mountains that rise up behind the Spanish ladies' property. The whole valley is ringed by high peaks.

"Oh sure! You think it isn't dirty? Do you want to take a bath in that filth, then?"

He comes up menacingly and begins to shove her with his shoul-der. Ximena takes a few steps back from the edge of the ditch and quickly bends her knees, keeping her feet close together as she takes the jump that will land her on the other side.

Edmundo is left with his mouth open and his staff raised high. Cintia stops where she is with her eyes round, her lips in the shape of the "o" of the "ox" in the alphabet book. Bracing herself against the wall, Ximena takes a deep breath and then keeps on walking.

"Pure luck!" he yells. Then, just before the next gangplank boards, without any space in which to get a head start, Ximena gives another leap that lands her at his side.

"Now it's your turn," she dares. Edmundo does not look at her. He stalks along in front waving his staff back and forth in front of him as though he were blind. Ximena runs up behind him and pulls on his sleeve repeating, "It's your turn!"

"What for?" he answers, ignoring her. "I don't feel like it."

Cintia catches up with them and plants herself in front of her brother, cutting off his way. She is red and panting; her eyes beseech him.

"Jump, Edmundo! Jump! She is going to think that you can't."

He keeps walking on. He has put his free hand in his pants pocket and he spits like a grownup. "Let me pass, idiot. I don't want to."

He speeds along galloping on his staff. He has never before used it as a horse. He steps with the points of his shoes and raises little clouds of reddish dust, then, imitating how old men walk, or maybe just clowning around, he hobbles and limps along the other side of the ditch after crossing on one of the gangplanks.

Cintia yells at him from behind. "Edmundo, for God's sake, jump!" Two big tears are perfectly suspended on her cheeks. She doesn't get ugly when she cries. Her eyes shine more when they fill, and her sweetly pointed little nose retains its nunlike wax color.

"Big deal!" the boy mocks loudly, "Big deal, jumping over a filthy ditch!"

In Indian file, they arrive at the plaza. He goes off, leaving them alone, so he can stroll around, erect and serious, like a dwarf-size gentleman. The two girls go over to a dark kiosk, where they are waited on by a smiling Japanese woman. They buy sugar cookies and a Sublime chocolate bar which they share in silence. Still uncomfortable about what has happened, they sit down on a rustic bench. Edmundo disappears down a narrow alley and they wait for him for a while. Since he does not come back, they decide to return home.

"Aren't you scared of falling into the water?' asks Cintia.

"No. It's the water that gives me courage. There are elves that live in the bottom who sometimes come up to the surface to scramble up the plans human beings have made. They do it to play, though sometimes they can be mean, but they already know me because they baptized me in a magic grotto that appears and disappears depending on what they are dreaming."

Ximena remembers that baptism very vaguely, but she completely hides her father's intervention. Feeling out of place in the valley, a poor companion on Grandfather's and Uncle Jorge's expeditions, and completely excluded by his wife's transformation into an Amazon when she goes horseback riding, her father has taken advantage of the improved health of his daughter's lungs to show her how to run greater and greater distances, timing her with his watch. He teaches her how to jump over brooks and ditches, showing her when and how to bend her legs, insisting that she should concentrate fully on the exact place where her feet will hit the ground. On very cold days the two of them go into the living room where the piano is. He moves the armchairs, the end tables, the Chinese screen, and the various antiques; he spreads open newspapers on the rug and exhorts her to jump, instructing her in all the movements, even in how and when to breathe.

Cintia walks along the very edge of the ditch. She peers at the water every once in a while, calculating the distance, absorbed in thought. When they get to the gate, she pulls on Ximena's sleeve. "Hey," she murmurs. "Do you think I could jump over the ditch?"

"I don't know," she answers, surprised. "Why?"

"I don't know; I don't know, either," repeats Cintia turning around to look at the water once more before she goes into the house.

That night Ximena dreams about labyrinthine gardens. She is on the balcony of a strange, unfamiliar hotel and she wants to find her way through the tangle of paths under tall well-trimmed cypress trees, but the nearby roar of the ocean distracts her. Someone wakes her up, shaking her shoulder gently. "Wake up, Ximena."

It is Cintia, who is standing next to her bed. Ximena thinks that she is part of her dream and that the two are spending the summer at a house on the coast.

"Wake up, Ximena."

She opens her eyes again, and still lulled by the roar of the sea that lingers in her ears, she focuses on her cousin. The curtains are open and the light of a full moon low in the sky falls directly on Cintia. Rather than pajamas like Ximena wears, she has on a long pink flannel nightgown. A white ribbon shirrs the embroidered lace neckline. Her corkscrew curls, half unwound, swirl around her shoulders and catch the light coming through the window. "You look like an angel," murmurs Ximena.

Cintia gets impatient and her voice rises. "I don't want to be an angel. I want to jump over the ditch."

Ximena wakes up completely and is alarmed. Guessing what she is thinking, her cousin calms her.

"My mother is snoring. She has taken two sleeping pills because she wants to look well rested for the party tomorrow."

Then Ximena remembers that there is going to be a dance at the

Cosíos' house the next night.

"I want to jump over the ditch." she insists again, whispering. "What do I have to do?"

"You have to please the elves with a sacrifice."

"Kill another duckling?"

"No. Cut your hair."

Ximena is startled by her own words. She hasn't meant to say them, they have come flying out all by themselves from someplace else. She turns her head and her eyes are caught by the moon that keeps on shining, mercilessly.

Cintia does not answer. She gets off the bed and stands next to it, like before. The windows are closed, but the moonlight floods her nightgown with the shimmer of water. She goes off silently and vanishes into the darkness. Ximena calls her to no avail.

Before going back to sleep, she thinks that this has been an apparition risen out of her dream, and when she remembers the episode in the morning, she is quite sure that she has dreamed about her cousin.

After breakfast, Cintia rebels and refuses to practice the piano. She has a huge argument with Aunt Constanza, who is still lethargic as an aftereffect of the pills, and worried about the details of her hair style for that night. She complains interminably about how in this miserable town there is only one poor excuse for a hair salon, where Indian women go in with their braids and come out with their hair frizzed into a reddish permanent. That day all efforts to keep Cintia in line are cancelled.

The two of them go to the garden. For several days they have had a tacit agreement not to go over and look at the animals. Without talking to each other, keeping together, they head for the summerhouse, climb up the creaking steps, and sit quietly on the bench. In the bluebells, a bee buzzes tenaciously.

"Ximena, I want to jump over the ditch."

Cintia's voice bursts a bubble. It was not a dream after all. She would like to tell her that she will need practice and that her father is not there to train her. But she does not say anything when she sees the muddy waters of the ditch flowing in her cousin's honey chestnut eyes. "Cut my hair, Ximena."

To hide her anxiety, Ximena follows the bee's flight. Cintia touches her arm.

"Listen to me. I'm talking to you. Listen, you, Ximena. Cut my hair."

The bee hovers over Cintia's blue ribbon, but she does not move to brush it away. She waits, pressing her fingers into Ximena's arm.

Reacting more to the rhythm of the words that ring in her ears than to what they mean, Ximena murmurs, "Look, if you want to do what the elves say, you have to cut it yourself. I can't do it."

Cintia does not hesitate.

"Go quickly and find some scissors and then let's go to the ditch."

The only ones Ximena can get hold of are the large rusty shears for cutting flowers and herbs that she sneaks out of a kitchen drawer at a moment when the servants are not paying attention. From her own room, she brings a round box that originally held cookies, and she starts emptying out its contents: her magic stones; feathers she has chosen for their perfection; little eucalyptus cones, which, just the opposite, are precious for their imperfections; shiny *lúcuma* seeds that a Campa Indian girl had given her, on one of their trips, in exchange for her medallion of the Virgin of Sorrows; all the treasures she has accumulated during the last two seasons in the valley. Edmundo must have gone out with the men or else he has gone out all by himself to walk around the town. Aunt Constanza and Ximena's mother are in the sewing room fixing their party clothes, searching eagerly for delicate artificial flowers and lace collars, so they will look fashionable, mixing laughter and whispers, tweezing their eyebrows, rubbing egg white on their faces, doing up their hair with hair pins and scraps of paper.

Ximena and Cintia head for the secret place in the garden. Suddenly, its magic takes hold of them again; it becomes a newly created space. It is a hot morning, and the finches are making a racket with their twittering. The breeze is heavy with woodsy smells and Ximena breathes in with so much pleasure that it makes her dizzy. Cintia also seems to be affected by the mood of the place and her nostrils open wide while she half closes her eyes. The scent that always perfumes her clothes mixes with the air, makes it sweet, enervating, and for a few instants they both give themselves over totally to the pleasure of listening and smelling, under the nervous flutter of their eyelids.

Ximena thinks, hopes, that Cintia will turn back. She is on the brink of confessing to her how important her father's role had been in developing the skill that has so impressed her, but once again the shadowy current of water running in the depths of her cousin's eyes stops her. She hands her the scissors.

"Turn around," orders Cintia. "I don't want you to see me do it."

Ximena is gazing at the yellow broom bushes when she hears the first raspy sound of the rusty old shears. A few second later, she hears another, drawn out, ragged sounding, unsure. Cintia complains. "I have to pull on my hair and yank it out because it has gotten stuck! But don't look at me because it would be worse!"

Ximena listens to the rusty blades opening and closing, and to her cousin's uneven breathing. Little by little she must have gotten the hang of it because the closing snaps of the scissors follow each other more closely and without a hint of a pause between them. She has tried to count out the thirty six sacrificed curls, but emotion has made her lose count. Labored panting lets her know that the task is coming to an end. Cintia is trying to cut all the curls gathered by the ribbon in one slash of the scissors.

"Now you can look at me, but don't laugh."

She turns around very slowly. She is not afraid of laughing, she is afraid of choking in a coughing fit. Her throat and her chest burn as though she had thousands of threads erupting in knots. In a first blaze of impression, Ximena thinks that Edmundo is standing in front of her, in a blue organdy dress. The image does not amuse her, but rather the contrary, it horrifies her to the point of hurling her into the coughing fit she had dreaded. While her body is shaking in spasms, she has a chance to size up the change in Cintia. She has cut her golden corkscrew curls off almost at the roots. Her hair, a darker shade right close to her head, sticks to her skull except in a few places where a curly lock has escaped the cruel onslaught of the shears. The curls, scattered on the ground, have taken with them the passive roundness of the cheeks and have made her features sharper. The absence of the bejeweled arrangement of curls hardens her face, giving her the look of a street urchin. It makes her dress look ridiculous.

"Help me with this," Cintia asks, and she points with the tip of her white shoe to the pile of hair at her feet. Ximena thinks of the drawing of the decapitated Medusa. She would swear that the curls undulate slightly as though they were alive, and for a few seconds, she is reluctant to touch them. "Don't stand there like a dummy. Help me!"

Cinta bends down first and with horror Ximena discovers that she has left two round patches that are almost bald. She is about to say the Aunt Constanza is going to kill them, but her cousin's resolute movements startle her and she remains silent.

They gather up the hair with both hands and put it into the metal box, decorated on the top and sides with snowy Christmas scenes, sleighs full of gifts, and plump Santa Clauses.

"Can I keep one curl as a souvenir?" asks Ximena. The soft texture of her cousin's hair warms her hands and moves her as it did before.

Cintia lifts her eyebrows in surprise. "Won't the elves mind?" she asks in turn.

Ximena has forgotten about the elves, and with a sudden shudder she realizes that the moment of reckoning has come.

In order not to cross through the house, they climb the wall, go out onto the unpaved coast road and, running, they double back toward the irrigation ditch. Ximena, terrified, with her heart thumping, runs with her mind a blank. Cintia trots along beside her making an effort to keep up. Neither one looks at the other, and Ximena feels desperately alone. An Indian is walking along the road by the ditch, urging along a burro loaded with bundles. He is one-eyed and smells of liquor. "Good morning," he greets them, nodding his head. Ximena observes him while he goes by. She does not recognize him. He does not look like one of the field workers on their hacienda and that relieves her. They both wait until the Indian and his burro disappear in the direction from which the girls had just come.

They halt at the edge of the ditch. There are days when the water level is low and it flows quietly, without making waves. Today it is rushing by faster and the ditch is full; the water is lapping at the weaker parts of the channel, and it looks more like a brook than a drainage canal. Its splashing noise is in synchrony with Ximena's pounding heartbeats, and to her it seems deafening and vengeful. And now she is gripped by the fear that she herself will not be able to make the jump she has made so many times before without even thinking about it. She wants to believe that she is having a nightmare, that she will wake up any minute in the warmth of her bed, that she will remember with relief that Cintia's hacked off curls were only a dream, and the round coffin box that they have not yet buried is a dream, too. But the sharp sensation in her lower abdomen, her legs that have turned into noodles, her uneven gasps for breath, and above all Cintia metamorphosed, Cintia alongside her almost bald-headed, all these inform her that no, it is daytime, and somehow she has to help her get to the other side.

She tries to repeat all the words she remembers, and her father's tone of voice, but neither the words nor the tone are quite her father's any longer. They flow out of her mouth snaking into the air and the water. Nevertheless, her own advice helps her to calm down and jump without difficulty over to the wall side. With the ditch between them, facing Cintia, she looks at her again. Cintia seems to have gotten slenderer; perhaps it is the intensity vibrating in her body that strips away her old cherub curves.

"Step back in order to get a head start, count, think of just what you have in front of you and not about anything that is behind or below," she manages to say to her and she closes her eyes because to her astonishment, and as quick as the blink of an eye, she has seen the little white shoes lift off the earth and the blue dress open up like wings; an awful fear forces her to not look, to not hear her terrible fall into the ditch, to not see the brown water churning over the naked head. She thought Cintia would take longer to get ready and now she is the one who has to leap back because her cousin has taken such an enormous jump that she almost knocks her against the wall as she lands.

They look at each other in recognition for a moment as though they were meeting after not seeing each other for a long time, and then they embrace and laugh giddily.

"Let's cross by that bridge," suggests Ximena.

However, Cintia, red-faced, wiping off the sweat that dampens her forehead, turns down the suggestion and indicates that she would prefer to jump from where they are. In vain Ximena tries to convince her that to jump from the wall side is much more difficult because there is not a big enough space to get launched.

"You jump and I'll follow you," insists her cousin, "Show me how."

Ximena jumps and Cintia follows her as though she had grown springs under the soles of her white party shoes. In a festive zigzag of hops, like two young goats, they crisscross the ditch, playing, until way down on the road to the town. And they climb back up to the house the same way, zigzagging, laughing. Sometimes Ximena goes first, and other times it is Cintia who leads, without hesitating.

When they get close to the door, their laughter dies out. While they catch their breath they try to compose their faces into the expressions they put on to deal with grownups in these situations. Perhaps they don't have time to get it right; perhaps the appropriate mask fell into the water while they were jumping the ditch and neither of the two is able to arrange herself and feel ready. They have not thought about how to confront the grownups; they have not managed, in the midst of their rejoicing, to make up a plausible lie. Without smiling at each other, without looking at each other, without even a gesture that would silently lock those moments of transient happiness into their memories, the two cross the threshold and enter the patio.

Aunt Constanza's scream must have been heard throughout the valley. It was a wailing "Ay," sustained and screeching. It carried through the thickest doors, the most massive walls, it bounced turning cartwheels above the tops of the trees, it smashed against the braids and hats of the servants, against the cages of the animals who lifted their beaks and ears in expectation, and there are even some who say that that cry cracked a lightning line down the center of the mirror in the sewing room where Cintia's mother saw the reflection of her daughter with chopped off hair. Ximena does not remember this detail. She does remember what the others, shocked, later denied or were silent about: when her anguished scream had run its course, Crazy Grandmother's laugh was heard clearly, and was heard so close by that her mother ran as she had when the old woman was alive, to see if she could possibly have escaped and come to spy on them.

Ximena takes refuge behind her mother's skirts, since her mother was so astonished that she did not at first intervene in her cousin's fury. Aunt Constanza shakes her daughter as though she were a rag doll, and Cintia makes her body go limp to better endure the impact of the assault.

"What have you done, wretch? What have you done, you idiot? How have you dared, you stupid fool?"

When she finally stops shaking her, Aunt Constanza collapses in a fit of hysterics. She is still white as a sheet and with her hair up in rollers that start to slip out of their hair pins, she is converted into an out-of-control marionette. Ximena, hiding her fear, looks out of the corner of her eye at her cousin who, without blinking, maintains her imperturbable calm. Ama Grande appears with a glass of liquor to soothe Aunt Constanza's nerves. "It's a magic potion," thinks Ximena. In any case her aunt has pulled herself together somewhat and turns furiously on her niece.

"You! It's your fault! Scrawny, jealous, vicious little sneak, this is your work all right. You should get a real beating for what you've done!"

She takes a few steps and falls on her, and her long red fingernails that she polished for that evening seem to stretch out like a wicked witch's. Cintia, her mother and Ama Grande intercede.

"It was me!" shrills Cintia above the uproar. "I cut it myself to be able to jump over the ditch!"

Ama Grande carries Ximena out of the room. She holds her close against the old apron that smells of herbs.

"Now, you, see if you can make yourself invisible," she advises her.

From the kitchen, where Paulina offers her bites of fresh-cooked tamales, Ximena listens to Aunt Constanza's raging grief. A little while later, Cintia comes in and sits down next to her. They eat together, blowing on each other's fingers after they have tried clumsily to unwrap the cornhusk bundles that are still too hot. The heat of the kitchen has begun to curl the jagged tips of Cintia's hair.

"You're my best friend," whispers Cintia secretly, right close to her ear. They do not look at each other, and Ximena knows that she should answer something, but she is silent as she always is when affection caresses her with words. Also, she feels like a traitor. Probably her cousin could have jumped the ditch without the elves' help, and probably the sacrifice was not necessary. Fear, longing, and remorse are twining their thorny branches throughout her body. She is not afraid of the possible reprisals of her mother and aunt. Sheltered in Ama Grande's generous skirts, she has learned the consolation that time goes on, and that grownups forget, too, that their memories are patched full of unimportant matters. But she so much liked that head of curly hair! To look at Cintia was to believe that one of the fairy tale characters had escaped from the pages that she so loved. Just looking at her made you happy! Now, where could she focus that envy that pushed her into dreaming? Something has broken beside her, leaving her with the fluttering wings of a dream in full color that she will not be able to recover. So that, even though she is happy that her cousin is sprouting up like the Indian princess, reaching to embrace the sun, shedding the layers of her old self, Ximena misses the fragrance of the organdy dresses which perfumed the wild corners of the garden and the dim musty recesses of Grandfather's house.

From the kitchen, they see Edmundo crossing the patio. Ironically, he has just come from town where he has gone to get a haircut, and he doesn't know about anything.

"He's going to rip me to shreds," says Ximena resignedly.

"I'll help you," offers Cintia, taking her hand. Ximena pulls her hand away quickly. It has felt as though knife petals were scraping against her skin.

Her mother obviously feels terrible about all of this. Her eyes are cloudy with blame. "Ximena, did you do it?" she asks.

"The elves and I," she answers without hesitating.

The recently manicured fingernails take hold of her shoulders and shake her two or three times. Ximena knows that she is trying to contain herself. When her mother is angry, her clenched jaws make her mouth into a thin line. She calms down without her having to recur to the stratagem of tears. "Why, Ximena, just explain to me why;" it is the white pleading tone of the usual question.

And because she knows that her mother, totally unlike Ama Grande, does not believe in the existence of elves, Ximena has to lie and as on other occasions, tell her that she doesn't know why, that she is thinking hard about it, that she is really sorry, but that she doesn't know why.

Ama Grande has broken the promise she made to the grownups and she comes to wake Ximena up at dawn. "They are about to leave," she tells her as she kneels to put on her socks. For a while now the old woman has not been able to bend over or squat on her heels, and it hurts Ximena to see her shrunk to child height that way, very close to the floor. But she does not protest and she lets herself be dressed by those hands that know every inch of her body so well. They will wait until her aunt and cousins are settled in the van before they go to the doorway to see them go. Ximena listens behind her bedroom door to an interchange in hushed voices. Her mother is still trying to make peace, but Aunt Constanza does not listen to her; her voice breaks when she speaks of Cintia and predicts a dire future for Ximena.

Finally they hear the van motor, the happy whistling of the chauffeur who strides through the lugubrious gloom of the patio and Aunt Constanza's tense voice as she tells him where to put the suitcases. The sound of words stops and now they only hear the giddy chirping of birds in the garden and in the distance the bleating of a flock of sheep being led out to pasture. The door must be wide open because the music from the van radio is even louder than the sound of the motor. Ximena and Ama Grande go out into the patio silently, tiptoeing as though they were fleeing.

It has rained the night before, and the paving stones shine because of the dampness that darkens them. It is a radiant morning and the whitewashed walls are tinged with the orange still coloring the clouds. The smell of freshly made coffee wafts from the kitchen. Ximena sees her mother standing by the gate with Paulina. She lets go of Ama Grande's hand and runs over to them because she is afraid of not getting there on time. Her mother does not have the energy to scold her and, on the contrary, hugs her tight. Her arm smells of the cologne she always uses; it is smooth and warm and its light apple blossom perfume, as always, consoles her.

Aunt Constanza and the cousins occupy the back row of the van. The driver has picked them up first so that they can choose the best seats. They picked the back because there is more space and they have windows behind them and on each side. Edmundo is sitting by the window facing the house, but he does not want to turn his face toward them and he looks toward his mother who is sitting in the middle between the two.

The van pulls away. It will go quickly down the hill towards town. Ximena thinks about it and her eyes start filling with tears. They will go away and she will be left all alone again. And she knows that when she does see them, it will not be the same, not even with Cintia. They both will have changed; they will look at each other suspiciously; it will be like starting all over again with their first encounter a few weeks ago. And it will be worse, because together they have so much to remember and to forget.

The van begins to descend. Cintia and Edmundo turn their heads and look at her. They both look alike, and Ximena would confuse one with the other if Edmundo did not still wear his severe expression as mayor, and if Cintia were not smiling openly at her, without regret or blame, and despite Aunt Constanza's efforts to hold her arms down, as they drive away down the length of the ditch, Cintia waves good-bye to her.

IV / ALCINOE II
OR THE WEAVERS

From her room she can hear someone knocking on the kitchen door. She pushes herself up on her palms and lifts her body a little higher to see if she can identify the voice of whoever has come. But the effort makes her cough and her own noises echo off all the surfaces in her room, obliterating any sounds that originate beyond her door. Not only is she confined to her bed, they have also closed her in so that her lungs will benefit from the steam of the eucalyptus branches that are boiling close to her. Propped up on the feather pillows brought by her mother from the house in the valley, Ximena tries taking a deep breath to see if she can free herself from the cat purring that has invaded her chest. She can make out the sound of Ama Grande's footsteps shuffling painfully from the kitchen toward the dining room. Now she can clearly hear the two women conferring in her parents' room, and a little later, she can make out every word of her mother's voice, greeting someone in the kitchen.

Ximena cannot make up her mind. She knows that by sitting up like this she can probably figure out more easily who it is who has just arrived, and that these voices she hears may entertain her for a little while, distracting her from the sad words and images that had her on the verge of tears just a few moments ago. But she can't decide whether to give in to her curiosity about the visitor or whether to sink back into the nostalgia of her melancholy daydream. For a few moments Ximena tries to resist the temptation to obsessively replay the episodes of the film based on *Wuthering Heights*, not because the memory makes her suffer, but on the contrary, because she fears that if she reruns the scenes in her head too many times, she will end up feeling indifference instead of pain. But she senses that, despite her efforts, some scenes are beginning to slip from her memory. She suspects that she is filling the blanks with her own imagination, with her own words and colors; the fear that she is losing her first impressions of the film also makes her suffer, but suffer in a different way, without tenderness and with a tinge of anger. She calms down when she thinks about how her mother is reading the novel and in the evenings, tells her about certain episodes. When they are not very long or complicated, she even agrees to read her sections of that brown book, so thick and filled with tiny print, which Ximena, without a scrap of remorse, envies her resentfully every time she sees it or thinks of it, held by those delicate hands that look so fragile. She consoles herself even more when she dreams that someday, when she is grown up, she can see the film and read the novel as often as she likes; she will be able to cry over it all she wants without feeling guilty that she cannot make herself feel as distressed about children who are dying of hunger in the world, who are real live children.

Ximena holds onto her grief so as not to squander it, and she decides to guess who it is talking with her mother. It can't be an important visitor because although they might have come in through the kitchen, they would have gone into the living room. So it must be someone who works at the Company or some place like that. She would go over to the door in order to hear better, except that the fever makes her head spin when she stands up. If she has a sudden fit of coughing, they will rub Capsolina Vapor Rub on her chest and on her back. Following Ama Grande's advice, her mother will wrap strips of red flannel all around her, under her pajamas. Capsolina burns her skin, sometimes it even makes blisters, but her mother has faith in the powers of that medication, and although the American doctor has laughed at the red flannel, her mother still trusts the old woman's advice. When her father is at home, Ximena is reprieved from that torture. He makes a fuss, alleging that the practice is sadistic and medieval; then her mother answers in a sweet voice, "Never mind, it's all right," but as soon as he leaves and goes back to work, if Ximena coughs a lot, she rubs the pomade in mercilessly.

The door to the dining room begins to open slowly. Two heads, one above the other, squeezed into the crack between the door and the wall, turn in her direction. They are Sami and Beto, the weaver's sons. They look at her for a few moments without saying anything, without even smiling. It bothers her that they have been allowed to barge right in and stare at her propped up on her bed pillows. "We can't come in, because you're contagious," says Sami, the older of the two.

"I know, go away and close the door: you're letting the steam out," her voice dries up with the shame of knowing herself to be sick.

"Where do you hurt?" asks Beto. His lips are so red, Ximena thinks for a second of the color of red wine in a glass. But his lips are also chapped and split with the cold. His two front teeth have come out, and Ximena is both disgusted and nervous as she watches the way the boy automatically flicks the tip of his tongue in and out of the gap.

"Nothing hurts; go away."

Ximena turns her back to them and pretends to be looking out the window. Although it is only around lunchtime, the day is very gray;

it looks as though it is about to get dark. The rails of the fence around the house and the telephone post gleam where last night's ice has accumulated on them. Tensely, she waits in the same position for a few moments, until she hears the sound of the door closing.

Now she can make herself comfortable, close her eyes, and think about Heathcliff and Catherine. After lunch she will think about how mean Hindley was when he was a boy, and later she will choose whether to come back to the main characters when they meet after death, or to Isabelle's suffering. And then, without being aware of it, or knowing how or in which moment, her thoughts flow along by themselves and she finds herself remembering Sami and Beto. Her anger fades because right now no one is humiliating her by gazing at her helplessness, and she thinks of the two boys as unreal and distant characters. Perhaps because the weaver, too, comes wrapped in a mysterious story. They have not told her or read her this story; patiently Ximena has patched together, insofar as she can figure them out, the bits she picks up from grownups' conversations. She knows all too well that she cannot and should not ask questions about the weaver's life. They will either be totally silent, or they will look at her sternly without letting their eyes give away the least hint of the secret. Everything she knows, she has heard through the cracks of doors or by pretending she is asleep while the others are talking in whispers.

The weaver is small and dark. She wears her black hair in a short permanent and she wears lipstick. She does not dress in Indian-style layers of heavy wool skirts and a shawl, a *lliclla*, like the others who come to the house to sell the cloth they embroider or weave. She dresses in dark colors and wears cheap high heeled shoes, maybe because she is so short. Her mother commented once that she is "a little piece of nothing" and she doesn't understand how Samuel Robertson lost his head over her. She looks ugly to Ximena. Her eyes are uneasy and evasive, and her face reminds Ximena of the old guinea pigs in the valley. Robertson, they call him by his last name, is just the opposite, blond and good looking. They talk to him in the kitchen, too, as though he were one of the ordinary smelter workers, although by his appearance he could be one of the many gringos who work with her father. A while ago, he was a Company mechanic, but after the scandal with the weaver, he lost his job.

Ximena recalls clearly, still with a trace of astonishment, as though it were yesterday, the time that Robertson and his wife came to plead with her father to intercede in their favor. She was in the pantry with Ama Grande, having fun picking out the bugs and the little stones that turned up like freckles in the translucent pallor of the rice, while her parents and the others spoke in low voices in the kitchen. They had forgotten to close the door, and the tension she heard in their voices made her fingers clumsy, annoying the old woman, who scolded her under her breath. She remembers clearly that her mother kept saying "What a shame!" every little while as Robertson went on talking slowly, stuttering, correcting himself, repeating the same sentences that crept along until they arrived and died at Ximena's feet. Her father seemed to be staying out of it. When he insisted that he had no influence in the workshop, his tone lacked the cordiality that it usually had when he talked to employees, however lowly they might be. Ximena was distressed by this unexpected severity, even more so when not a single sound inside the house or from outside broke the long silence that followed his words. It was then that the weaver got up her courage to speak and begged, losing all sense of shame. That same night at dinner her mother commented that he had been too hard on Robertson. Without lifting his eyes from his plate, he answered tersely that what that woman had done was unforgivable.

There is laughter in the kitchen and Ximena knows that the door is about to open because grownups talk louder when they are saying good-bye, as though it were time for applause before the curtain falls.

Ximena thinks of the silent good-byes that children say, and of the terrible awkwardness of separations, when close friends are supposed to kiss each other and other acquaintances have to repeat the polite words dictated by smiling grownups. The door closes and the two women talk for a few minutes in the kitchen. Ximena hears Ama Grande's rolling Quechua tones and her mother's short Spanish answers. She lets herself slide down until she is almost flat on her back again, and she feels the peacefulness that finally lulls her to sleep.

As long as she can, she holds off the pleasure of thinking about the film. She cuts paper dolls, makes some drawings, looks at the bright pages of a storybook. If she wants, she can ask them to bring her a volume of the encyclopedia, the book of *Universal Myths* with its colored illustrations, or the photo album. But she prefers to save them for another time. By midafternoon, after the cough syrup that leaves her feeling as though her body were foam, she gathers up the books, papers and colored pencils scattered on her bed, and carefully stacks them neatly at her feet in order to be able to stretch out and find a comfortable position in which to remember. Lying on her side facing the window, she closes her eyes and sees Heathcliff, surly and disheveled, on the day when he first came to the Earnshaws' house. She no longer clearly recalls Heathcliff's face as a child; it is getting gradually blurrier, his adult features overlay those of the child and when she makes a conscious effort to reconstruct the diffuse fragility of her memory, her effort fails because she keeps remembering other children's faces, and at that instant, Healthcliff fades in and out, wearing Beto or Sami's features.

Her images of Catherine and Hindley when they were small are also dissolving little by little into mist. She blames herself for having used them up too soon. On various occasions she has asked her mother to read her the descriptions of these characters in the novel, but it is no use, they are not like those in the film and she suspects, mortified, that her mother, when she carefully reads and explains these descriptions to her, is imagining them herself, in her own way. She clearly remembers how the movie shows Heathcliff and Catherine when they are young. But she knows that she will eventually lose the clarity of this image, too, and that there is nothing to do but resign herself to the double betrayal of memory and of words. Catherine is extremely beautiful; she is a little like the Japanese girl in the El Rocío shop but, as her mother has said, beauty does not protect you from a broken heart.

Ximena sighs; she likes the sound of that sentence, she will have to repeat it a few times out loud so that its intriguing but intangible quality will last a little longer, hovering around the furniture in her room. If she knew how to write, she would spell it out with clear, well-formed letters using purple ink on an unlined page of a small notebook with leather covers. Heathcliff's sunken and saddened eyes make her squeeze her own tight closed: he did not know that Catherine had always loved him, until it was too late for them both. Ximena covers her eyes with her arm and concentrates on Heathcliff's pain. Gradually she gives in to short sobs which shake her chest intermittently. Before giving herself over entirely to grief, she thinks about Catherine's death, about the open window of her room from which she gazed out at her beloved marshes for the last time. The spasms make her cough and her mother rushes into her bedroom.

"For Heaven's sake, Ximena!" she reprimands, exasperated. "You're never going to get well if you insist on crying on purpose. Taking you with us to see that movie was the worst idea in the world. There was a good reason why it was rated Adults Only, but between you and your father, you with your silly notions, and he wanting to please you, you stuck me with the whole burden of struggling with your whims and your lungs. If you don't stop carrying on like this, I'm not going to tell you about that book or read you any more of it."

Ximena does not answer. At the beginning, when they were still in Lima and she had not gotten sick yet, she had first started to remember things and cry, without doing it intentionally. Later, when she started to remember and weep intentionally, so that they would leave her in peace, it was easy to invent fake reasons for her grief. Afterward, when they had returned here, and she had gotten sick, they let her ask questions about the film because it seemed to amuse her. When the answers made the screen images vivid to her, without being able to bear any more, she started to cry when she was alone, huddled in different corners of the house, and sometimes even in front of her mother. Pretty soon she could no longer deceive her with her subtle ploys, because her mother had learned how to distinguish real tears from the ones conjured up by remembering the movie. She explained to Ximena that crying on purpose was worse than lying.

"All right. I won't cry any more; bring me the photo album."

However, despite her promise, Ximena does not desist. When her mother leaves the room, she closes the album and vows to herself that she will only let herself think about two characters. She has become aware that imagination does not function as well with just one, that it takes two to achieve whatever effect she seeks. She casts her eyes around and this time she sees herself gazing at her own image in a mirror, recognizing her ordinary everyday face, and then the other, the face that changes in a flash and is deformed when she impatiently conjures up certain scenes from the film.

As a child, Hindley detested Heathcliff. He made him suffer in the same way big sisters or stepmothers make the youngest daughter suffer in fairy tales. But in fairy tales, invariably the ones who start out by suffering are happy by the end. In *Wuthering Heights*, Ximena has discovered the pleasure of tragic endings, the open gap in the circular journey of written stories through which one can move in and out of the drama, leaving it unfinished in order to sustain the pleasure of suffering at will. Ximena thinks that, just like in fairy tales, Heathcliff arrived at the Earnshaws' house without any past, surrounded by mystery. He left there to confront the trials that life sent him so that when he returned, rich and powerful, he could finally win the hand of Catherine, his princess. However, Catherine did not know how to wait, and she chose Edgar Linton, which made happiness totally impossible. In his embitterment —the word *embitterment* is a new one, and Ximena insists on it because it warms her bones with a vegetal caress she has not experienced before—Heathcliff avenges himself upon Hindley, and later, although this does not appear in the film, on Hareton. Wiping her tears with her pajama tail, and doing everything possible to heave a deep sigh without being punished by an incriminating coughing fit, Ximena decides that the hour has come to put an end to her sorrow. She will return to her memories later, and will suffer from now on because she knows that however hard she tries to keep them intact, the next time they will no longer be the same.

Ximena is feeling better. Sitting at the dining room table, she looks at the illustrations in the *Universal Myths* book. Sometimes at night, her father sits her on his knees and explains to her who Pallas Athene is, what Hercules did, and what Zeus is like. In a calm voice and very patiently, he tells her the stories that correspond to each illustration. When Ximena asks him if these stories are true, he answers that they are true for the imagination, and Ximena accepts that, just as she accepts some of Ama Grande's strange pronouncements about the power of certain plants or of some people's gazes. One time her father was telling her about the seduction of Leda, when her mother interrupted, her lips tight with tension: "How do you think Ximena is going to be able to interpret that?"

"She will interpret it in accord with what she knows," he had answered her, "in the same way she comprehends the Divine Conception of the Virgin."

Her mother had turned red.

"You know perfectly well it is not the same thing," she had murmured before closing herself up in her bedroom, slamming the door. As though jumping down from his knees might hurt her, her father had lifted Ximena gently to set her down and go calm his wife. Then Ximena had looked closely at that drawing, full of curiosity.

Now, several weeks later, she is again absorbed in contemplating that colored illustration which gleams and is shadowed in places depending on how it is illuminated by the dim light coming through the windows on her left. Leda appears semi-naked, reclined against the fragile trunk of a flowering shrub by the shores of a violently blue lake. On the lake's horizon, the sky is lit up in shades of orange like those Ximena remembers from the sunsets on the coast. Leda has light, curly hair, pulled back with diminutive flowers on her head and her eyes are too big in comparison to the minuscule strawberry-colored mouth. A huge white swan covers part of her body with his wings and sticks his beak into the bodice of her tunic. Leda caresses his neck without knowing that he is the fearful god transformed.

Ximena does not doubt those miraculous changes. Ama Grande's daily language is full of all sorts of transmutations so when Ximena sees a stray dog on the street she is sorry for him because it could be a man who is being punished, and she, in turn, is careful never to swallow the seeds of fruit because they can carry within them the germ of some rebellious elf or of some underhanded god. She is terrified by the idea of being like Dina Medina and becoming a mother at her age. The day they had the argument about Leda and the swan, her parents made up quickly, but other similar disagreements would keep happening in the future. Even so, for years her father continued, with the same patience, to tell her about the stories that matched up with the illustrations in that book with its old green binding and exotic gold lettering.

She is entranced, oblivious of everything around her, staring with new interest at the picture of Psyche and Aphrodite, about to kiss each other, when her mother receives a telegram. The boy who brings things from the post office has gone off, waving his hand in a clumsy salute, and her mother's hands are trembling as she opens the little yellow envelope. "Oh God, don't let it be bad news," she murmurs in a husky plea. As she reads, her expression changes to one of joy.

"Ximena, guess who is coming to visit us for a few days? Your Aunt Alejandra with a friend of hers. They will arrive tomorrow. We'll have to set up the camp cot and make them some space in your bureau drawers."

Ximena barely remember her mother's cousin and she runs to get the album. There she can identify her because she knows which names go with which faces in the photos. Although she knows there is no point to it, she starts at the beginning, looking at the little girl with bangs and a big smile, standing next to her mother. The two of them are five or six years old and her mother is almost as slender as Ximena. Like her, she must also have felt self-conscious in front of the camera because not only does she not smile, but you can tell how timid and fidgety she is. The two are holding hands and are sitting on the edge of a fountain in some park in Lima with a lot of trees. Ximena still feels a kind of vertigo when she sees her parents or other relatives as children in the pictures in the album. At first it was hard for her to accept that once upon a time they had been so little; now it's more that the blood rises to her face when she thinks about how her body has within it the outline of a grownup. She turns the pages until she comes to another photo that shows the two cousins together. They are riding a horse, maybe on one of the paths near the house in the valley and they must be about seventeen years. Ximena thinks her mother is the prettiest. This time she smiles directly at the camera. The other one, who still looks just the same as she had as a child, is laughing so hard the picture caught her with her eyes closed and her mouth open. Her short straight hair frames the strong bones of her face and you can see she is thinner and taller than her mother. Impatiently, she looks for the photo of the wedding.

It is a large picture; it fills up a whole page of the album and it is a sepia color like the ones that Ximena likes best. It is very dark in the back of the elegant room where the photo was taken. Uncle Rafael is a little off to one side and turned toward the bride, but he is looking at the invisible photographer with a serious expression. Vaguely, Ximena remembers that he was a relative, too, although more distantly connected, so that the couple never had to negotiate with the Archbishop of Lima or with the Pope in Rome as others in the family had had to do. Her mother's cousin also leans toward him a little, but she is smiling at whoever looks at the photo because the camera has caught her in such a way that however Ximena moves from side to side, Aunt Alejandra's eyes follow her. Ximena is hypnotized by the bride. She barely notices the elegant dress, with its long train like a lace waterfall, or the delicate headdress of orange blossoms and pearls. That expression, where has she seen it before? She is on the point of giving up—like when in the morning she tries to tell Ama Grande about a dream that had totally filled her mind only a minute before but that just a few seconds later, evaporates irretrievably as she tries to tell about it—when, suddenly, the dreamy quality that Isabelle and Catherine have when they think about Heathcliff provides her with the key. Ximena has just identified the expression of someone in love.

That night, after they have finished supper and are having coffee, Aunt Alejandra and her friend arrive. They had been expecting them for several hours; they have left their places set at the table. They only have one suitcase, but they are carrying all sorts of packages, satchels and a tripod made of wood and metal. Aunt Alejandra still wears her hair short and straight. She has black bangs over her forehead, and dark wings of hair on either side of her face. She has dark almond-shaped eyes, and when she focuses on Ximena for a few instants, her gaze is so intense, that her niece instinctively looks away. Her friend Gretchen is shorter and has sharp, small features, except for her eyes which are round and very green. Ximena thinks she can see a certain resemblance to the drawing of Athena's owl, but she admires the red mass of rebellious curls that flow down over her shoulders.

While they all drink coffee, Aunt Alejandra and her mother laugh as they reminisce about old times. The anecdotes follow one after another amid hilarity, hugs, and sentences left incomplete because the peals of laughter cut them off, and the two of them, accomplices in the past, are the only ones who know how the stories turn out. Ximena feels a twinge of uneasiness because her mother's voice takes on a tone which is new to her; it rises stridently and a little crazily over the smoke of Gretchen's cigarettes. Gretchen and her father watch them, casting sidelong looks at each other every once in a while. Exiled from the magic circle of the two cousins, they don't dare to say anything.

Later, they go to Ximena's room. Turning to Aunt Alejandra, her mother said, "You can sleep with your niece because her bed is wider, and Gretchen can sleep on the camp cot which is narrower, but quite comfortable."

The friends shoot a quick look at each other and Ximena thinks she catches a smile barely suppressed in time.

Since they do not answer, her mother adds rapidly, "If this arrangement does not seem all right, Ximena can sleep with us. She never bothers anyone at night."

To her disappointment, the others do not accept this offer and Ximena watches them walk back to the living room and bring back a blue vanity case. They leave the rest of their bags there, scattering their disorder on the pristine red of the patterned rug. And it is as though an unexpected and discordant note had just shattered the peaceful symmetry of the household.

Aunt Alejandra wants to be a professional photographer. Her interest in this began as a hobby to keep her busy during long boring days in Lima where Uncle Rafael is a lawyer and where they have properties that always need attention and personal overseeing. "He is never at home, not during the day or at night either," she says, taking a cigarette out of Gretchen's hand. "And I'm not one to stay home darning socks or watering the plants."

She tells how she met Gretchen at an art exhibit and through her, became acquainted with various other artists. She discovered that she was talented at looking at the world deliberately, the way you look through a camera, and that light and shadow, her companions, have gradually been showing her the best way to focus on shapes. Gretchen is a painter and has shown her work in two galleries. She spreads out her recent charcoal drawings on the dining room table, so they can all see them. Most of them are studies of faces and nudes. Ximena recognizes Aunt Alejandra by her hair and eyes; in one of the drawings she is crouched down and holding an apple in her hand as though she were about to throw it. In another, she is lying on a couch.

"Gretchen's Maja," says her aunt, putting a fingertip on the curve of her waist in the photo. As Ximena could have predicted, her mother pretends nonchalance while trying without much success to hide her embarrassment.

The next evening, at Aunt Alejandra's request, Ximena and her mother hunt for the old family photographs, the ones they always intend to put in an album but which continue to pile up in two cigar boxes and a big manila envelope. Ximena stays right with them even though her father has offered to play checkers with her. She has hardly ever had a chance to see these photos because her mother feels guilty about their being in such disorder, and prefers to not even think about the dark corner of her closet where they have been for years. Her aunt especially wants to see the pictures of Crazy Grandmother because she is writing some short pieces about her.

"I don't know why my mother kept so few of these. I want to see all the ones you have, from the time she was little until the very last pictures."

Her hands search through the pile of various sized photos, some already frayed and others which have held up better over the years because they are as thick as postcards or were artistically framed in cardboard by the studio. Her aunt's long, slim fingers make her think of her mother's, but her aunt's are stronger and more agile, and Ximena, staring at them, imagines that they are like the outstretched wings of roosters at dawn. Gretchen looks at the backs of the photos. "But there are no names or dates here. How will you be able to recognize her as a child or as a young woman?"

"I'll recognize her by the look on her face. When you come across one with a rebellious expression, looking as though she is yelling a decisive "No!" to the whole world, that is our grandmother."

Ximena wishes they would look at all the photos one by one even if they were not of the grandmother. She would like to see all the other relatives, too: ladies with parasols, with very narrow waists and heart-shaped bustles; boys who look just like their sisters because they have the same haircuts and because they are all wearing baggy blouses or sailor suits; several of a naked baby sleeping face down on a big shiny, dark cushion; men dressed up in their Sunday suits, with sideburns that connect with their beards, mustaches with pointy tips, their jackets unbuttoned in a gesture which is clearly meant to show off the gold watches hanging from their vest pockets. Sometimes Aunt Alejandra makes them laugh by imitating the exaggeratedly erect posture and the patriarchal seriousness of these relatives. "Just look at this couple! As though they had gotten dressed and had forgotten to remove the coat hangers!"

But she does not linger long on these. She hunts for the ones she wants and puts them to one side. Crazy Grandmother, whom Ximena remembers only as a shadow by the window of the room where they had her locked up, at the house in the valley, is easy to identify because she does not pose like the other girls and young women. Even in pictures of her when she is younger than Ximena is now, there is something defiant and mocking in the way she stares.

"She was a real character, an exceptional woman," sighs her aunt. "Imagine the stories she could tell us if she were alive!"

"She was totally out of her mind," replies her mother. "Why do you think they had to lock her up first in Lima and then on the hacienda?"

"They locked her up because she wouldn't let herself be tamed, because from very early on, she threw away all regard for proper manners and the family reputation in provincial society, in order to live as she pleased."

Ximena observes her mother's increasing tension. The skin around her mouth is stiffening the way it does when they contradict her and she gets mad. "You may see her as a literary character, but she was a woman of flesh and blood and caused the family lots of problems with her bizarre behavior and her temperament. They should have taught her a lesson early on and put her behind bars. All it got her was that they excluded her more and more often and when they did invite her to social events it was only because of her family name or because they knew she would play the eccentric clown and liven up dances. They laughed at her. And you know full well," she adds, speaking in a louder and louder voice, faster and faster, to Ximena's dismay, "that she never settled down, and she was a bad wife and a worse mother. If she had any excuse, it was that she suffered from her nerves, and there were all those entire days when she would close herself up and not see anyone. Remember how we used to spy on her during those strange spells when she filled her room with incense and, wrapped in a sheet, prayed to Hindu gods as though she didn't have a religion of her own? And why so much mysticism? It just put everyone off. If people felt sorry for her, it was because she was out of her mind."

Ama Grande, as though she were connected by threads of premonition, without anyone having called her, comes in early from the kitchen to put Ximena to bed. While she tries to escape, without anyone noticing, from the big rough hands that, in a gesture her body knows all too well, are trying to push her toward the bathtub, Gretchen stares at her openly and Ximena feels ashamed. She would have liked to protest, and plead to stay up for at least a few more minutes, but she feels found out and exposed, and she snuggles up against the comforting embrace of Ama Grande's layers of skirts, until she almost disappears in the sheltering folds.

Before she falls asleep, she thinks about Heathcliff and Catherine, but the laughter and voices from the dining room distract her. She is rocked back and forth by the three women, each of whom is trying, in her own way, to resurrect her fragmentary memories of Grandmother. After listening to the rhythmic rattling of the train passing, she succumbs to sleep. She has just gone into her room and her aunt is photographing a couple dressed like the olden days. The woman, seated in a chair with a high back, is heavy and imposing. Her huge bust is even more conspicuous because she is wearing a white lace blouse and an onyx medallion that has an amethyst and topaz pansy in the center, ringed by tiny pearls. Her hands rest on the chair arms and Ximena discovers in surprise that the bracelets of little gold chain links are wrapped not only around the velvet of her sleeves but also around the wooden chair arms.

It is then that she looks closely at the woman's head and horror dries her throat, because that is not a tall hat that she is wearing. In the woman's open skull, enormous numbers of white eggs are piled up into a pyramid. The man by her side, the part in his hair precisely centered between the two halves of his long mustache slicked into points, has placed a hand on the back of the chair and with the other he raises his jacket lapel to show off the chain of a gold watch. Ximena hears its loud tick tock. Tossed onto the rug, as though it were the lid of a sewing box carelessly dropped to the floor, is the top part of the cut-open skull on which a three-tiered coil of hair still trembles as it begins to fall apart into wavering strands. Ximena wants to yell and run over to her aunt and hide behind her, but her aunt is intent upon getting the angle in exact focus and is unaware of her presence. Then a smoky shadow comes in through the window and assumes a more definite shape as Ximena draws closer. Her aunt has waved her hand in greeting although she continues to concentrate on her work. The shadow—which is opaque and transparent at the same time—takes Ximena by the hand and leads her out of the room. "It is my *ama*, my nanny," she thinks a second before waking up and confirming that the face of smoke and flesh has left behind an aroma of dried flowers and incense that she smelled once in her crazy Grandmother's bedroom.

The weaver comes at noontime to deliver the crocheted tablecloth her mother had ordered. They take it into the dining room to spread it out on the table and admire the detailed perfection of the repeated design with more than a thousand rosettes in fine thread. Sami and

Beto have come, too, and Ama Grande sends the three of them out
to play in the patio even though Ximena protests.

Embarrassed by being hustled outside so quickly, and awkward
because it has been a while since they have played together, the boys
head for the wooden fence and Ximena sits down on the cement steps
that lead to the kitchen. The three of them stare off into the distance
where they can just make out the workers' camp and where the train
goes through, its tracks cutting across the flat open fields. The boys
talk to each other while they spin around with one hand holding onto
the fence. Their brown hair looks even lighter in the sunlight. They
are both very white, and do not look anything like the weaver. "Lucky
children," her mother has commented more than once, "they took
after Robertson." Sami comes up to Ximena.

"Get out your red wagon and let's take turns with it," he suggests.
Ximena would have preferred to play with the old wheelbarrow they
use for hauling wood because it only has one wheel and its wobbly
dance from side to side both scares and excites her, but she knows
she is alone on this and that giving in is her only choice. She also
knows that the brothers are very stubborn, especially the older one,
and that they will not give up until they get what they want. When it
is their turn to pull Ximena, they run really fast, knowing full well
that the wagon jolts on the stones and that Ximena has to hang on
very tight in order not to be tossed out. Frustrated because they can't
make her cry, they leave her alone and start climbing on the fence rail-
ings again.

Samuel Robertson comes by to collect his wife and sons when it is
already lunchtime. The boys run to meet him and climb into the old
two-colored van their father uses to pick up and drop off passengers
in various places along the road to Trujillo. He is not the owner of
the van, and as a driver, he earns a lot less than he did as mechanic
for the Company. Besides which, "who knows if it is not God's pun-

ishment, making him travel the same route as before," the weaver, drying her tears, confessed to her mother one afternoon when Ximena was spying on them through the crack of the pantry door, which had been left ajar. Robertson came to a stop in front of her.

"They are incorrigible," he said, gesturing at the van. "How long have you had to put up with them?"

Ximena doesn't dare to answer. She had never looked closely at Robertson's features. His eyes are sunken like Heathcliff's, but they are very blue and big. With anxious curiosity, Ximena notices the blond hairs visible under his unbuttoned shirt and pullover.

"Are you coming in with me?" Robertson asks her as he knocks at the door. Ama Grande opens it. He stands aside and lets Ximena enter first, and as she is about to cross the threshold, he runs his big hand, smelling of cigarettes, through her hair. For just a moment, her eyes fog with emotion and her legs feel about to collapse. Without paying any attention to the women who are chatting about the new tablecloth, she goes to her room and sits down confusedly on her bed. The tick tock of the old clock in the dining room and of her own heartbeats mix up together and vibrate throbbingly in her body. She hardly breathes and does not move until Ama Grande's scolding voice calls her to lunch for the third time.

Aunt Alejandra keeps asking questions about Robertson and the weaver. Ximena is very aware of the grownups' evasiveness, and of their use of double meanings which are meant to protect her from the truth.

"What a pair!" her aunt exclaims, laughing. "They are the worst matched couple I've ever seen!"

Gretchen, who has not participated in the conversation, shrugs her shoulders. "You are forgetting that love is blind," she says seriously.

Ximena remembers the drawing of the naked child with wings and a blindfold over his eyes who is shooting arrows at both those who are paying attention and those who are not.

"Well, he has really played havoc under that pretense of being blind," remarks her father. "Robertson is a good man and that woman has been a plague in his life."

Her mother casts a sidelong glance at Ximena before she ventures to answer. "She's not a bad person; she works hard and keeps her word and takes good care of her two sons..."

But he does not let her finish sketching out her defense. "Her two sons? And the others? What about the others?"

Aunt Alejandra wants to know more. "Others?" she asks curiously. Ximena lowers her eyes to make herself invisible, but her mother's silent admonition has already had its effect. They talk for a long while about Gretchen's aristocratic family in Trujillo, about her German mother who is a descendent of a noble family, and then the conversation takes different turns: they discuss the war, mention Hitler, prices, the smelter, the miners, the valley, their relatives. Only Ximena dwells reflectively on that couple.

"What's wrong with you, that you aren't talking or eating?" her aunt asks her, flicking a breadcrumb at her face. A suffocating anxiety knots up her body and she cannot answer. Her mother reaches out rapidly and automatically to feel her forehead, and then pulls her hand back, relieved. Ximena lifts her eyes and finds Gretchen staring hard at her, forcing her way into that innermost center where her thoughts tremble.

That night, after dinner, the grownups talk about a biography of George Sand. Her mother gets very embarrassed when she has to confess that at first she had thought it was a book about a man. They discuss her novels, and the time in which she lived. Every once in a while Gretchen peers sharply at Ximena. There is no mockery or hostility in her eyes, but Ximena is uncomfortable because, in the gaze of those green eyes, she recognizes the same impertinent spying and the same eagerness to understand that she herself feels when she stares. Anxious to get away from it somehow, she bursts out suddenly: "Last night I had a really strange dream."

She tells it, complete with details, because the images have haunted her all day, and Aunt Alejandra bursts out laughing when she finishes. "Divine! How revealing!" she applauds. "I can hardly wait to develop the film to see if it is the way you dreamed it!"

Ximena and her father are amused by her aunt's reaction. But it makes her mother uncomfortable. "It's the whole business of the photos last night, and the memories of grandmother. She was always afraid of her."

"That's not true," protests Ximena. And she would have liked to add that although in the valley, they had gotten her to eat by threatening her with the scary ghost of the old woman, her curiosity had always been much stronger than her fear.

When she gets up from the table so that Ama Grande can bathe her, her aunt hugs her, laughing. "Dream whatever comes next and tell me about it tomorrow," she whispers in her ear.

Curled up in a ball, waiting for the rattle of the last train going past, Ximena tries to think about Healthcliff and Catherine. Their images hover around the rough edges of her semiconsciousness as she drifts towards sleep, but it is Robertson who appears to her. Those are his eyes, the blond down of his chest hair, his hand, his odor. It is Robertson who leads her by the hand into sleep, past the algae and the sea urchins along the edge of a stormy precipice against which the waves are breaking in rhythmic cadence before opening out into foam flowers. But it is not her the way she is. It is her in her Aunt Alejandra's pulsating, vibrant body.

She is sitting on a little bench next to the pantry window listening to

Ama Grande's marvelous stories. She has been well behaved all morning, and Ama is rewarding her with her favorite tales. They exchange stories. Ximena tells fairy tales, splicing in pieces of myths and films, and adding details that occur to her—seemingly all by themselves—as she is speaking. Sometimes she hears herself sighing unexpectedly; she loses track of the most familiar words, and she finds herself gazing out through the yellow-flecked gauze curtains at the dreary patio and leaden sky that shows some promise of letting pearly, misty sunlight filter through. The Robertsons live over on that side, to the right of the bridge and farther down, in the most dilapidated buildings in Pueblo Viejo.

"Why did Robertson marry the weaver?" she asks in one of the old woman's thoughtful pauses.

"They aren't married," Ama Grande answers dryly. She picks up a round potato with smooth skin, almost violet in color. Then she adds, without any change of expression: "They are just living together."

Ximena does not understand, but something in Ama Grande's voice warns her that she should find out more about the matter some other way. She wants to know why the Company fired Robertson. The old woman has begun to peel the potato and seems completely absorbed in the skillful movement of her hand. Then, as though she were saying it to herself, her voice rises, bitter and resentful. "That is what this is all about, their not being married."

The paper-thin peel curls down in a spiral like a snake.

"Then why don't they get married?"

"Because they can't. He got involved with the weaver in Trujillo years ago, before he got his job as a mechanic, when he was a van driver like he is now. She had a rooming house and he stayed there. One fine day he brought her along here and a little later he began to work for the Company. Then people found out and the bosses got rid of him."

"But why?"

"That's how the bosses are, that's how things are. I haven't said a word to you. Your head is still young and it should be like this potato, without eyes to see people's troubles."

Ximena does not insist. She imagines the colored threads that bound Robertson and the weaver together, and she is tangled in the warp and woof of her own confusion. The potato gleams white and smooth in the gnarled red hands of her *ama*. The peel, all in one piece, has fallen onto the oilcloth table cover, in purple whorls, and it moves as though it were still alive.

One afternoon Robertson comes to collect some thread that her mother has gotten together for another custom order. He waits for a while in the kitchen, and then is shown into the dining room. Ximena, who is looking at the pictures in the book about myths, sees him come in and she is startled. Her mother goes into the big bedroom to look for the package of thread, and Ama returns to the kitchen. Gretchen and Aunt Alejandra are taking a nap in the other bedroom. It is totally silent and Ximena wishes the radio were on, or that there were sounds of voices, footsteps, the wind blowing, or the river, to hide the accelerated rhythm of her own heartbeats that deafen her in this silence. He comes up behind her and greets her. He leans over to see the book and Ximena gazes at the hand he has rested on the table and again she smells the odor of cigarettes, this time mixed with a trace of gasoline. The ends of his fingers are blunt and his nails are dirty. He is asking her if she already knows how to read when her mother comes in. They exchange the polite phrases that grownups always say to each other so automatically. Ximena would like to escape to the kitchen, but the van driver is still standing right behind her, so close that she can feel the echoing tingle of his words on her skin when Robertson pauses in the conversation and is silent.

The door of her bedroom opens and Aunt Alejandra appears, yawning. She is wearing casual pants and a white bed jacket that is so transparent that her lacy bra is clearly visible. Her eyes, still heavy with sleep, look around with surprise at her surroundings, trying to adjust to the sharp outlines that things have when contemplated from the other side of sleep. When she recovers herself, she begins to smile and comes over to Robertson to shake his hand. The man's embarrassment hits Ximena like a sudden wave of heat. While her aunt engages him in conversation, Robertson's fingers drum nervously on the table. The blond fuzz between his knuckles is splattered with shiny black dots of oil that smell of gasoline. Way in a distance, although she is only on the other side of the table, her mother clutches the bag of thread and Ximena observes this gesture which only later may translate into barely contained recrimination for that seemingly natural interchange.

Robertson's hand has remained there, has calmed down, without suspecting anything, like the relaxed hand of a beggar waiting for alms. Some sign from her mother, perhaps the gesture of handing over the bag of thread or something even more subtle, puts an end to her cousin's laughing monologue. The three head for the kitchen door. Ximena, surer of herself now because of the distance that separates her from the others, dares to turn around and look at them. Before crossing the threshold, Robertson turns around, hesitates a second and then words spill out all of a sudden, in a gush. Blushing slightly, he offers his services to take the visitors in his van wherever they would like to go anytime when he is not away on a trip. In leaps and jumps, Aunt Alejandra's voice and laughter invade and take possession of the house.

Ximena closes her eyes and takes a deep breath. She is afraid that if she had to speak, she would not recognize her own voice. To keep the memory of Healthcliff or of Robertson from making her burst into tears right at that moment, she tries to concentrate on the book of myths. Nevertheless, the drawings lose the serenity of their fixedness and undulate like rushing water; they spill out beyond the pages, clouding her eyes. "The smell of gasoline has made me feel sick," she thinks while the faces of Psyche and Aphrodite loom closer and closer and in the growing dizziness of the engraving, Ximena imagines that she sees a kiss.

She maneuvers it to go play with Sami and Beto at the Robertson's' house. Her mother has been indecisive until the last minute, but the weaver has kept insisting and Ximena knows that, caught unprepared, her mother will not been able to find a proper excuse and she has no wish to risk offending the woman who has so often felt the town's contempt. The brothers do not seem particularly interested in her visit, although just in case they should oppose it, Ximena deliberately did not reveal the end of a story that she told them at teatime. She has named the two princes Samuel and Alberto, and she has described incidents in places the boys had mentioned on other occasions. Although they seemed indifferent at first, they were finally seduced by the personal parallels Ximena described and they fell totally into the trap. But now they have gone outside to play and they are energetically trying to strike a fire with two flintstones they have found in the patio.

Even when it would be shorter to go by the riverside, they go through the field near the houses the Company has built for important employees. Sami and Beto run on ahead. They have picked two switches out of the woodpile of cut-off branches, and they amuse themselves by dragging them over the white fence posts while they imitate the intermittent popping sound of machine guns. Every once in a while they jump in front of each other and fight with the sticks as though they were swords. Ximena does not mind being left out of these games. She is thinking about Robertson, looking at the two boys and feeling the weaver's hand as an almost tangible continuation of the van driver's. Besides, she views everything she sees in a new light and although she focuses on things with her usual curiosity, always eager to see something new, the surroundings seem different to her, as if they were another color. "My eyes have changed," she thinks as they draw near the bridge. The weaver calls her children. There is none of her usual meekness in her tone; the cry does not come out of just her throat but from her entire body, from her gray dress with its pattern of faded daisies, from her worn-down shoe heels.

All four of them hold hands as they cross the bridge. Ximena mentally compares Sami's hand with his mother's. It is like gripping a warm live bird on one side, and on the other a bird which is barely tepid but which cannot make up its mind to die. The voice she has heard a few seconds before does not correspond in any way to that bland inert hand. When they get to the center of town, they head in the direction away from the shops and they walk toward the side of Pueblo Viejo where the poorest houses are, almost as shabby as those in the Company's camp for workers. The people who recognize her do not hide their astonishment when they see her with the weaver. It is the first time Ximena experiences in her own breathing how hostile stares can thicken the air.

The Robertsons' apartment is very small and dark. Ximena looks around for the source of the lemony smell that fills the place. At first she cannot locate it, but then she realizes that it is the walls that give off that slight but clinging aroma. There are just two rooms. In the larger one, next to a chipped old sink, they have put in a gas burner and a table with four chairs that do not match. All the kitchen things are in that corner. Farther along there is a very old sofa patched with a series of crocheted circles made to look like doilies. The walls are decorated with pictures cut out of magazines, a photo of the Pope in a gilt frame, and odd tapestries—perhaps made with the odds and ends of threads and wools left over from custom orders—which combine a delirious mixture of colors. Half hidden in a shadowy corner is the loom, which has made the weaver well known in the town. On the floor behind the armchair, Ximena sees a mattress covered with two or three blankets. Unembarrassed, Beto tells her that he and his brother sleep there.

"Where does your father sleep?"

Beto points to the only other room in the apartment. Instead of a door there is a kind of curtain hanging on several hooks. The weaver is wringing out something in the sink and the boys are still playing with their sticks. Ximena fully understands that even if they were—perfectly reasonably—to want to stop her audacity, her desire and need to cross to the other side impel her as forcibly as the compulsion to turn to the next page of a book. She enters, and her eyes have to adjust to the semidarkness because the window is only another dark frame. The room is so tiny that the bed, the same size as hers, fills almost the entire space. On a dresser, there is an image of the Blessed Virgin, a wooden crucifix, several religious pictures and in the center, a tin candlestick with an unlit candle in it.

Ximena looks for traces of Heathcliff in the room. Something brushes against her hair and she discovers a shelf bracketed to the wall holding a clock, a wooden box like the valley craftsmen make, a few toilet articles and a soap dish with a shaving brush. Stepping softly, she goes over and smells the soap, but the lemon odor doesn't let her get a full sense of it. Then she picks up the brush with her fingertips and runs it over her face. Without returning it to its place, she takes two steps toward the clothes hung on hangers on big nails in the wall. She leans against some denim overalls with faded black oil spots on them. For a few seconds she smells Robertson's hands on the rough blue cloth. She would like to linger in that bedroom, touching, recovering the feeling of languidness and anxiety that have filled her since she saw the movie, intensified since she noticed the van driver, but the weaver is calling her. With the curtain as backdrop behind her, and with her hands hanging at her sides, the woman looks the perfect image of a martyr resigned to her sacrifice.

Because it is impossible to play hide-and-seek or tag in such a small space, they take a skein of red wool and one of them hides it for the others to find, with the hider saying "hotter" or "colder" as the seekers move closer to or farther from the wool. Maliciously, the boys trick her and confuse her by giving her false information, and Ximena, frustrated, goes over to the weaver, who is embroidering a white tablecloth. She admires the elegance and confidence with which her brown fingers aim the thread as they dart in and out of the cloth, as flowers and leaves, also in white, begin to grow and swell and take on the quality and substance of butterflies trapped and pinned onto a mounting. It is hard for Ximena to believe that that hand is the same one that rested so lightly in hers when they crossed the river.

"Why does your house smell of lemon?"

"Because I cry so much," answers the woman without changing her expression. "Before I came here, I had several lemon balm plants in my patio and the smell has followed me, not in my body but in the walls that look at me when I feel sad."

"And why are you sad?"

"Because I am condemned."

Ximena has almost never heard that word, although she thinks she understands what it means; it is not only having nothing: it means to be nothing. In vain she tries to find some words of comfort in response to that alarming confession, which, with the weaver's sighs, has intensified the aroma of the walls. "My mother says no one embroiders or weaves as well as you."

"The embroidery needles and loom are my punishment, but they help me to live."

In jumbled order, some images and episodes from the book of myths suggest a dangerous fate to her. She thinks of Athena and she feels cold. To protect herself from what she does not understand and which drags her irreversibly into confusion, Ximena goes back to see what the boys are doing. They have stopped making the uproar of a few minutes before, and they are playing with a wooden top. She would like to go over to see and hear the magical humming and spinning toy. From where she is, she envies them a little resentfully. Her own top is not one of the real ones; it is imported and hardly any bigger than a nut, enameled red and carved to look like an apple. It doesn't have a steel tip and the wooden point doesn't make music like the bigger ones do, even when they are crudely made.

Sami and Beto lift their heads suddenly. They have heard the motor of their father's van pulling up next to the sidewalk. Ximena feels a river thundering through her temples and flooding her voice. She pulls her knees up to her chest and wraps her arms around her legs so that no one will notice that her body is trembling. Robertson comes in and does not see her. He spends a few seconds with the boys, who tell him something that makes him turn in surprise toward the kitchen area. He comes up to her and like the time before, he runs his hand over her head and, smiling, holds it out to her in a gesture of greeting. Ximena is slow in giving him her hand, but at the moment when she knows it to be within the grasp of the van driver's big rough fingers, the room begins to spin around her. She would like to faint for once and for all, but she is restrained by her fear that, upon recovering consciousness, she would have a coughing fit. Robertson has knelt down by her and is peering at her worriedly. "Do you feel sick?"

Ximena does not answer. The weaver brings her a glass of water, which temporarily soothes the hallucinated flow of an uncontrollable current that makes her burn with fever and shiver with chills. Robertson comes even closer and lifts her chin, searching her eyes for the trace of an illness. Holding her breath for fear of shattering the image, she concentrates on the two shades of color in his irises, on the light and dark sparks flaring up in the blue explosion of his enormous pupils. The pattern of rays she can see in his eyes reminds her of the drawing of the sun in an astrology book.

The weaver insists that the boys have not done anything to her, that until just a few moments ago she was at her side talking with her, that perhaps the angel of another child has strayed through her body by mistake. "In any case," she adds, resting her hand on her forehead and then adjusting her hair clip, "it would be a good idea for you to take her home."

Ximena rides along seated between Robertson and the boys, on the front seat of the van. She has calmed down a bit although she still doesn't feel all there; it seems to her that from some distance off, she is observing the scene where a blond driver is sitting behind the steering wheel whistling while a skinny girl sits beside him. Suddenly Sami jabs her in the ribs with his elbow. "Hey, finish telling us the story."

"I don't want to any longer."

The boys complain and Robertson makes them stop. "Don't pay any attention to them," he tells her and puts a hand on her knee to reassure her.

Ximena dares to lean over a little, very stealthily, so she can look at him. His profile is Heathcliff's, his way of furrowing his eyebrows is the same. That night she will ask her mother to read her a bit of the book. She looks forward to being able to think about him before falling asleep, and she derives comfort from this anticipation, even though she already senses that it will be heavy with grief.

Robertson accompanies her to the kitchen door. Ama Grande

comes out to meet them, surprised that Ximena does not run to hug her legs. Gretchen and Aunt Alejandra, who are sorting photographs in the dining room, come over smiling. Ximena notices the man's confusion, this time knowing to watch for it.

"Why so early? Here we were just having a good rest from all your questions," her aunt tugs her hair gently and Ximena aches with awareness of how ridiculous it is to be her age.

"I don't know whether she is just shy or whether she is coming down with something," says Robertson.

Aunt Alejandra bursts out laughing. Ama Grande laughs, too, and even he joins in. Only Gretchen, with her round eyes, stares at her without blinking and remains serious, without a smile.

"Timid? This little character? On the contrary, she does some pretty odd things, especially when she gets wound up or goes into her Scheherazade mode and tells incredible stories non-stop."

She is too embarrassed to pay attention to the other things they say, but her legs do not comply when she orders them to take her to her bedroom. Before he leaves, Robertson shakes hands with the two women and closes the door after himself without remembering her or Ama Grande.

When Ximena is heading for the refuge of her room, she hears her aunt's strong, clear voice. "Don't you think he would be a perfect model for your Apollo? If Isabel has no objection, I'm going to see if I can take a series of photos of him. And I would certainly pay him so that his wife won't think we're up to anything else."

Ximena sits down on the edge of her bed and does not know what to do to free herself of the distress which has invaded her body, or how to stop herself from feeling, at the same time, so remote, so distanced from herself, as though her affliction were due to that very doubling, that distancing, that unknown and nameless breach between herself and everything else that no matter how hard she tries, she cannot seal up or close.

When she wakes up it is still dark. She is clinging to the edge of the bed trying to keep her distance from the heat of her aunt's body even though she does not really remember having bumped into her at all with her arm or legs. She stretches a little to get comfortable without disturbing her aunt and she reaches out her hand to try to measure the space which separates them. She doesn't find anything and her foot moves more freely, only encountering the cold softness of the sheets. There have been other times when she has half wakened at night and has also been aware of not feeling her beside her, but she has heard sounds, as if from far away: murmurs, moans, a rocking that makes the bedroom vibrate, something like the cadence of the train which comforts her before she falls asleep.

She turns over and looks across at the other side. In the dim light that is barely beginning to diffuse through the window, she can make out her aunt's back over on the camp cot. Gretchen's arm is resting on her slender waist, and her hand, small and rosy, is visible against her friend's smooth brown hair. Their bodies are so close together that from where she is, they look like just one person and only the hand and the copper curls resting against her aunt's dark hair let her know that they are sleeping with their arms around each other. She sits up in bed without making a sound and contemplates them with curiosity. They breathe in unison and so gently that if it were not for a slight trembling that shakes them both at the same time, in the opaque light of the room, they would look like a photo blown up to life size. Disconcerted, and nevertheless filled with a new happiness that bubbles in her chest and warms the cold dawn air, Ximena lies back down.

She yearns for a body next to hers, someone like a sister, or a good friend, someone at her side with whom to sleep without having to think. Even the enormous stuffed bear would be company right now, but she would have to get it out of the cupboard where she has put it, and she does not want to wake them and interrupt their sweet and peaceful sleep.

Something terrible has happened. While Ximena was enjoying herself looking at the illustrations in the encyclopedia and listening closely for the first time to the sad words of a tango on the radio, her mother has tried over and over again to telephone Ximena's father. Nervously she paces through the living room and the dining room, her lips tense and her eyes shiny. When Ximena has asked her why she is that way, she has snapped at her not to bother her, that it is none of her business. Finally she manages to get through to her husband and she tells him that she can't explain over the phone, that he has to come home right away even if he can't stay long. No, it can't wait until evening. Yanking furiously at the telephone cord, she yells exasperatedly that he should come home now, right away.

There is no one in the house. It is Ama Grande's day off, and the two friends have gone to visit a nearby town. Ximena is reassured by the fact that the van the Company uses for errands has come to pick them up, and that they have not had to call Robertson. She does not know if they are still thinking of using him as a model. It has not seemed like a good idea to her mother, who thinks that this kind of relationship can cause upheavals in such a small community and not only affect them but also the driver's family, and they have problems enough already. Ximena thinks about Robertson before she goes to sleep; she thinks about him when she hears love songs like now; and at last Sunday's matinee, for the first time she felt overwhelmed by emotion during the movie's final kiss scene. She also thinks about him when she mentally browses through the episodes of *Wuthering Heights* and even more when her mother agrees to read to her or to answer her questions about the characters, and later she rearranges these impressions as she wishes.

She no longer despairs when she cannot recover her initial memory of the episodes. An invisible but definite bridge crosses her over to labyrinths of new sensations where she herself is involved in the mystery. Even in the illustrations and in the fantastic stories of the myth book, the ones that get so mixed up in her head without her being able or without her even wanting to remember them separately and in order, there are constant traces of Robertson and Heathcliff who gradually have begun to lose their individual characteristics and to be identifiable only by their names.

When her father arrives, they send her out to the patio. Ximena obeys because she knows that arguing will do no good. She watches them close themselves up in the big bedroom and she walks across the kitchen, opens the door which leads to the patio and slams it hard without going out through it. She waits a few seconds and on tiptoe she returns to her room and goes into the bathroom. As she expected, her parents' door to the bathroom is closed and, lowering her pants just in case they catch her by surprise, she puts her ear against the keyhole. She can hear her father's voice clearly.

"Calm down, dear; maybe it isn't the way you think."

A sound of buzzing bees answers him. Taking great care not to make a sound, Ximena leans up closer to the little opening to try and make out some of the words. She can hear the sharp and broken tones of her mother's voice but not the separate words; it sounds like crickets caught in a sudden rainstorm. Once again her father's voice comes through clearly. "And even if it were true, why should it affect you?"

The buzzing sound gets louder, bouncing off the walls, a humming which ricochets back and forth in harsh scratches. Ximena hears the rattling of branches being tossed about by a gale force wind that is crashing against the furniture looking for an exit. She knows that all this fury is unloosed in the bedroom by her mother's blind and violent pacing.

"Calm down, they aren't hurting anyone. Artists are like that, eccentric, and tell me, how can Alejandra possibly respect that womanizer of a husband she's got?"

"It's contrary to nature!"

This time the incomprehensible words have reached her clearly, carried by that strident screech that pushes her backwards.

The storm seems to be fading, moaning its departure, ceding before the insistent sobriety of that other voice. Despite the uncontrollable wobbliness of her knees, Ximena calms down, too, and even feels sympathy for the continued sobbing in the other room.

"They kissed on the mouth, on the mouth, like this, on the mouth! Oh Enrique, I want them to get out of my house! I saw them hugging each other, I saw them...on the mouth..."

Ximena does not wait longer. Confused, she pulls her pants up and stepping noiselessly she goes into the kitchen and then out to the patio. She sits on the cement steps and gazes through the fence rails at the expanse of the field, the blurry spot of the distant camp. As so often before, she feels forsaken, and she is cold. Pulling her knees up to her chest, she folds her arms around them and hides her face from the afternoon light that hurts her eyes.

That night, the two friends do not return home to sleep. They have called to say that they will be back the next day. The three eat in silence even though her father has tried to act as usual and has even joked with her every once in a while. Ama Grande has still not returned and her mother busies herself bringing in supper and taking the plates back out to the kitchen. Her eyes are swollen and sometimes turn glassy and distant, as though she had left what she wants to look for in some inner part of herself. She walks back and forth,

sits down, takes a deep breath and seems disconnected from everything around her. She doesn't even scold her when Ximena barely
tastes the piece of bloody steak they put on her plate.

Before she falls asleep, when her eyes have adapted to the darkness
of the room, Ximena looks at the cot opened out beside her bed.
Narrow and flat under the wool blankets, its narrowness reveals its
temporary status. It seems ready to be folded up at any moment and
returned unprotestingly to the storeroom off the patio. Ximena
thinks about the two sleeping, embracing bodies she had watched in
the peaceful dawn, and she misses them. She would like to see them
sleeping that way even if it could only be once more.

The train goes by right on schedule, just when Robertson is leading her by the hand across an infinite open meadow. Ximena knows
that if they keep on going straight, the grass tickling her feet through
her sandals will turn into sand because they will have come to a
deserted beach where there are neither rocks nor trees. She breathes
in the smell of the sea, listens and matches her breathing to the ebb
and flow of the waves she still cannot see, and she would like to pick
the little purple flowers that she can barely make out in the dim light
of the evening, but he leads her on toward the sea and she cannot run
and get ahead of him because she is older and young women are not
supposed to rush even when their bodies and desires yearn to burst
out. Her short hair, black and straight, hangs in folded wings on
either side of her face and when it brushes against her cheeks, she
smells the light almond perfume that Aunt Alejandra wears.

They do not reach the beach. Thinking her asleep, her mother has
tiptoed into the room. She turns on the lamp on the night table and
begins to look through Aunt Alejandra's and her friend's things.
Ximena, her back to the light, pretends to be asleep. By the sounds
her mother makes, she can tell that she is turning the pages of a book
or a notebook. Then she hears her sit down on the other bed and

move the lamp farther over toward her side. Ximena hears the murmur, clear in the room's quiet, that her mother makes with her lips when she reads. Little by little the words begin to reach her more distinctly because, feeling herself to be alone, her mother's whisper rises, since there is no one around making fun of her, saying she can't read anything without spreading the story to the four winds.

"I don't know how they had let me get in, but I was not afraid that they would find me. Grandmother was smoking a cigarette in an ivory holder carved with delicate swirls. The smoke rose in blue puffs and mixing with the smoke was incense burning in a tiny Aladdin's lamp. The walls were covered with tapestries and paintings and on the floor there was a mattress covered with a brilliant bedspread, with several cushions of various sizes and colors on it. On the wide sill of the window overlooking the garden there were photographs in silver and wood frames. Grandmother, who was wrapped in a Manila shawl with a black background and yellow and purple flowers embroidered on it, put her arm around my waist. She stretched out her free hand in order to show me the photos, one by one, with her long hooked index finger.

"That one is me when I was queen of the Carnival when I was eighteen. Here I am the following year, in my wedding dress. See what a hangdog expression I have! This naked woman under a veil that doesn't cover anything is also me, a lot happier here. The photo was taken right after I married, by my first lover. He was such a gloomy man; he tried to weigh me down with guilt, wrote poems with terrible rhymes and one night in April, shot himself to death. I keep the photo so I can keep him company for a while in death since in life I was never able to pledge him eternal love. This is the bullfighter with whom I ran off to Andalucía for a few months. They gave me up for dead even though I wrote them a letter from Tunis, and when I got home they all met me with funereal faces. This is my husband, your grandfather, many years later, smiling as though he had won a battle, with one foot on a king-size puma, handsomer and worthier than he is. He ambushed him with the help of Indians who were frightened and obedient because the animal's roar had kept them awake during his nocturnal prowls that began when my husband began to fence in his property. This is the best friend I ever had. She is very young here, and the photo does not do her justice, but it is the only one I have. Through years and years we kept up a friendship that was a true union of body and spirit, passion and charity. In her, the essence of trees and of larks fused together effortlessly. Here am I, in my forties, drinking a toast with some diplomats in the Hotel Crillón and that man with the profile of a Viking staring at me, was the Norwegian ambassador who, in flawless Spanish, was reciting the most obscene limericks I had ever heard. In this one I look like a ghost because I had just come back from one of those terrible seclusions forced upon me by the family at regular intervals. This time they locked me up with a nurse and two servants for several weeks in a little house in Chosica that was like a dollhouse. This boy with a dreamy expression is your uncle, that giant with gray hair you know so well, before he got stuck with the burden of the inherited and futile message that he and all the field workers should spend their lives maintaining the family estate forever for the benefit of its heirs. This is your aunt, my only daughter, who died of terrible astral fevers when she was twelve; in her delirium, like certain salamanders, her color changed to many different hues and before she died, I discovered her floating like a silk butterfly in the rarefied air of her bedroom. They accused me of not weeping when she died, but I always knew, ever since she was born, that she was not firmly grounded in this life, that her voice only reflected the shadow of the things she saw, not the things themselves. She was weighed down by her skin, her chestnut braid, the rosy pallor of her breasts. That little girl in a party dress is your mother at her fifteenth birthday celebration. See how much she looks like your grandfather? Just like him, but without his spitefulness; she was embarrassed by me from the moment she became aware of anything. She lived decorously and she died decorously, confessing her little sins, the trivial slights that made her suffer so as a good society lady.

"But I don't want you to feel sad. If I am telling you these things it is because I know how much you like stories and even though I've always preferred life itself, I preferred it to the extent to which it was like certain stories, only certain ones, because since we live through words, it is necessary to select which role we want to play whenever we can. Alas for the multiple Dianas and for the goddess of Ephesus. Why are you looking so serious? Come, I also know how much you enjoy sweets and before you go, I want to give you a candy and also a ring that was mine for a very long time."

Grandmother glides across the room as if her feet were not touching the floor. Her body gives off an aroma of dry flowers and of musk powder. She takes a little coconut ball out of a box wrapped in tissue paper and puts it into Ximena's hand. It feels weightless. By the door, she leans over a little, just enough so that her face is on a level with Ximena's, and she whispers to her, "Help them, Ximena, you can do it, help them."

When she opens her eyes, it is day, and it is a struggle to recognize the familiar surroundings of her room. She remembers the candy because her bedroom smells of coconut and vanilla and one of her hands, closed into a fist, opens to show her a ring with a tiny ruby set so deep into the gold that it barely sticks up at all. The smell of incense still clings to her, pulling her and enticing her back to the other side of the dream. She opens her hand again and she sees that she has clenched her hand closed so hard while sleeping that her nails have left a curved dent in which a drop of blood has dried, red and round, perfect in its smallness. She looks at the palm of her hand again, but just then she hears Ama Grande's footsteps coming toward her and she closes her hand to hide the ring that she has again glimpsed and felt, hard and warm against her skin.

Gretchen has come back alone. It seems that Aunt Alejandra has decided to stay for a day longer on the high plateau of frozen lakes where the two of them had gone to paint and take photographs. As she crosses the threshold, she barely greets them. She does not take off her green wool jacket, she does not look straightforwardly at them as she had before; her eyes are irritated and she looks exhausted. Her mother has gone out to welcome her and they both come in wearing the desolate look of people who have lost something. Ximena is afraid that her mother will break the silence with the cutting words she has been polishing up during their absence, but no, she holds her tongue and does not say anything while Gretchen walks slowly to the bedroom to pack up her things. Ximena follows her out of curiosity and because she feels bad that she should be alone that way, looking so hunched over and orphaned. Coming up to her, she asks her if she would like to try the coconut dessert that Ama Grande has been preparing since before breakfast. Gretchen does not answer her, but when she kneels down to pick up some shoes, she puts her arms around her.

"I didn't want it to end this way, Ximena, but Alejandra is very obstinate and won't listen to reason," she murmurs in a faint voice.

From the dining room, Ximena watches the two women, who do not know how to say good-bye to each other. Her mother's dress rehearsals for a planned confrontation seem to have gotten her distress under control, and she seems even calmer after making the arrangements for a Company van to take Gretchen to the station, where she will be able to arrange long distance transportation.

"There is no point in my waiting for Alejandra because I know that right now any effort at reconciliation would be futile," Gretchen tells her mother. She is clearly making a big effort not to seem upset. "But, please Isabel, when she gets here tell her that I am waiting for her in Lima, that we have to talk more about things, that everything that happened is a misunderstanding. There is no point in my waiting for her today, so I have no other choice than to go, but knowing her, if we let the days go by, it will be too late for us both. Tell her that I am waiting for her in Lima; she knows where. Please, tell her that from me."

Before leaving, she turns toward Ximena and looks at her again as though she would like to delve into her bottommost thoughts. When she opens the door, from inside the house, Ximena hears the purr of the motor that echoes the sustained, harsh thumping of her own chest. She realizes that without the insistence of that gaze that some-times confused her so, she is more alone than ever, because in a way Gretchen, too, carries off something of Heathcliff and Robertson with her as she leaves.

Aunt Alejandra does not come back that night. They wait for her for a long time before having tea and her place at the table is still set at dinnertime. She has not sent any sort of message and her mother begins to worry about her as the hours go by. She has calmed down a lot since the day before, but Ximena knows that she has not changed her mind about what upset her so violently the previous day, because she continues to be distant and even cold to her husband when they are both in the same room. As usually happens when they are quar-reling, he tries to mitigate the tension of the silences by playing with Ximena. But this time she does not feel like going along with this, and instead, she takes refuge in the memory of her dream. Breaking into the uncomfortable silence that isolates them, the cuckoo of grandfa-ther's clock points out at regular intervals how alone the three of them are. When Ama Grande comes in to take her off for a bath,

Ximena is a little cheered by her aroma of the valley, of herbs, and of spices. She is also consoled by her familiar gestures, rough and tender at the same time, the predictable movements of her body and the tone of her voice while she puts her to bed. And that night she is grateful to hear stories about condors and elves instead of the sad *huaynos* she sometimes sings to her to entertain her while she is in the bath.

She is wakeful and she pleads for a book, any book, so she can look at the pictures before she goes to sleep. Her father hands her the myth book and Ximena turns the pages to find the colored illustrations, trying to recall the stories that go with them. She is exhausted by the emotions of the last two days, but she knows that sleep will elude her, that it will be of no use to close her eyes, to wait for the sound of the train passing, to invent games, or to think about Robertson because now his image, much to her grief, is inextricably linked to the absence of her Aunt Alejandra. She would like to find her way to sleep by returning to Grandmother's room, by getting the ring out of the treasure box where she has hidden it, but she is afraid of not finding it, and she is equally afraid that if she does see Grandmother again, she will see her as she did last, small and in a death sleep in the ebony coffin, dressed in black, a black mantilla on her head and a missal attached to her translucent hands by a rosary of alabaster beads. She does not want to remember her this way and she seeks help in the book illustrations, although she is too tired to even want to sort out the myths that always end up by getting tangled up in her imagination and that go off on their own in new directions.

When her mother comes in to pray with her and turn off the light, she lies in the darkness thinking about the weavers in the book and about the terrible punishments they suffer at the hands of the goddess who should have been looking out for them. And what would happen if Robertson's wife, like the spider in the myth, were condemned not only to be nothing, as Ximena had thought to begin with, but rather to weave and knit, to weave and knit all her life long as retribution for what she had done, her part in that scandal that not even her own father would forgive? Maybe at night, when everyone else was asleep in that little apartment that was so dark anyway, the weaver turns into a spider and as a spider learns the labyrinths of her art so that when she turns into a human again, she can continue to weave together all the invisible threads in which the image of Robertson has been kept captive. Perhaps the lemon balm smell that invades her house is part of her punishment or, who knows, maybe it is a benign spell created by another goddess to alleviate her sentence. But there is also another weaver and in the midst of her tiredness and confusion, Ximena turns the light on and looks for the figure in black and white on one corner of the page that depicts a woman about to drown herself in the waves of an angry sea. She finds her and knows that she is that one, although she doesn't understand the role of the weaver in this myth. The only things she can remember is that Athena has intervened again and that once again a woman has been chastised.

It is much later, when she is on the verge of falling asleep, when her mother comes in and scolds her for still having her light on and takes the thick book out of her hands, that the image of Alcinoe looms up tragically in the twilight of her dream.

Aunt Alejandra arrives in mid morning. She throws the bundles she has taken on her excursion onto the rocking chair in the living room and goes into Ximena's bedroom without even saying good morning. She, too, begins to pack her things, but in marked contrast to Gretchen, her movements are brusque and angry and she seems to be battling with everything she stuffs into her enormous canvas bag. Since she hasn't put on makeup and she is very pale, the bones of her face are clearly visible within the frame of her dark hair, making her face look like a mask. Ximena does not dare to offer her anything. From the door into the dining room, she watches those frenetic movements with alarm. In another part of the house, and without consulting Alejandra, her mother is phoning for someone to come take her to the station.

While they wait for the Company van, there is an oppressive silence. Ximena knows that her mother is wishing she could find the words in which to say a conventional good-bye and that perhaps she would manage this except that there is nothing usual about her cousin's tense figure. Ama Grande comes in shuffling her feet and bringing a box lunch so that the traveler will have something to eat on the way. Then it is the old woman who offers to carry the strange baggage to the van.

It is only when her Aunt Alejandra, still without having said anything at all, heads for the door that her mother speaks to her in an almost inaudible voice: "Gretchen left a message for you. She asks you to wait for her, you know where, in Trujillo."

Ximena's chest gives a great jump. Although she thinks she remembers that it was not a weaver who threw herself into the sea after having lost her mind over a foreign guest, she has a premonition—in clear black and white—that Robertson's weaver, forsaken by him, will drown herself, abandoning her children for the second time. Then Ximena's thoughts are invaded by a tangle of colored threads that suggest to her that her Aunt Alejandra will take Robertson's van to Trujillo and that they will go off, the two of them, to live together, and that on a certain evening, under a rosy sky, against a backdrop of a very blue sea on the Huanchaco beach, under the shadow of a small flowering bush, he will recline his head on Alejandra's chest and then raise it and move his lips up to hers.

"No! She hasn't gone to Trujillo. She is waiting for you in the place you know in Lima and she says that everything has been a misunderstanding and that what she most needs in the world is to talk to you."

When she hears the crash of the door slamming, Ximena runs to hide herself in Ama Grande's skirts. She is trembling, more because of what she has just done than because of the inevitable punishment she will receive from her mother. "What mess have you gotten yourself tangled up in now?" her Ama murmurs, caressing her.

Ximena does not answer her, and although it is forbidden, she lets her pick her up like a baby to hug her. The smell of the kitchen and of the old woman's body gradually have a calming effect. She realizes that she feels distanced from the self that is trembling, as though she were able to observe it from a little way away from where it is located. It is as though she were herself and yet separate, strange, other with the otherness that the memory of Robertson holds for her when she manages to conjure him up without effort by closing her eyes. Now, however, his image appears to her stripped of the delirious agitation of the last few days. She is not surprised, even though it is painful for her to realize that no matter how much effort she makes, she cannot remember what Heathcliff looks like, and even less how his voice sounded. As she hears the rhythm of her mother's footsteps approaching, each tap an implacable harbinger of the next, Ximena understands that in order to keep dreaming, she will have to open her mind to new Healthcliffs, she will have to invent new woven images with the help of who knows what shadows and words, as they make their warp and weft out of the letters and sentences of the books that will open to her when she finally learns how to read.

V / THE COAST

And such was the spell that those who descended
to decipher the signs that sang on the sand,
lost their previous path, confused
the times, and were no longer able to say
whose voice they heard.

A'isa bint Tàsfin (12th century)

The main gate was closed, but Ximena had no difficulty sliding open
the iron bolt that gleamed in the sunlight and felt almost painfully
hot to her cold fingertips. As always when she crossed to the forbidden zone, on the other side of the patio, her chest thumped furiously
in anticipation of daring to look at the crazy girl tied up to the giant
ficus tree in the back. There she was, sitting silently, motionless, on
the dry earth, hugging her long skinny legs with her needle-thin arms.
Only this time, she didn't make her usual fuss or even seem to take
notice of the new arrival. The sound of running water distracted
Ximena. Without completely letting go of the gate, she turned in surprise in the direction of the old washtub where María Eugenia had

told her Don Serafino scrubbed the hotel sheets. She saw a head dripping with water and at first, because the person was tall and the hair
very short, Ximena thought it must be a boy. But no, it was a young
woman. She was wearing tight pants, faded into different shades of
green and tied around the waist with a thin rope. She was semi-naked
and, Ximena, astonished, stared for an instant at the erect breasts
exposed to the bright light of day without thought of modesty.
Reaching out, the woman grabbed a white towel like the ones in the
hotel and only after wrapping it around her head like a turban, did
she notice the presence of Ximena, who continued to watch her in
amazement from just a few steps away.

The girl said nothing, and barely smiled. Ximena stayed there
transfixed, staring at her eyes. "They are like the sea," she thought
and then, a second later, the first lines of Gutierre de Cetina that she
had heard so many times popped into her mind: "Oh light, serene
eyes..." Ximena was so enraptured by the vision that she felt dizzy for
a moment, and clung even tighter to the gate, because her knees felt
wobbly. This was the most beautiful woman she had ever seen in her
life, more beautiful than the ones in pictures in her mother's magazines or any of the actresses she had seen in movies, far lovelier than
the most beautiful women in the family albums or in the illustrations
in her books of fairy tales.

A big hand grabbed her shoulder. "I've told you over and over
again, missy, that you shouldn't be here. It gets the crazy girl all
upset."

It was Don Serafino with his face as yellow as papyrus, wearing his
old straw hat. Ximena resisted. She wanted to keep watching the
woman; she wanted to keep absorbing that unexpected image with
her eyes. Don Serafino did not give in, and pulled her away toward
the patio. With the sun shining in her eyes, it was hard to make out
the medal that hung on a fragile gold chain on the stranger's damp

chest, but Ximena managed to see the outlines of a starfish that glinted whenever a ray of morning light caught on it and lifted it out of the shadow of her neck.

"Who is that woman?" Ximena asked him.

"What woman?"

"The one washing her hair in the laundry tub."

Don Serafino smiled.

"You're quite a joker, aren't you!" he answered. "They're right when they say you make things up. Trying to fool me, when I'm as old as that tree! Go on inside. Your mother is sure to be looking for you."

Ximena kept on asking questions even though she knew it would not do her any good. No, there was no one there except for the poor crazy girl, the hotel owner told her, while he refused to let go of her shoulder. There was never anybody else in the back lot at this hour. Never. No one, not even the people who lived in the hut in the back, used that laundry tub. Never. No one except him and Anacleto, and she should not tell lies like that to adults.

They passed by María Eugenia's room, separated from the rest of the hotel rooms because it faced onto the patio. A smell of burned milk pried her body loose from the remains of the daydream in colors she had managed to cling to until then. She made an effort to rescue it, closed her eyes so as not to forget the woman, her tranquil expression, the starfish against her naked chest. When she opened her eyes she saw her mother and Libertad Calderón, who were waiting for her in the hallway with the bags all packed up, ready to go to the beach.

It is a short trip to the little town where they spend summer vacations, not more than two hours from Lima, but this time it is an uncomfortable trip for Ximena because they have put her in the back seat with Libertad Calderón, whom she hardly knows. Her father drives and some of the time he sings tangos and the Spanish songs he still recalls from childhood, in his warm tenor voice. Her mother accompanies him, as usual, more in silence than in song since she has brought a book of poems along to read on the trip. When he falls silent, she reads a poem that she likes, out loud and passionately, and then Ximena, looking sidelong, notices the girl's mocking smile. They ask Ximena to tell a story from her ever-changing repertoire, but this time she refuses; it embarrasses her that her parents are putting together a whole entertainment program no one has requested. Trying to isolate herself, she keeps pressing her face against the opaque glass on the window. She would have been much happier if Ama Grande had wanted to come with them, but the old woman was unmoved by all of their pleas, even hers. She has never liked the coast, and even though it is the rainy season and her poor bones suffer so from the cold, she has preferred, as on other occasions, to spend these weeks in the highlands.

Ximena looks out and does not see the desolate landscape her father is complaining about, using long, difficult words that she does not know. On the contrary, she has always liked the enormous expanses of sand on both sides of the highway better than the valley's green hills, with little rivers winding their way along, and ochre-colored trails. As she has every summer, she pays reverent attention to the marks carved by the wind on the surface of the dunes, tracings which look permanent but keep shifting around. She amuses herself by opening and closing her eyes, and trying to guess at possible objects that the play of shadows suggests on the sand. Pretty soon she stops doing this because by now, she has realized that it is easier to fantasize about imaginary shapes in the clouds than in the sand patterns. Depending on how they are reflecting the light, the colors of the dunes vary, and Ximena feels them both as salt and as thirst in her mouth. Anchored in her silence, and rebelling against her father, she thinks about how all these shades she cannot even name attract her much more than the concrete colors of mountain vegetation.

Every once in a while, she leans over into the center so she can see out the front windshield and watch the shining pools that suddenly appear in the middle of the highway and then disappear, magically, as they get close to them. "They are sea mirages," her father has explained to her as he often has before; however, she does not understand the connection between the sea which she still cannot see nor smell, and those puddles of light that vanish between one heartbeat and the next.

From time to time, she can spot a diffuse blotch in the distance that looms up unexpectedly in the middle of the arid plain, and Ximena's enthusiasm never dims when they come to one of the towns strung out along the length of the highway. Because the streets are narrow and the car has to move along slowly, sometimes her eyes meet those of other children, and then she shivers just like she did the year before, and is again surprised that people on the coast stare in a different way than mountain people. When her mother requests it, they get out of the car to walk around a bit in the little plaza in front of the church and they let her choose the leafiest tree and the least shabby bench to sit down on and drink a soda. The air has a special aroma and the sun warms her skin with an exquisite stinging sensation. Ximena breathes in deeply, drawing the softness of the breeze into her lungs, and if no one is looking at her, she closes her eyes to better enjoy the heat on her face and arms.

When they stop like this, she whimpers to get them to stay a few minutes longer before they get back in the car. She could spend hours watching the heavyset women in their close-fitting dresses of flowered cotton, gazing at the ragged children with round eyes who laugh so openly and kick a ball around skillfully while they play and yell back and forth. She could spend hours feeling a yearning curiosity to plunge her fingertips into the thick curly hair, like metallic shavings, of men with dark skins and thick lips; hours being astonished over and over again at the insistent—impertinent, her mother has sometimes remarked—way in which almost all of them look directly at her without trying to avoid eye contact. So she pleads with them for a few more minutes, and to herself, she repeats "thank you, thank you, God" while she consciously lets herself be swathed in that sugar-sweet air and those disturbing sensations that she only experiences on the coast.

The town where they usually stay has a gray street that seems interminable to Ximena because they always enter from one direction and never drive the full length of the street to see where it ends on the other side of town. This summer, she gets reacquainted with the familiar places: lots of big and small restaurants, tiny dark sweet shops, the only bakery where they also serve food, modest hotels with half-illegible signs, two barber shops, the movie theater, the dentist's, the pharmacy and the same old stores with dim lighting on the same corners. There are cross streets, very narrow and unpaved, where there must be houses, but looking out the window, Ximena can see that the streets are very short, and she guesses that they end in empty lots rather than in cultivated fields. She does not know whether there is a main square like in other towns and she has not yet figured out where the church is. On the coast, her mother stops going to mass because she says that the heat and peoples' sweat make her feel faint. Nor are there any trees, shrubs, or palms. The town is smaller than the Company town. The buildings and the sidewalks look dirtier, and although the main street and the others are straight, it has a chaotic and rowdy quality to it that Ximena has never felt in her town nor in the valley, except on festival days. In the Company town, there are very few cars and the sounds that can be heard are those of the smelter, the train, and the wind which whistles through the streets, sometimes blowing off the corrugated iron roofs of the poor houses that are beyond the field back of her house.

Her father answered one of her questions, saying that this coastal town is known as a customary truck stop and wayside rest stop for all sorts of passenger vehicles that run along the coast from one place to another. The beach is quite a way from the center of town, and there are big old mansions and more recently built villas with elaborate flower gardens visible behind their fences. Her father has also told her that although there is a water shortage in the region, some of the rich people's houses have swimming pools. This whole area faces onto a boardwalk lined with palm trees. It is a wide beach, but tents and umbrellas rarely appear there because the sea on this side is rough and it has a dangerous undertow. Since they like to swim, they go over to the beach at a another nearby town every day.

They have always stayed at the San Cristóbal Hotel. Her father likes the big rooms even though the floors are made of rough wood and the furniture is shabby and battered, set out haphazardly and not always arranged the same way as the summer before. When they enter the room assigned to them, they are hit by a wave of the insecticide Don Serafino sprays everywhere in his eternal war against mosquitoes. Whenever Ximena comments that there is something different about the room, he scratches his chin.

"Who could have moved that bureau? Not me, not Anacleto, but sometimes these strange things happen around here."

It does not bother her father that the rooms have no baths; it is a very old hotel, so they have to use the shared toilets and showers just off the patio. Her mother complains that the rooms do not have windows, and that the only light bulb, suspended from the high ceiling, hardly gives off any light. Every summer, Don Serafino solves the problem by bringing in a lamp which is very ugly but serves its purpose, making it possible for them to read at siesta time and at night.

This summer, Ximena is resentful because her parents have put her in a separate room which she has to share with Libertad Calderón. Without asking anyone, without even asking Ximena's mother to intervene for her, all on her own, the girl requested a lamp. When Don Serafino comes back to place it in the room, Libertad is already unpacking her suitcase. At first Ximena is pleased to see that she has brought very little clothing but lots of books and notebooks. But she soon loses interest in them. They do not have drawings or colored illustrations in them, and Libertad tells her that they are not stories for dumb kids and that she is not to touch them. Right from the first day, Ximena misses the close relationship she had with her *ama*. Libertad Calderón is not a relative, not even a goddaughter, but her family is poor and Mr. Calderón has recently been fired by the Company for subversive activities. Ximena's father has told her, choosing his words carefully, that these activities are a form of dreaming, although the dreaming is dangerous for the person living it. Sometimes Ximena tries to understand the girl's generally grim expression, and she peers at her narrow forehead, her eyes that are too close to her nose, and her hair pulled straight back and up into a long, heavy pony tail. She forgives her habitual sullenness when she thinks of the girl's father, whom she remembers not only for his small-pox scars but because, even though he is very short, he holds himself up so stiff and straight that he always seems to be standing on tip-toe. She also remembers that he speaks Spanish mixed up with expressions in Quechua. She shivers when she thinks how they have threatened him with jail for dreaming and she tries to find out whether a scrap of those dreams might have slipped by chance into his daughter's surly expression. Ximena watches her but still cannot understand why they have brought Libertad Calderón with them, when they could have brought any one of the girls from the valley. Her parents' reasons seem evasive to her, and seem to have to do with the fact that her mother, in addition to appreciating a helpful hand, is also pleased to be able to talk to someone who studies Law at San Marcos University in Lima.

On the afternoon they arrive, in an attempt to head off a temper tantrum that threatens to turn into one of those kicking fits that leave her blue in the face from the effort to hold her breath, her father finally agrees to take her to the town beach. They leave the boardwalk in order to walk barefoot on the rough sand, stepping around greasy wrappers and scraps of food scattered on the beach. Ximena does not mind the litter. The strong smell of the beach air wraps her in a humid blanket of mystery, and her senses, focused on their own pleasure, reject anything that is not ocean. The water, sometimes green, sometimes gray, rushes up dangerously now and then in an unpredictable rhythm. It breaks into waves close to shore, and sprays up foam that silences the raw cries of seagulls and other sea birds. Ximena pleads so, that her father agrees to walk out to the water's edge so she can get her feet wet. They have to step over algae, long dark or golden ribbons twisted like snakes around other aquatic plants, uprooted and still-living ferns, gelatinous stalks heavy with small oval fruits that may be like little marine cactus fruits for fish and elves or the mysterious beings that inhabit the ocean as well as living at the bottoms of rivers. The sand is very cold and she really likes the rasping roughness that tickles and scratches the soles of her feet. Without warning, a delicate fringe of foam surges up to her heels and when it retreats, the current is so strong that Ximena is pulled off balance; she feels herself sucked out toward the waves and her feet sink deeper and deeper into the sand in her effort not to fall and be lost forever. She holds on tight to her father's hand and tries to resist the powerful tug of the surf, shivering in excitement, in a mixture of fear and pleasure as each successive wave washes out to sea.

As it begins to get dark, the wind picks up and intensifies the motion and the clamor of the waves. Even the birds seem to fly faster and more frantically. Her father's impatient voice tells her that it is time to go. They have both gotten their rolled-up pants wet and they walk back toward the car on reddened, sore feet. They are the only people on the beach, and from the boardwalk, some young couples point at them and laugh.

Libertad Calderón refuses to read to her, or tell her stories at night, or get her dressed in the morning. "I am not your servant, and you are old enough to dress yourself," she has told her cuttingly without taking her eyes off the book she is reading and on which she is taking notes. Before she goes to sleep, and when she wakes up, Ximena watches her study, sitting very close to the lamp with its dim light. Generally she has to call her several times before she pays any attention. Only when her parents are present does the girl hold her hand to cross the street, tie her shoes or help her to eat.

"You should be ashamed of yourself," she says when they are alone, "acting like a baby in front of the whole restaurant."

The first time they went down to the beach to swim, Libertad Calderón simply said she did not want to go, and something must have gone on between the grownups because Ximena, to her embarrassment, notices that her mother is frowning and looks very annoyed, while the girl seals herself up in a stony silence all morning. She does not put on her bathing suit, and she goes down to the beach with a huge book. Only when Ximena shouts at her to come with her, while her parents are sitting on the terrace having a beer, does she stop reading, but she still does not speak a word to her, except when she answers questions in monosyllables. Her mother must have scolded her again, because the next day, Libertad Calderón wears her bathing suit down to the beach although she does not go swimming.

At times when Ximena gets tired of looking at the pictures in the story books she has brought, if Anacleto is not around, she walks through the hotel hoping to come across a door that is not closed, so she can peer into the room. Just off the lobby, a big space with lots of light, are Don Serafino's and the Raimondis' rooms. Don Serafino's does not interest her because it is just as shabby and dimly lit as the guests' rooms, and has only calendar pictures stuck up on the walls. They are all pictures of women who are very white and semi-naked, with big light eyes and very long legs. There are brunettes, redheads and blondes. Very few have black hair and almost none of them wear their hair cut short. They wear transparent clothing, except for the ones dressed up as cowgirls, with tight fitting bright-colored pants, their shirts open so their breasts show. And there is one with a towel, who is different because her hair is slicked back and she looks as though she just got out of the water. They all look a lot alike and they all seem to have been done by the same artist.

In the Raimondis' room, every bit of the wall space is covered with paintings, oils of goddesses or nymphs in tunics like the ones in *Universal Myths*, hunters with big mustaches, medieval castles, country scenes and some still life scenes. Among these there is one that shows two fish with shining scales on a board splashed with blood; beside it, catching the light in the pictured room, is a basket of lemons, peppers and onions. A huge knife with rust spots on it is lying on the red and white oilcloth of the table. Both fish are shown in profile and while their mouths are gaping for air, they stare at her with their immobile but very open eyes. Confused by her uneasy suspicion that that picture is out of place, that it is one of the room's tricks, and feeling herself watched, Ximena always turns her eyes toward the old family photographs, less menacing behind glass, and like almost everything else, set out in crudely carved bronze frames. The bed in one corner also serves as a sofa. There are two armchairs and several little tables and shelves full of knickknacks: porcelain figures, crystal and all sorts of statuettes.

On some afternoons, Mrs. Raimondi invites her mother for tea. Very parsimoniously, she opens a cupboard and takes out a box of English biscuits, her silverware, and her pretty Limoges cups. She pours the tea with a serious and ceremonious air. She is always dressed in bright colors and she wears a lot of makeup under her now lusterless hair, tinted a jet black that contrasts with her pale, withered skin, which seems even paler and more like a mask because of the light powder and vivid red lipstick she wears. She has told them that she comes from an old Arequipa family, and Ximena does not understand why her mother does not say anything when Mrs. Raimondi tells them yet again about her distinguished ancestors, since she has heard her mother saying afterward that those are pretty farfetched stories. But her mother comes to have tea with her once in a while because "the poor woman, marooned in a poky little town like this, must suffer a lot." Don Serafino has told her parents that a few years ago, Mr. Raimondi lost his cotton ranch in a lawsuit against a foreign company, and that now they live very modestly on the rent coming in from some vineyards in the South.

Her mother has not had to explain to her more than once that when she goes with her to tea at Mrs. Raimondi's, she must sit very quietly on one of the chairs and not move except to leave the room. She would really like to closely examine and touch each one of the accumulated ornaments in that asphyxiating world, but Ximena realizes that it would be impossible to do this without bumping against the little tables covered with fragile antique objects. She usually accompanies her mother because she has not given up hope that one day they will finish the biscuits, and then she can ask Mrs. Raimondi if she can have the handsome tin on which there is a sumptuous carriage, with the Queen of England descending from it, smiling, surrounded by her pages.

Mr. Raimondi is very quiet. He wears thick glasses that make his eyes look small and that seem to keep him at a distance from what he sees. Exiled from the room, he smokes one cigarette after another in the lobby or standing up near the street door. He coughs often, as though his lungs were bothering him, and Ximena flees from the smoke and from that cavernous sound which reminds her of her own afflicted lungs. From a distance, and hiding her interest, she examines him on the few occasions when Mr. Raimondi talks with her father. She feels the same tenderness for him that she has always felt for taciturn and worn-out old people. Despite their white hair and their experience, these people always react to her with alarmed surprise, as though the presence of a staring child could scandalize them over and over again, so much that they hurry to turn away their gazes in order to avoid her. Ama Grande says that some evil eye blocked part of their souls with fear when they were children. In a weak moment, Ximena told Libertad Calderón about her sympathy for Mr. Raimondi, and she said, "You have to have your head in the clouds not to see that he is a hypocritical old bully like all men of his class." Indifferent to the girl's cutting tone, Ximena only picked up the phrase "head in the clouds" as though she had just discovered a gleaming coin in the sand. It sounds to her like a flight of fantasy, like images of the Virgin floating up into the sky, surrounded by the scenery of the heavens, as she repeats it over to herself before she falls asleep.

Anacleto is shorter than any of the grownups, shorter than even the shortest Indians she knows. For a man, he has unusually large buttocks, and when he walks, it looks as though he is going to fall headlong. His face is unusual, too: there is something about it that does not fit, that does not look right even though his features are regular and even pleasant. Ximena scrutinizes him and thinks that it is because he has wrinkles despite his boy-like stature, or maybe because his expression is so different from anyone else's.

"Why is Anacleto the way he is?" she asks her father one morning, when they both watched him go by with his mops and pails without looking them in the eye, in his usual way. His clothing is so clean and starched that it rustles when he walks. His hair is piled high and shaped with hair gel above his forehead, and he leaves a swath of cheap cologne behind him as he moves ahead, pitched forward at an acute angle.

"He is retarded," he had answered her after thinking for a few moments. "You probably already know more than he does."

Since then Ximena watches him with more curiosity. She begins to discover the care the dwarf takes with everything he does so as to disguise the natural clumsiness of his movements. She senses that if Anacleto does not avoid eye contact but also never looks back, it is because he is aware of his condition, and that his impairment is not sufficient to cancel out his vanity. Don Serafino says he has never had a better employee, that no one has ever been as punctual, as hardworking or as responsible as he is.

"I found him half dead, bruised and bleeding from being beaten up, at dawn one day here in the hotel entrance. I patched him up as much as I could but even though his body healed, you could see that he had lost the will to live. It look a long time for me to get him to eat anything, or to get him to say anything that would let me help him return to the place he had come from. Even when he was well enough to walk around the hotel like a small ghost, he wouldn't open his mouth except to sip a little broth. After several weeks, when he was beginning to help me and learn his job, he told me that after they kicked him out of the orphanage, he just stumbled along from one place to another. He has been an unpaid servant and he has put up with hunger without a complaint, as long as he had soap and water. Somewhere along the way, he became obsessed with cleanliness.

When he did not have anywhere to go, or anyone to turn to, he would take refuge in a church. But who can understand these things? Anacleto doesn't seem to like priests; he says it is not right that men should wear long skirts. He has been beaten up more times than a losing boxer, and since he does not go looking for trouble, it has to have been because somehow, these things happen in our shitty world."

Anacleto does not inspire confidence in either her mother or in Libertad Calderón. "May God forgive me," murmurs her mother, "but that man makes me really nervous."

The girl has never said anything but Ximena can see the visible repulsion in her body and in the way her jaw tightens, when they come across him in the hallway. Her father jokes with him, often offers him a sweet roll, a chocolate, or an ice-cream on the occasions when they buy something on the street. Anacleto lowers his head and thanks him without smiling. He closes himself in with his sweet treat in his little room near the bathrooms. When he has finished it, he comes out and goes over to the washbasin in the patio and cleans his hands and teeth carefully. Ximena feels an unhealthy curiosity about the dwarf. She would like to know all about how his child-size brain thinks, and what it thinks, after being beaten up so many times, and she keeps coming back to that idea that she may know more than this old, clean-scrubbed, deformed creature who moves from place to place in the hotel without a word of greeting to anyone, and despite this, manages to not seem insolent. If Ama Grande were with her she could clear up this confused feeling that upsets her, and she would relieve the feeling of guilt that fills her when she thinks about him. In the bits and pieces of her stories, the old woman would dig to the root of her discomfort with well-chosen words and then she would be enabled to imagine him in a context of tree, river, stone, the very earth he walks, and Anacleto would become all that and someone else, too: a complete self, not just the Anacleto who ended up in the hotel by chance.

María Eugenia is sitting in the door of her room in the patio combing Fátima's hair. As usual, Fátima is wearing sandals and a short white dress. Little Lourdes, barefoot and cranky, is standing beside the chair, sucking from a bottle listlessly, whimpering whenever she stops to take a breath. Ximena goes over to them. "María Eugenia, do you know a young woman who uses the washtub out in the back lot?"

"No one ever goes out there, and you'd better not go out there either. You've been warned enough times. One of these days the rope will break and quick as a flash, the crazy girl will jump on you and scratch out your eyes."

Ximena does not pay any attention to her. "But haven't you ever seen a tall woman with green pants and gray eyes who wears a starfish on her chest?"

"Is she pretty?" she asks, intrigued.

Ximena nods. "She is the most beautiful woman in the world," she says impulsively. Her whole body feels uneasy as though she had just betrayed the unknown woman, given away her secret.

María Eugenia finishes tying Fátima's white ribbons and walks heavily over toward her room. She is very fat and her calves are covered with varicose veins. There are big grease spots on her shabby black skirt, and her flesh bulges out above her bra, under her brown arms. She emerges a minute later with an *Ecran* movie fan magazine which, like Lourdes, smells of sour milk. "Let's see if we can solve this big mystery. Tell me which of these movie stars she looks like."

She sits down, wearily picking up little Lourdes who has started to cry, while Fátima and Ximena sit down on either side of her. She turns the pages slowly. "Is she like Ava Gardner? Ava is tall and well built."

Ximena looks closely at the actress' eyes, at her dimpled chin, and at the perfect contour of her bones. "Her hair is different," she explains. At that moment she realizes that she has only seen her with wet hair. Without taking back her words, she continues: "She does not have a permanent or curly hair. Her hair is short, but straight and natural. And her face has a sweeter expression."

"Ah! I know, she must look more like Leslie Caron," exclaims María Eugenia enthusiastically. Wetting her index finger in Fátima's saliva, she flips through several of the pages that stick to each other. She stops at another photo.

"No, that isn't her. Her hair is even shorter, without bangs," she explains, "and her mouth is not like that."

The woman gestures in exasperation. "But you can't tell me that Leslie isn't charming, even with those buck teeth. And she is a good person, you know? Her soul is so pure that in her innocence, she even talks to puppets. And she is an orphan, and poor."

She shows her two more actresses. Ximena has known right from the beginning that they would not find her in the magazine.

"She is tall and has light eyes and has a starfish on her chest," she repeats.

María Eugenia looks pensively at the magazine cover. Her youngest daughter has fallen asleep and is drooling milk in a thread running down her dirty cheek. Fátima is nodding off, leaning against her mother, sucking her thumb between sighs. "Light eyes?" María Eugenia asks, recovering her usual high spirits. "My husband has light eyes. You'll see him when he comes around. And he is tall and well built. When he comes, we are going to move to a little brick house near the beach."

Ximena has heard this story several times. Discouraged, she starts to walk back toward the hallway.

"Don't go," pleads the woman. "Maybe it is one of his sisters, his younger sister, they all have light eyes in that family..."

Ximena waves good-bye without turning around. Before she reaches her parents' room she hears María Eugenia's radio, and the sound of her harmonious, melancholy voice flows across the cement of the patio and through the gardenias that don Serafino grows in old clay pots.

The first time Ximena heard the crazy girl, she thought they must be keeping a wild animal behind the big gate and that that was why they had forbidden her to cross the patio. She put her ear to the wooden door to see if she could hear better, but a long hoarse cry gave her goose pimples and made her retreat. They had just returned from the beach and at that hour, the grownups were getting ready to go have lunch. María Eugenia's door was closed and Anacleto was busy cleaning on the other side of the hotel. While she was thinking about it, as though her hand were operating all by itself, she found herself lifting the latch. Little by little she opened the gate cautiously, trying to see what was there without making a sound that would give away her presence.

In the back of the lot, she saw a huge ficus tree, and tied to it was a girl just a little bit bigger than herself. She was running back and forth at the end of the tether that held her to the tree, and was moving her thin arms around violently, beating them up and down as though she were trying to fly. She was barefoot and her legs were two long dark sticks barely covered by a ragged gray dress. On one side there was an adobe hut and on the other, cages of rabbits and guinea pigs. A few hens pecked at the dirt next to the cages and moved off unhurriedly when the girl leapt that way as she went around and around the tree. As she circled around, the tether became shorter and shorter as it wrapped around the tree trunk, then she pounded the tree furiously with her fists and without a second's rest, kept on with her frantic jumping until the rope was wound tight and she couldn't move. Her labored panting seemed in synchrony with her jumps and every little while an inhuman screech shook her body and shattered the midday peace.

Trembling, Ximena watched the strange rite for a few seconds, frozen by terror and by desire to remain immobile, invisible, even absent, in the presence of the other's tireless delirium. She heard, as if from a great distance, that someone was calling her. Her name seemed alien to her at that moment, both unrecognizable and as though being spoken for the first time. She closed the gate without bothering to do it silently, and crossed the patio, clutching at things all the way in order not to fall, repressing as best she could an unexpected desire to screech herself, but without any vestige of fear.

Ximena did not tell anyone about her discovery. Sometimes on the beach, sitting on the damp sand and making castles with her red pail, she thought about the prisoner and had to make an effort not to tell Libertad Calderón what she had seen. She did not trust the girl to keep her secret, and she sensed that the others knew about the existence of the child in the back lot although for some unknown reason they were hiding it from her. At other times, in the silence of their room during siesta hour, while Libertad Calderón was studying tenaciously without a whisper of distraction, Ximena wondered whether they did in fact know about it; maybe it was possible that even the permanent guests were somehow unaware. But how could they possibly not know about it when her screeches could sometimes be heard even in the hotel lobby? Just recently, while she was with her mother and Libertad, hanging up the towels in the patio, Ximena had heard her howl heartrendingly. The other two hardly reacted at all; their backs stiffened for just an instant, and for a second they seemed to hold their breaths. "What is that?" she asked, to force them to answer.

"What is what?" her mother had responded serenely.

"That cry."

"What cry? Did you hear anything, Libertad?"

Without raising her eyes, the girl kept on shaking out the towels. "No, I didn't."

Whenever she could be certain that there was no one around, Ximena repeated her daring act again. She did not hear anything on these occasions and her intention had pretty much been to make sure that the girl was still there. There was one particularly silent afternoon when not even the trucks could be heard rumbling past, honking their horns furiously, making their brakes squeal, amidst all the turbulent noises that generally reached them from the street at that hour. She pushed open the gate and at first she did not see her. She could only make out the tether rope, loose on the ground, and when she looked closely, she realized that the girl was almost hidden behind the tree trunk and was wrapped around it. For a long time she could not see any movement at all. Ximena did not move either, and cautiously, she stayed right next to the gate in case she needed to escape. Suddenly the girl began to move her feet slowly, so slowly that she almost seemed to be staying in the same place. She continued to hug the tree, one side of her face resting on the rough bark and pressing her palms against it, inching them forward until her arms were encircling the trunk. Still embracing the tree, she moved her body around it so gradually and quietly that she seemed almost immobile. Sometimes she would pause and, with her body still pressed against the bark, she would turn her face, lift her chin and lick the wood unhurriedly.

The second time Ximena went over to the gate to spy on her, it was curiosity about the howls that drew her there. More confidently daring, in a definite act of provocation, after she looked over at the tree, she defiantly crossed to the other side and left the gate closed behind her. When she allowed herself to turn toward the back of the lot, she saw the girl sitting on the ground a few meters from the ficus tree. The rope was lying in a tangle behind her, and although because she had her legs drawn up to her chest, it was not possible to see if she was still tied around the waist, Ximena was sure that they had not let her loose. Her hair had been cut since the last time. Bleached by exposure to earth and sun, it hung down straight to just over her ears, the bangs almost the same length. The same ragged dress she had been wearing before, which exposed more than it covered, was now tucked under her legs so that she gave the impression of being almost naked. She reminded Ximena, despite her skinniness, of the jungle Indian children she had seen in Oxapampa.

Neither of the two moved at first and Ximena thought that she was going to suffocate, not because she could not breathe, but because her heartbeats thundered so in her throat. They looked at each other without moving, one sitting in the shadow of the big tree and the other standing in the glaring afternoon sunlight. They both kept their eyes wide open as though they had agreed to play a game of who would blink first. The silence and the tension were unbearable and it occurred to Ximena that they were playing at statues; only this time, as punishment for her audacity, they would remain like this forever, frozen in place.

It was the ficus branches that broke the spell. The animals in cages came to life again and the hens went back to scratching in the hard soil. Other sounds began to reach them more clearly, not the inevitable street sounds at that hour, as much as a general hum that seemed to surge up from the very center of all their surroundings. Still in a trance, Ximena remained motionless until the other's jump took her by surprise and made her jump too. It was an extraordinary jump, as though she flew up into the air without having stood up first. She did not take her eyes off her and she did not move from her place. Suddenly, pushing up with her arms, she gave several more leaps, as though she were getting ready to fly or as though she were inviting her to imitate her. Ximena jumped in turn, and without having to agree on the rhythm, one would touch down just as the other was jumping up. She, too, began to bend and extend her arms and even believed that with each jump she was going higher and higher.

They kept this up for a long time, playing in an invisible seesaw alternation, flying in vertical flight without moving from their places. The sterile empty lot filled with life; the leaves of the old ficus shone green against the brilliant gray of the afternoon; the hens were more than hens, they were joyful reddish notes in their slow movements; and even the hut took on a rustic and serene enchantment. Ximena wanted to smile, even laugh, but something told her that the slightest change would be an infraction and would break the magical spell of the moment.

It was Don Serafino who pulled them from the game. Ximena did not sense his presence until the girl, without giving her a single sign of warning, suddenly stopped jumping. She put her feet on the ground and instead of leaping up into flight, she let out a scream that pierced Ximena's body and startled her so much that she fell down. Before she could manage to get up, she realized that someone had opened the door and was trying to help her. In front of them, the fearsome cries began, and the terrible circling, rapid and violent, along the rutted track.

Don Serafino did not seem to be angry. He did not threaten to tell her mother, as Ximena had expected. He warned her, certainly, choosing his words very carefully, that she should never again open the gate, that real danger lay on the other side.

Libertad Calderón does not like the beach. She tenses up when they begin putting towels and bathing suits into bags in the hotel, and she only calms down again when her mother calls out to them from the terrace overlooking the beach that it is time to go back to town.

"Don't you like the sand?"

"I couldn't care less about sand," she answered angrily.

"Are you afraid of the waves?"

Libertad Calderón does not answer. She turns her face away, pretending to be indifferent, and looks out at the water for a few seconds. The tide is coming in and the sea is rough. The waves are breaking noisily on the beach, one right after another. "I'm not afraid of them," she says without much conviction.

"Then come with me when I go in, at least as far as the foam," says Ximena, deliberately provoking her. She knows perfectly well that Libertad Calderón is afraid of the sea. Her father was the first one to realize this and, jokingly, and very frequently, he has tried to encourage her. He has offered to go in with her past the breaking surf, to where the water is quieter and they can just rock in the swaying rhythm of the big waves.

"Come on," he has said over and over, "come on, I'll show you how to swim."

Libertad Calderón has not wanted to accept her mother's help either. "The water is really cold," she says each time, "and the sea gulls and terns are unbearable."

On these occasions, Ximena pleads with her parents, exaggerating her courage. "Take me, I'll go in with you; take me."

She goes in with one of them, and out of pride, she goes all the way out to where the bottom drops off under her feet, and she struggles to resist her urge to race back to shore when a giant wave covers her mercilessly. Sustained by parental hands, she braves the torture of the terror and the salt water she swallows along with her fear.

A beach ball, big and lightweight, bumps against Libertad Calderón's feet. Even though the sky is clear, the wind is blowing hard and overturns some beach umbrellas and scatters the scrap paper from ice cream bars and cones. A boy comes over to collect the ball. By accident, his foot knocks over part of the wall of the castle the two of them are building. "Sorry," he says and when he bends down, he smiles at them.

Libertad Calderón does not move a muscle, and the boy, without saying anything else, goes back to the group of young bathers who are waiting for him. Ximena knows them by sight; sometimes the girls come over to her, call her by name, and talk to her or touch her hair. One of them, the most outgoing, the plump one who laughs so contagiously, has fastened Ximena's bathing suit strap for her and once even offered her a Good Humor bar. Ximena knows that they are people from Lima, who have summer houses in this beach resort, because her mother chats with the families of the group and her father plays volleyball with the boys when they get out the net.

Libertad Calderón has not wanted to be introduced, and seeing that she is mortified by the idea, her mother has not insisted again. "I should have thought to buy a bathing suit for the girl," she commented one night. "The one she has is very old and is too wide for her."

Libertad Calderón does not take off her wrap except to go into the surf with her for a few minutes, and her parents say that it is a shame because she has pretty legs.

"Why do you act that way with them?" Ximena asks, nodding her head at the group that is playing and fooling around right close by.

"Because they are idiots," answers the other in a low voice. "They act as if they were ten years old."

"That's a lie," Ximena contradicts her perversely. "Some of them are couples, and ten-year-olds don't go around holding hands or kissing."

"They are irresponsible imbeciles," answers Libertad Calderón, "and don't talk to me about them and don't keep staring at them like a dummy or you'll end up looking like them."

Ximena wouldn't mind looking like them. Almost all of the girls are pretty, and look happy. They walk or play nimbly and freely, as if the beach and the summer had been invented for their bodies. They dive into the waves just like the boys and are just as brave about swimming way out there, so far out that the grownups yell at them in vain from the beach, and beckon them, unheeded, to return to shore. "They haven't done anything to me, and I like the way they swim," says Ximena with pretended innocence. She doesn't need to look at her to measure the effect of her words.

"What a joke!" responds Libertad Calderón. She has said it trying to laugh but her mouth twists into a grimace. "Why not; it's not as though they are good for anything else."

Ximena does not insist any more, but she is not the least bit sorry to see her pained expression. She purposely rubs her sandy hand against her cheek. "You have to take me down to the water," she demands and grabs her hand. "I'm getting sand in my eyes."

"Go by yourself. You don't need me with you in order to wash off."

"I don't want to. You have to come with me."

They look at each other in silence for a few moments. Ximena brushes off her cheekbone with the back of her hand and screws up her face. She can feel and see the little glittery dots of sand on her lashes. She spits, making a lot of noise.

Libertad Calderón does not argue any more and obeys, but when they reach the water an unexpected shove tumbles Ximena down face forward. The sandy foam splashes over her, even wetting her hair. Dripping wet, still on her stomach, she lifts her face to look at Libertad, wishing she could spill water over her so that the old strawberry colored bathing suit would sag down even more, but the girl's defeated expression restrains her, and then Ximena begins to splash her arms and legs as if she were swimming.

The two are alone in the lobby. It is very hot and in the windless still-ness of the afternoon, even the flies have settled down on the win-dowsill. They don't even fly off when Ximena and Anacleto come up to look at them. There are seven, they have counted them out loud, of all different sizes. Unhesitatingly, she has decided which ones are the parents, the children, and even a grandfather. Anacleto accepts these relationships, although it makes him nervous when the insects confuse him by changing location. They look closely at the cere-monies taking place, at how they meticulously clean their front legs first, and then their back legs, and at the clever way they move their wings. The light catches on the blue metal flecks that glitter on their bodies and on the transparent silver tones on their wings. "They are pretty, aren't they?" whispers Ximena very softly, so as not to startle them.

"Yes, but they are filthy." answers Anacleto. "They walk around on dung ."

Ximena laughs and the flies scatter.

"That's a lie that grownups tell," she asserts while she walks over to the large broken-down armchair where she has left her storybook.

Anacleto follows her and sits down right next to her. His old child's shoes are well polished and they dangle against the faded upholstery without touching the floor. Ximena is with him because Libertad Calderón has given her permission to leave the room at sies-ta time. The girl never sleeps at this hour. She makes use of the time to study, and since Ximena's parents read and rest for a long stretch, they won't find out that she has disobeyed their order that Ximena should take a nap to recover from the beach. Recently, her mother worries that she is spending too much time with Anacleto. "I feel uneasy around the poor man; he makes me nervous," she confesses, although Ximena and her father both protest. "He may be just as innocent as you think, but he is still a man, for all that."

She has also spoken of her concern to Don Serafino, without taking care that Ximena is out of hearing, but Don Serafino answered her with a guffaw. Removing his straw hat, as he always does when speaking to her, he assures her that there is nothing to fear. Despite her mother's threats, Ximena manages to spend a good deal of time with the employee during the secret siesta hours, while her parents are off on walks, or at gatherings at the dentist's house at the beach, and during the evening each time a new film is shown. At first, she is the one who seeks him out; she is the one who tags along after him, interesting him in her stories and in the colored pictures in her books. Pretty soon, Anacleto hangs around in the hallways or in the patio in hopes of seeing her alone, and then Ximena enjoys exercising her power and getting him to beg. "I don't feel like it now," she tells him, even when she has the books in her hands. "I want to read them by myself, lying on my bed."

Anacleto looks at her pleadingly.

"Just one little story," he implores. He has the sweet, refined voice of a woman and Ximena is pleased and intrigued, hearing this voice come from a child who is old, who is not old and is not a child.

She opens the big book of Andersen's tales. "Which one do you want me to read you today?" she asks, knowing that Anacleto cannot remember the titles even when she makes him repeat them over and over, as many as fifty times.

Anacleto is not deflected. "The one about the girl."

"Which girl? Because all the stories have at least one girl in them." Ximena observes the rapidity with which his tranquil expression changes to one of affliction. To mortify him even more, she doesn't say a word and just waits. Through the open door of the entryway, they can hear the torrents of conversation of people passing by along the street, and the loud honking of big trucks. The flies are no longer on the windowsill; they have flown over to explore the newspapers on the little table behind them, next to the armchair.

"The one about the girl who is a princess who can't stop dancing?"

Anacleto says no, that's not it. "The one about the princess who sleeps," he adds vaguely. Ximena knows that the story he prefers is the one about the little mermaid, and that if he does not ask for it, it is because she almost always refuses to read it to him. She maintains the privilege of offering him that story whenever she happens to feel like it.

"And what did the princess sleep on?" Ximena asks him in a tone of authority.

"A bean," he answers without vacillating.

"I've already told you that in the story it is not called a bean. In the story, it is a pea."

"You told me yourself that it was a bean," his voice rises higher in anxiety.

"I told you that because you didn't know what peas were, but in the story it says a pea and that is how it must be said. Beans don't exist in the story. Look and see."

Ximena picks one of the stories, and opens the book on her knees. Anacleto comes over closer to her. She thinks that the book is like a talisman, and that its attraction pulls him despite his own will. Full of respect, he stretches out a hand to touch the cover. "No," says Ximena, pulling the book away from him brusquely. "Today you cannot help me turn the pages because you couldn't remember the word I taught you."

Anacleto does not reply. Rapturously and reverently, he contemplates the pages where the letters are arranged, looking very black against the thick shiny paper, with the pictures sharply outlined in bright, precise colors to show various scenes from the tales. Ximena knows that Anacleto likes the illustrations as much as the stories, and that at first he was more interested in gazing at the pictures than in finding out about the tales. Little by little, the repeated plotlines have worked their magical effects, and now she can tell him the same story over and over again without his tiring of it. "See," she says, pointing to a word with her finger. "Here it says *pea*, not bean."

Ximena does not know how to read yet, but she never makes a mistake when she points out a word. And when she pretends to read the stories, she does not change them or use any tone of voice other than that of reading. Once she told one in a conversational tone, in her everyday voice. "No, that's not right," Anacleto had cried out in outrage. "It's not the same!"

And after that, Ximena adopted the other voice, and she ran her finger along the lines, as though she were going to lose her place. Sometimes she pretended to be spelling out a word. She lowered her face right close to the page, pondered some long word, bit her lips and then sounded out all the syllables one after another. Anacleto observed her with his eyes wide, holding his breath in admiration. He did not seem embarrassed to reveal his fear and his anticipation. Only when Ximena had resolved the challenging syllables, and the word emerged round and complete in the air, would he give a sigh of relief.

After the story has ended and the prince has claimed the princess, and they are sitting there thoughtfully, before Anacleto can ask her to tell the story again, Ximena asks him confidentially, "Have you asked Don Serafino what I told you to ask?"

Anacleto does not remember and he is bewildered. Then she clicks her tongue and rolls her eyes in a gesture of impatience.

"Didn't I warn you that if you didn't worm out the secret of who the girl with light eyes and the starfish on her chest is, I wouldn't tell you any more stories ever?"

"I have asked him," smiled Anacleto. "I have already asked him, and he said I must be having drunken fantasies."

Ximena closes the book, while Anacleto stands up, and with a neatly pressed blue striped handkerchief, he blots the sweat on his temples and neck.

"Don Serafino does not know, Miss Ximena, or perhaps he has forgotten, but I have never seen her and it is not that I don't remember. Yes, I would remember. If I had ever seen her around the hotel with a starfish on her chest, how would I forget that? Most likely you didn't really see her either, and it was the morning light playing tricks on your eyes."

Ximena does not answer because it does no good to insist. No one believes her when she describes the woman. Something she does not herself understand keeps her from confiding in her parents and in Libertad Calderón, so she has been asking the hotel people. But Don Serafino has laughed openly and Mrs. Raimondi has listened to her, lost in a haze of other landscapes, and from a great distance has said, "There is no one like that here, dear." Whenever they take the car to go to and from the beach, when they walk to the Chinese restaurant, go into sweet shops, or see crowds of people at the movies, Ximena has searched for her. She has tried to spot her on the beach itself, peering at strangers and keeping an eye on the group of girls she knows by sight. All in vain. No one looks a bit like her, and no one wears a starfish on her chest.

"I know!" Anacleto says suddenly. "She must be the pharmacist's daughter. He has light eyes."

Ximena remembers the sad old man in the pharmacy, tall and stooped, in a shabby dustcoat, patched and mended from years of use. A few days ago she went to the pharmacy with Libertad Calderón and although the pharmacist knew perfectly well who she was, because he knows her parents, he did not greet her or ask about them. He handed over the little bottle of eye-drops without wrapping it and he gave back Libertad Calderón's change to her in the same hostile silence in which she had paid him. Despite this indifference, Ximena feels an inexplicable sympathy toward this sad figure and now, in the midst of the humid afternoon heat, she remembers that there is a quality of fresh water in his faded blue eyes. The possibility of a clue dances within her body and in an explosion of generosity, to recompense Anacleto for this afternoon, she allows him to touch her books.

One day Ximena thinks she hears voices behind one of the doors across from the guests' rooms. As you enter from the street, after the lobby and Don Serafino and the Raimondis' rooms, there is a hallway that leads to the patio. To the left of this hallway are the big old-fashioned rooms that Ximena has seen, and to the right, the original layout has been changed by the addition of a series of rooms which are very small, to judge by how close together the flimsy doors are. She has always thought that Don Serafino must store the hotel's supplies there, and she has never been curious to know what lies beyond that thin partition painted a cream color that doesn't even have a proper ceiling.

She goes closer and realizes that one of the doors is closed, but that it does not have a padlock on it like the others. She sneaks up on tiptoe and puts her ear to the wood. She hears the monotonous tones of a very low voice, a kind of buzzing sound interrupted by another voice, a man's, in a tone of weak protest. Sometimes she hears the two voices speaking together and the sound of a lament rises up over the partition. Ximena does not understand what they are saying; she thinks she can recognize some of the rich consonants and typical diphthongs of Quechua, but no matter how hard she concentrates, she can't manage to isolate any of the words. They are speaking very quietly, as though they were protecting the sleep of someone else in the room.

She pushes the door gently. If it is Quechua that she hears, it does not seem to her that it would be a rash act to find out who they are and why they are there. However, something stops the door from opening completely, and she feels, in the gap of space she has just created, a sudden silence and a warm smell of humid wool, of hay, and she is instantly filled with nostalgia for the highlands. She shifts around, trying to find a position from which she can peer into the room; from the doorway, she can barely make out the outlines of the shadows.

Little by little her eyes adapt to the dim light and the first thing she sees is the light cloth of the man's shirt and the white blouse that the woman is wearing under her striped *lliclla*. She had not made a mistake. They are two young Indians who are sitting in front of her on a bed which, despite being very narrow, fills most of the room. A small table is located at a right angle to the bed, and on the other side, piled one on top of another, are two wool-covered bundles. There is hardly enough floor space for two people to stand embracing each other.

The couple has become so totally silent that Ximena thinks for a second that she is dreaming, but her reaction to that beloved familiar smell squeezes her throat into a nostalgic sob and because it is her own gasp that breaks the silence, she knows that the bizarre whispering and those out-of-place Indians are not a dream. She wants to talk to them, but she does not find her voice. She wants to ask them how they got lost in this hotel on the coast, but her body shakes her in a muffled roar. They are still looking at her without speaking, very seriously. The girl has begun to smooth down her skirt in a tranquil, slow gesture. She is sitting on one side of the bed with her feet doubled under her, half leaning against the wall, and when she looks closely at her hand and her skirt, Ximena realizes that she is pregnant. He is sitting on the edge of the bed facing his wife, and in order to look at Ximena, he turns his head. They both observe her with the same curiosity, although without the emotion that she feels as she smells, more than sees, an unexpected fragment of her other life.

Someone laughs and chatters in the lobby. Very carefully, as if any sound at all might shatter this unexpected vision, Ximena closes the door. She waits for a few seconds without moving, so that she can feel they are speaking, to assure herself that they are still there and that her inopportune presence has not interrupted their conversation. She would like to wait there as long as necessary, but footsteps in the entryway are coming nearer. Because she knows she is guilty of spying behind doors and sneaking around trying to overhear grownups' conversations, Ximena reacts automatically and runs to her parents' room. Once there, facing her mother who is peacefully reading one of the novels she has brought, she can't hold it in any longer and she starts to cry.

"What are you crying about, Ximena, who has hurt you?" her mother jumps up from the bed and hugs her all in one motion.

"Two Indians, a couple," she manages to say.

"Two Indians have hurt you? What have they done to you? Where?"

Ximena pulls away, annoyed. "They haven't done anything to me; they got lost on their way somewhere, and they have ended up here, and Don Serafino has them shut up in a closet."

Calmed down now, her mother cannot suppress a smile. "Oh, Ximena, the things you make up!" she says, trying to hug her again. Ximena pulls back, and her sobs give way to frustration and impatience.

"Come with me," she says, tugging her by the hand. "Come with me, and I'll show you."

They go down the hall together. Her parents' room is the last one before the patio. On this side, there is sunlight and in the afternoon the strong aroma of gardenias cancels out the smell of the disinfectant that Don Serafino and Anacleto use daily in the bathrooms. As they move away from this side, the corridor darkens in a dim brownish light; with each of their steps on the creaking floorboards, and with each of Ximena's heartbeats, they are more aware of a closed-in moldy smell, old furniture and insecticides that characterize the inner parts of the hotel. They get there and the door is just as Ximena left it, closed but without a padlock. She is about to shove it open when her mother grabs her arm.

"What are you doing, for God's sake! You should at least knock, even though surely it is impossible that there should be anyone here."

Ximena knocks and there is no answer. She knocks again, harder this time, and again, she only hears her own rapid nervous breathing. Without waiting for permission, she leans against the door, which cedes, and she gestures to her mother to look inside. Her mother comes closer and standing behind her, peers into the shadowy depths of the room. A low, almost inaudible cry, escapes her and makes Ximena tremble. She feels pressure on her neck, but because she is planted there solidly, holding onto the door frame, her mother would have had to really shove her to move her aside, so there is a moment's delay before her eyes adjust and she can take in the minuscule scandal of the room.

The silence is irresistible and then her mother asks them where they are from. They do not answer her, they do not move, and Ximena again has the impression of a dream. The other body pressed against her back, the softness of breasts against her head and her perfume mixed with the odor of the couple's bundles and clothing, is proof to her that all this is happening on the side where odors and emotions originate and in hues that are very different from those of dreams. Without shifting tone, her mother asks them the same question in Quechua. The two of them exchange a barely perceptible look and without changing his expression, he answers that they are from Ayacucho. She asks them other questions and the boy thinks a lot before answering or smiling; he asks her to repeat what she has just said, because he has some difficulty understanding her.

"We're going to look for Don Serafino," her mother says abruptly and with one yank, she pulls her out of the doorway.

They find him fixing the plumbing of the patio sink. Fátima is scratching her back against the wall, balancing herself rhythmically on her feet without taking her fingers out of her mouth. Like her clothing, Fátima is also very white, with silky curly hair. Although her clothes are not new she is always clean, with her hair combed, and now, seeing her doing this pendulum dance against the wall, Ximena remembers that on a certain occasion her mother and Libertad Calderón were talking about María Eugenia, commenting in low voices that Fátima was very attractive, and that if in some cases, one could put faith in appearances, it did seem that the youngest had to be someone else's daughter. While Ximena mentally recreates that conversation, she notices Lourdes, who as usual is crawling around the cement floor barefoot and with dirty diapers. Even though she has reddish hair, she is much darker than her sister and Ximena does not understand why or how the certainty strikes her, too, even in regard to a baby, that Lourdes' features are coarse and that she is not as pretty as her sister.

"Don Serafino," from her tone Ximena knows that her mother is trying to calm down, "what is this story that you are about to throw those Ayacuchans into the street when the poor people have nowhere to go?"

"Don't fall for that line, madam," he smiles his enormous smile, showing his large even teeth. "I'm not saying it about you, because you are different, but people from the highlands are very shrewd: they whine that they don't have anything, and all the while they do have things; they pretend they don't understand and of course they understand. They owe me money, ma'am, and even if I were sorry for them, I can't let them stay if they don't pay me."

"Not all the hotel guests pay you, and some of them seem to stay indefinitely," her mother has intentionally looked in the direction of María Eugenia's room. The music from her radio reaches them clearly through the closed door.

Don Serafino laughs loudly. "She pays, ma'am; she pays with what she has."

Her mother's fingernails dig into her shoulders and hurt, but Ximena does not complain, because the confrontation she is witnessing is intensely exciting to her curiosity. "Well, I am going to speak to my husband immediately about paying any charges they owe you." Her voice is defiant, and although Ximena can't see her face, she knows that she is maintaining her composure, even though she is disconcerted by Don Serafino's mocking attitude.

"Don't even dream of it," replies the hotel keeper. He excuses himself mechanically, puts on his straw hat again, and scoops up Lourdes, who is half asleep under a shrub. "They would all get to hear about it, and they would be chasing after you to do the same favor to all of them. Believe me, ma'am, you wouldn't want that."

"What do you mean?" Her mother tries to keep her voice from rising. "You mean there are more of them? Are you telling me that there are other rooms like that little hole in the wall? There should be a law against it! It's really terrible!"

"But I'm doing them a favor, ma'am. Don't I give them time to find work? And when they leave, they always go off owing me, but they're stubborn as mules and they don't believe it even when the situation they're in is staring them in the face."

"But you don't speak their language; how can you give them any advice?"

"They play dumb, ma'am, like I just told you, those yokels understand a lot of things perfectly well."

María Eugenia opens her door. Her eyes are still full of sleep and her hair on one side is damp and stuck to her face. She lifts her arms to yawn and Ximena is disgusted by the rolls of fat and sweat marks on the blue cloth of her blouse. Fátima runs over to hold onto María Eugenia's skirt and when they go by them, Ximena notices her own mother's gesture, a slight movement of her body, a quick dip of her chin which is barely a greeting.

Her father is not in the hotel that afternoon. He has gone over to the dentist's house to play chess and her mother has to climb up on a chair to take what she needs out of the upper part of the wardrobe. "Go get Libertad, would you?" she asks her.

Ximena has to insist several times before the girl puts down her books. "You never believe me," she complains.

"Because you never tell the truth," Libertad answers.

When they get to the room, her mother is counting some orange bank notes. "Libertad," she says, "Ximena is going to show you the little room where there is a couple from Ayacucho. I can make out more or less what the boy tells me, although he does not seem to understand me very well. You have a try; your Quechua may be better, or maybe the woman will get up her nerve to talk to you because..."

"Why to me?"

Ximena is startled. Even when she is really annoyed, Libertad Calderón never interrupts her mother. But this time her face looks upset and the breasts outlined under her sundress heave up and down as she tries to get her breathing under control. "Ever since I went to Lima to study, I have forgotten that language. It's useless to ask me to talk to them," she replies, enunciating each word slowly. Decisively, she begins to walk toward the door. Ximena expects her mother to call her back, but she just clenches the bank notes and gets sadder and sadder.

While she puts the money back in her purse, she mutters to herself in a low voice: "All I was going to say to her was that the woman might trust her more because she is younger than I am. And even if I had said what she thought I was going to say, why should that be so insulting? Who does she think she is to give herself such airs?"

The two of them walk down a long, hot, dusty street. The sun is intense wherever there is no shade and with the lack of wind, the atmosphere is full of smoke from exhaust fumes from the heavy traffic. The sidewalks are narrow and the passersby don't step aside they way they do in the highlands; here, they charge ahead and sometimes brush against them or knock into them without even stopping to beg pardon. Ximena finally gets accustomed to the lilting sounds of the way people speak in this coastal town, although it is still an effort for her to get used to the loud laughter and strident tones. It is as though the moment she goes out the door of the hotel, someone turns the volume up on the one main street in town. Despite the heat, the noise, and the jostling, the two move purposefully along.

They go first to the store with the most variety of merchandise that they know of, but they do not find clothes for newborn babies. The woman behind the counter is a dark skinned Asian, and she gestures when she speaks, like everyone else in the town. Seated on a stool in a dim corner, a man is watching her mother through the smoke of his cigar, and when he realizes that Ximena is staring at him, he unexpectedly, inexplicably, between two puffs of smoke, sticks out his tongue at her. Surprised and embarrassed into blushing, Ximena turns away her eyes and looks at the little lead soldiers arranged in squadrons behind the counter. When her mother has finished buying some lengths of cloth and is paying, Ximena dares to look at him. And because his attention is still focused on her mother, she can gaze for a few seconds at that wide sallow face where all the features seem too round and excessive.

On their return walk Ximena breathes in deeply to see if she can detect any traces of sea smell in the suffocating afternoon air.

When they cross the hotel hallway, they notice that the door of the little room is just the way they left it. Hurriedly they put away part of what they have bought, and picking up the package of empanadas and tamales, they head for the Ayacuchans' room. They knock repeatedly and as before, no one answers. This time it is her mother who opens the door without scruple. The first thing Ximena sees is that the girl is spinning wool with the same dexterity she has so often admired in highland women. Transported to another landscape, for a few instants Ximena is absorbed in watching the dance of the spindle that rises and falls, capturing her in its rhythm. Only part of the man's back is visible, because he is bent over the bundles on the left. Her mother tries to squeeze the package of food through the crack in the door, and when he hears his wife speak, the man comes over to the door. In order to open it wider, he has to move the little table and set it down parallel to the bed. The woman keeps spinning while she and Ximena are eyeing each other and finally get up nerve to smile. After telling them that she will come back tomorrow with something for the baby, they leave them opening the package.

As soon as they get to the room, her mother starts cutting out the cloth with scissors borrowed from Mrs. Raimondi. Libertad Calderón helps her without protesting and Ximena is pleased to see that she is somewhat ill at ease. Lying on her mother's bed, battling the sleep that threatens to close her eyelids, Ximena watches them sew in the room's dim light. When she wakes up in the morning, she is in her own bed, and Libertad Calderón tells her that they stayed up very late hemming diapers and little blankets.

Ximena touches the cloth of the blankets.

"It is soft, isn't it?" says her mother, rubbing the flannel against her cheek. "Poor babies! So often I've seen them wrap newborn babies in a rough ordinary shawl, as though the skin of all newborns weren't equally delicate."

Ximena goes with her through the hallway, trying to control the impatience of her feet. Once again, they both knock together with their knuckles, and again, the door opens without resistance when they push it. A sharper cry than yesterday's shatters Ximena's chest. The couple is not there nor is there any trace of their bundles.

"Let's go ask Don Serafino," implores Ximena. But her mother shakes her head without answering. Tears are running down her face and she does not bother to dry them.

"It is useless, Ximena," she says, swallowing her sobs. "They left last night, or at dawn. Where will those poor people go? With no money and such a long road ahead of them!"

Her father tries to console them as best he can and he assures them that they are young, that they will have returned to their community, that they will be better off there. That morning it is he who taciturnly makes the arrangements to go to the beach.

For the first time, Ximena sees desolation rather than detachment or indifference, in Libertad Calderón's silence. Her neck, which is so firm and stiff even when she is bent down stubbornly over her books, has taken on a softer, more submissive look. But that night Ximena wakes up and surprises her crying, and sees her, with that barely suppressed rage she has glimpsed in her before, tear up, one by one, the pages of the novel which her mother has just given her.

Sometimes when the sea is very rough or when we arrive too early and it's chilly to be out on the beach, we go looking for mussels. There are hardly any beach umbrellas at that hour and only the mothers with small children are out on the sand, settling down in the same places where they were yesterday. The *amas*, whose bare feet contrast oddly with their typical uniforms, busy themselves changing the babies and rubbing Johnson's baby oil on their skins. Although all the nannies you see crossing the beach from one end to the other are young, and they do not look like your *ama*, they make you think of her, and you have to concentrate hard on the mixed fear and happiness that await you, in order to keep her memory from planting itself painfully in the center of your head, behind your eyes, in the very center of your throat, and which will ache then, with its sweet weight, a weight that spreads over your shoulders and ends up by being a butterfly whose fluttering wings fog your view and smell of the sea.

As we move farther away from the center of the beach, the sand has more and more seaweed on it. You used to ask if the water tosses it up on that side, or whether the town maintenance people, who come by in the afternoon to clean up papers and trash, just sweep the seaweed over toward the rocks where the beach ends. No one knew or wanted to answer you. There are bathers down there, too, but they are not like the people who frequent the other part, the area in front of the terrace with the bar and the changing rooms. They haven't had to explain to you that they are from another class, because you could figure that out on your own just by looking at them, and see that they are the people who live in the port all year round. They are all young people, a few children and a few women. With picks or with their hands, they dig along the waterline to find sand crabs, and when they have filled their baskets they cover them with algae and go back where they came from. When you found out that they used the poor creatures as bait you really cried. Libertad Calderón laughed at you: "What did you think, then, that they collected them just for fun?" Your father, somewhat distracted by a new poem that your mother was reciting as she walked along, explained to you again about the food chain in nature and stressed, impatient with your sorrow, that the seagulls, the sandpipers and even the smallest sea birds would have eaten them first if they had gotten the chance. His argument does not convince you and you suffer because you know how easy it is to dig up the sand crabs. When the wave recedes, leaving them mercilessly exposed, they scurry to hide, burying themselves in the wet sand, all in vain since they give their hiding places away by leaving a little hole with a bubble beside it on the surface. They are so defenseless, that even you can catch them easily by the luminous fragile gray edges of their shells, and you touch their white stomachs, and your father has shown you how to tell which are females, because they have a rose and blue tinge to their translucency.

Rather than gathering sand crabs for the pleasure of letting them go, you would like us to stay there for a while, watching the port people. Your father, even though he likes the green of the hills, often feels out of place among the valley people because he is different; but here on the coast, his personality opens up, and he is never inhibited about talking to anyone. Sometimes you follow him when he goes over to the group and asks them questions about fishing. The young women turn away, but the boys talk to him freely and naturally. Then the women come over, too, to see what is going on and pat your head consolingly with their hands that smell of algae, lemon and lapfuls of coriander. They talk with your mother, and like every woman in the world, they give her advice on what she should feed you so you will not look so sickly and malnourished. Taught by experience, you are ignorant of the double humiliation, yours and hers, and you do not pay much attention to what they are saying. You would rather watch the young men who, in shorts or bathing trunks, are jumping into the waves and playing around in the water for a while before they go on. The young women from the port keep on with their work or sit down on the sand without worrying about being scratched by the dry algae blackened by the sun. Laughing with their pretty white teeth, they chatter noisily. But you prefer to watch the young men. You enjoy their slender, elastic, brown bodies, their easy laughter, their evident rowdiness. You are in awe of their grace and agility in the water.

When they swim, their bodies and the sea seem to fuse as if when their bodies undulate they renew a green, deep, secret pact with the waves from which you feel inevitably excluded.

At first, the slope we climb when we leave the beach seems more like a hill than a mountain. We walk up a narrow path made by the footsteps of others, probably in the early hours of the day because we have never met anyone, either on the way up or coming down. When we start uphill, it is hard for us to move quickly because there is more sand than dirt and our feet sink in with each step. As we climb up farther and the slope becomes steeper, the mountainside on our right that faces the sea begins to lose its soft contours and turns suddenly into a rocky precipice. There is practically no vegetation near where we walk. Even when we have gone quite a way up, and the earth is less sandy, only a few scraggly plants can be seen here and there, sheltering in the shadows cast by rocks, struggling to survive the dryness. During the first excursions, your father began to reminisce about the north coast of Spain and told us how various trees and bushes of all kinds grew right to the very edge of the sea, but nobody paid any attention to him, and now he has stopped complaining about this miserable arid rock pile, and is walking along in front singing or whistling happily.

Libertad Calderón and your mother practically never talk during the ascent or descent. They both enjoy exercise and they are the ones who sometimes suggest the idea of the outing. You know perfectly well that your mother, always ready for mountain adventures, also goes along out of desire to spend a peaceful time with her poems or novel, away from the hubbub of people and music on the beachside terrace. You can intuit that for Libertad Calderón, the hike represents a respite from the martyrdom of the beach. And that's why sometimes, even when you aren't on particularly bad terms with her, you put on your theatrical act when someone suggests the outing, since the anticipation of pleasure does not eliminate either your rancor or your malice. You begin by opposing the excursion; you wheedle and bargain; you make them beg you, and encourage bribes; and you take great pleasure in seeing Libertad's face cloud over, without her being able to voice a single word of protest. At first, she insisted on taking not only a book but also her notebooks, in order to study, but you have done everything possible to make her give up that intention. Whenever your mother becomes deeply absorbed in her own reading, and your father endangers himself climbing down to cut handfuls of fresh mussels off the most accessible rocks, Libertad Calderón is supposed to watch over you, and all she can do is glance at her book, or half close her eyes, attempting to think her own thoughts, without altogether losing you from sight.

The ascent is not very difficult. Even you have climbed mountain ridges that are rockier, and certainly higher and steeper, on various occasions with visiting family guests in the valley. However, it is on this ridge where you have been more afraid than anywhere else, and it has been a very basic fear, deep-rooted, free of the twists and turns you tend to invent, to give more color to your life. With this awareness, even loving the beach as much as you do, there is never a time when you would not give it all up in order to have this same intense experience again.

There is a part right at the top where the cliffside on the right becomes concave and turns into a sheer drop. The trail narrows to the point of only allowing people to walk Indian file and you are convinced that the path is so narrow, that no adult could put one foot alongside the other. The first times you went along, your father carried you, and even so, your body trembled when you looked down at the steep precipice and the ravine way down below. Your mother tries to comfort you; she assures you that it is not dangerous, that she, don't you see her, walks along that six foot stretch nonchalantly, carrying her book and the beach bag. It is Libertad Calderón who avenges herself for all your past spitefulness. "Such showing off in the water and you get scared walking along a path my little sister could manage with her eyes blindfolded! All hot air and empty words, that's what you are!"

At night, after praying with your mother in front of Libertad Calderón's openly mocking expression, you say special prayers to the Holy Virgin Mary, to Saint Christopher and to the Holy Child asking them to give you courage next time. You don't call on your Guardian Angel because you think you are too great a sinner to deserve any help there. Little by little the images of the holy picture cards fuse together, and you find yourself in your *ama*'s lap, pleading with her to come to your aid in your time of tribulation. You conjure her up, calling her by her baptismal name and by the name you yourself gave her in order to distinguish her from all the others, but the names sound more and more distant to you, and you realize that you are only calling her by the name forged by your own voice, and not by the one that would count, the magic and true name which is hidden from you and which you still do not know. Without anything that designates her, except the memory that accompanies you wherever you go, you ask her to give you a sign, to command the spirits of the rocks, of the mountains, of the air and of the treacherous roads, in order that they should guide you. And you go to sleep in despair because you cannot fool yourself, and although you have confident faith that everything visible and invisible in nature breathes its own breath, nothing assures you that your *ama* has the power or the relationship with the mysterious forces that govern nature on the coast.

One morning, and you never will know why it had to be that morning, you walked unaided along the path you had so feared. Was it your parents' encouraging voices on the other side that gave impulse to the blind march of your steps? Was it the result of the prayers you uttered so fervently at night that finally led you by the hand to achieve your goal? Was it the presence of Libertad Calderón, who was right behind you and mercilessly spurred you on? Or was it above all an anticipation of the magic pond which lent strength and valor to your feet? Knowing that vanity is your weak point, your parents restrained themselves, and just smiled to congratulate you for the feat, and for the same reason Libertad Calderón made a big fuss over your triumph. That way you would not so easily forget your previous cowardice.

As the days go by, you become more confident of the terrain, and moments before or after crossing the dangerous stretch, you dare to look down at the little cove far below, at the bottom of the cliff. At times some of the young people from the port come to swim and play around there in that blue bowl you so envy. Your father has shouted down to them from above, "How did you get down there?" and they answer, laughing and waving their arms like wings, "Flying!" but you have spotted the two small boats, pulled up against the rocks, that reveal their true means of arrival. They are older and stronger than the young men from the other beach, but they move in the water and on the sand with the same gracefulness. Even from far above, you can see their strong muscles, their firm legs, the narrow line of their hips below their wide tanned backs. Without being inhibited by the presence of your parents, every time they spot Libertad Calderón, they call up compliments; they send invisible kisses with their hands, and they beckon her to fly to join them in the cove. Libertad Calderón's body stiffens and she refuses to even look at them.

"Why don't you at least smile at them?" you asked her once.

"Because they are ignorant show-offs," she answered you, without meeting your eyes. That makes you think about your mother's reaction when men stare at her or say complimentary things to her, when you are walking alone with her through the noisy streets of the town.

"Why do they stare at you like that?" you asked her one afternoon, wanting her to answer something that would reassure you and assuage your misgivings.

"Because men on the coast are really insolent," she answered you, squeezing your hand and walking faster.

Since then, you keep quiet about your curiosity, and you limit yourself to trying to control, as best you can, the turbulent emotions you associate with that forbidden zone. And there on the coast, you are even more intrigued, because you feel that the things that are hidden from you emanate from certain people and hang latent in the very air you breathe, including you in their menace.

When we get to the place that, over time, we have chosen as ours, before throwing himself into the adventure of the mussels, your father goes off, and standing on a rock, he contemplates the sea and is caught up in his thoughts about Columbus' three ships. Your mother takes refuge from the sun under an enormous sunhat; she stretches out her legs which have gradually changed color, and she takes out her book. Relaxed like that, she is lost in her world of pages and words. You explore around for a bit, mostly in order to prolong the suspense and at the same time to calm the anxiety of expectation. Then, with humility and a devotion you never have been able to feel in church, you walk over to your magic pond.

You discovered it one morning when the tide was low, and we decided to explore the part where the hillside narrows on both sides and descends to become an encrusted point in the sea. Waves never reach the place where the pool has formed, and at that point Libertad Calderón lets you go off on your own, so she is not there, and thus her presence does not destroy your silent pact with that small mystery of happiness amongst the rocks. On your knees, or sitting with your arms around your legs, you gaze at it and try to decipher its marvel. You touch the sun-warmed stones around the pool's edge, which are always dry, and you look at the water which, day after day, maintains precisely the same depth, alive, crystal clear, without the opaque muddiness of stagnant pools, and you cannot understand what magic keeps it full. Nor does it seem adequate to compare it with what you know on earth, although you tentatively call it "sacred marine garden" or "sacred sea forest." In any case, it is evident to you that it is neither a garden nor a forest, and you are left only with the inexplicable certainty of the strange power that it has over you. The first time you saw the pool, you could not suppress a cry that the others thought was a complaint and that brought them running over to you. Full of awe, you pointed to the watercolor transparency revealing its humid silence in the midst of the cries of the gulls and the pounding of the waves breaking far out to sea.

"Oh, how pretty!" your mother sighed, and your father warned you that you should take care going up to it because the water and the vegetation in these pools could trick the senses and hide their true depth. Libertad Calderón did not comment that morning, but on another occasion she came up next to you, so close that her bare arm brushed your shoulder, breaking your concentration.

"It's lovely, isn't it?" You asked her in a whisper, fearful that that bit of perfection might be a mirage that would shatter into nothing and vanish if profaned by the human voice.

"You've been infected by your mother's poems," she said with more indifference than scorn. "It's nothing more than a puddle of salt water with four clumps of seaweed in the middle."

The respect inspired in you by that pool of colors stopped you from answering her. However, you do know, without really understanding how you know it, that there is a spirit in that place that had been waiting for you to come, that claims you as hers and with whom you share an alliance created in the moment of discovery. So that now, when you walk toward the pool, you bring with you an offering that you allow to sink and be lost in its sinuous and untouchable depths. Without any regret, you give away your treasures: gleaming *lúcuma* seeds, perfect round *boliche* nuts, kidney beans with black designs on them, white snail shells, fragments of mother of pearl, little purple domes that had been part of sea urchins, and your gold medallions of the Holy Virgin and of Saint Teresita.

The rocks are light gray with dark veins on the outside, and seem to have been chiseled geometrically to produce these shapes. Where they are covered by water, they take on ochre and yellow tones, depending on the light . Only once have you dared to touch the water to see if it was as cold as the sea and then you also caressed the soft surface of the moss that covers the submerged edges. An invisible current ripples the ribbons of the algae and shakes the tightly bunched sea grapes whose luminous green contrasts with the lace of the marine lettuces and the dark rose that scatters its buds on the mirror of the pool. Fastened onto the moss, the scattered dots of tiny mussels are blue mineral specks among the vibrant colors of the plants. When the sun is reflected for a few instants from a certain angle on the surface of the water, shooting rays of luminous edges appear and disappear, swirling, moving, lighting up everything, and overwhelming your eyes, forcing you to close them because so much beauty and so much miracle is too much to bear.

Nevertheless, you cannot stop looking and you are surprised to see your own image mirrored by the water. Is that really you, trembling there on that quiet transparency? The girl in the pool has your bangs, your short limp hair, your fragile neck and the same skinny arms you have. In amazement, the two recognize each other and yet pull apart, both attract and deny each other, yearn to be a single liquid and corporeal being, yet both recognize that they are irrevocably separate. They pull apart, convinced that they will never manage to fuse into one, but then in that moment when the other one looks at you, you see the world contained in that pool where she floats, free and beyond your grasp.

During the intervals you spend beside your pool, the shadows that pursue you like a cloud of nocturnal butterflies dissipate little by little. Your burden of guilts and the certainty of your daily transgressions weigh less heavily on your chest, and by surrendering yourself totally to your pool, you manage to disengage yourself from your fear in a state of wordless communion. You forget the resentment you still feel about your *ama*'s voluntary absence. You forget Libertad Calderón's hostile scowl which protects her from the world like steel armor. You forget the feeling of uneasiness that you feel about your far from innocent relationship with Anacleto. You forget the anxiety of knowing that you still have not yet managed to tell your mother about the existence of the crazy girl in the patio, because the selfishness of your curiosity matters more to you than whatever help your mother could provide by separating her from you, and at the same time you forget your lack of courage to confront the grownups in your group about their tacit or unacknowledged awareness of the presence of the crazy girl. You forget the anguish that rakes you when you think about what might have happened to the Ayacuchan Indian couple and you even forget Libertad Calderón's hatred-packed words when she said you should give up your sentimental nonsense, and that your grandfather in the highlands did not treat his workers any better than Don Serafino was treating the Indians who ended up at his hotel. And you also forget your obsessive desire to seek the girl with light eyes and a starfish on her chest in every corner of each town and beach and in the labyrinthine alleys of your mind.

You don't know how long you spend absorbed beside your magic pond, but once you pull yourself away, you do not return again to it that same morning. If you did, its magic might be lost, or who knows, you might be transformed forever into a glass figure leaning over the

mirror of the water. Delirious and concrete, oscillating between feelings of joyousness that lift you up so you are floating in air, and the
sensation of a hot weight that pulls you down and makes you feel like
rock, water and moss, for a long time you neither want to nor can join
the group of the others. And you cannot imagine how it is they can
look at you without noticing the fish-scale wings that spring out of
your shoulders.

Without being able to do otherwise, you are retracing your own
recent footsteps, and while at first, you feel transfigured and everything you see seems new and radiant, little by little you are engaged
differently with the smell of the sea, the voices, the gulls, the crash of
the waves, the ashen blue of the sky after the morning fog dissipates,
Libertad Calderón's unavoidable stare. Pursued by those eyes, you
explore among the rocks, look for shells and, choosing patiently with
the hope of making yourself a necklace someday, you gather tiny crabshells that death and the sun have tinted orange and cream. Then
later, you help your father to sort out the tangle of mussels and seaweed; you listen to him sing; and you repeat the words of the songs
to yourself silently and stealthily and uneasily; you examine his back
and confirm that, like the crabshells, the pale freckles all over his
skin have gotten redder with the sun.

After that morning when you discovered your magic pool, the path
back to the beach never seems the same again, although it covers the
same ground as before. Even before that moment when you dared to
walk the path above the sheer cliff by yourself, your anxiety was less
solitary. And although the ecstasy was immediate, with each moment
that passes, your delirium is transformed into a hitherto unknown
calm. While it is true that this calm is gradually infiltrated by the routine of your days, the habits which you are taught, and your own inner
mazes and impulses, the unique image of that pool remains in your
body and your memory, and it becomes for you a talisman of water or

a jellyfish which trembles and accompanies you always.

As we get near the beach, the midday sun makes forms and colors stand out more clearly. A different vision fills your eyes and you rejoice in the garish cheerfulness of the beach umbrellas, the shouts of children and young people, the music from the terrace, the smell and general clamor of mornings at the beach. While Libertad Calderón and your mother busy themselves looking for a place to spread out the towels, and your father goes over, smiling, to give the harvested mussels to his friend at the bar, you take off your canvas beach shoes impatiently and with undulled eagerness, you run to the edge to wet your feet in the ebb and flow of the surf.

As she had so many times before, she went to the patio to watch the crazy girl. She instinctively knew which would be the best hour to avoid adult vigilance. Before she opened the gate, while she was walking past María Eugenia and Anacleto's rooms, besieged by the eternal blast of sound from the radio and the smell of bathrooms and gardenias, Ximena imagined to herself that the patio was a kind of anteroom of the forbidden area. She was sure that the hotel had certain spaces invisibly marked out. The entrance lobby, with Don Serafino and the Raimondis' rooms one on each side, was a well-defined unit, and separated from the long hallway with the guests' rooms on the left and the squalid little rooms on the right. However, that division, unmarked by doors or gates, was less clear that the one that could be sensed between the end of the passageway and the patio. Once again, and without any visible boundary, as she moved from the part that constituted the hotel proper into the roofless area, she moved into a zone that foreshadowed the strange world beyond the gate.

Her visits to the forbidden area were short. Sometimes it was a matter of only a few minutes in which they would both stare fixedly at each other without moving, or else Ximena would be a passive spectator of the other's frantic pacing . Neither time nor the frequency of her visits had appeased the fear the crazy girl instilled in her. It made no difference to tell herself that the rope was really strong, and that if she had never escaped before, there was no reason to think that she would do so at right that minute when she was there. She compared this fear with the apprehension she had felt before she dared to walk along the cliffside path, and she realized that while on the mountainside, her terror afflicted her when she got to the other side, here it paralyzed her or forced her to go back to the hotel. On only a few occasions had she managed to synchronize her movements with the crazy girl's, but when it did happen, then in the midst of the pirouettes and wild jumps that took over her body and will, she had felt exalted and carried away to the point of losing all notion of herself; during those moments, she was aware, as she had been, even that first time, that everything around her changed in proportion to the extent to which she became immersed in the crazy girl's agitated rhythms.

On a few occasions, before she opened the gate or when she was right in front of it, she was seized by the temptation to cross the distance that separated them to touch her, or even more, to liberate her from her captivity. But it was barely a shadow of a temptation because the desire evaporated in the very instant of its articulation, its fragility overwhelmed by the inscrutable expression in those other eyes. It had never been Ximena who had determined the way in which they stared at each other or played, and she never felt that she was the one who controlled the situation. She knew with certainty that she could not predict, or bend to her will, the actions or the will of that being, unpredictable and alienated by madness, and above all by the lack of words. And yet she returned because a dark and obsessive curiosity, unaffected by María Eugenia's recent information, was more powerful than her fear, and because the other, by just being there, corroborated the existence of the stranger with light eyes and the starfish on her chest. Each time she opened the gate, she felt both apprehension and hope that the woman would be there as she had been a few days before, glistening with water next to the old washtub in the back lot.

That afternoon, just like other afternoons, the two gazed at each other in silence. Ximena stood still, her arms at her sides, and gave herself over to an emotion which the cool afternoon air sharpened as it chilled her sunburned skin. Dusty from head to foot, squatting down, the crazy girl's legs were folded against her chest, and with her rags and her hair discolored by exposure, she looked like a stain projected by the light that filtered through the branches of the big ficus tree. What was she thinking about? What thoughts could fill her mind in that faded afternoon quiet not even broken by the hens' clucking, feather rustling, or strutting around like confused ladies? When or how did she eat? Why had Ximena never seen anyone entering or coming out of the adobe hut? And despite all the vague hints she had picked up, why did almost everyone insist on denying her existence?

María Eugenia, who often made general comments about Ximena's adventures, had made several attempts to scare her. "I know what you're up to," she had said to her recently. "But you be careful, be very careful, because that one doesn't recognize anybody and she even bites the hand that feeds her. That feeble little body is enormously strong. She will attack you by surprise and then, may God and all the holy spirits protect you. You won't have a single unbroken bone." Irritatedly, she had added, "You don't believe me, do you?"

Without answering her, Ximena had asked, "Who takes care of her?" and María Eugenia, shrugging her shoulders, had closed the door of her room. But then, one Saturday night, when the uproar on the street could even be heard inside the hotel, free of her parents and of Don Serafino and Anacleto, who had all gone out, and easily escaping Libertad Calderón's attention, Ximena had bumped into María

Eugenia in the patio. She was in the big wicker chair that she often dragged out of her room to sit in the light and page through her magazines. One hand held one of those cheap round glasses that made Ximena think of fat tonsured priests, and the other hand, resting on her skirt, held a beer bottle.

"Do you want to join me for a look at my *Ecran* magazines?" Her attempt to articulate the words clearly was unsuccessful. Even her voice, which was usually sweet and low, was unrecognizable now.

"It is almost too dark to see." Ximena answered her more politely than usual, because María Eugenia's wandering gaze disconcerted her, taking away her self assurance. It was a look from someplace else, inaccessible with everyday eyes, and that reminded her somehow of the crazy girl's stare.

"Come, come into my room. I have the last issue and you should just see how pretty Debbie Reynolds looks. And it has Tony Curtis on the cover. Don't you think he's handsome? Come on, the kids are asleep and aren't going to annoy you. I can offer you a Coca-Cola."

She refused, inventing an excuse. Although her mother had told her not to set foot in María Eugenia's room, it was not that prohibition that made her refuse the invitation that night. She had no qualms about lying to grownups, but when she peered in from the patio at the heavy darkness of the room, she did not want to go in.

María Eugenia stood up with difficulty and, with uncertain steps, she came up so close to her that her face lost its familiar features. Ximena moved backwards. "Come into my room and I'll tell you about the crazy girl."

And then Ximena did follow her in, because her curiosity was stronger than her repugnance. The room was dark except for a naked light bulb that lit up a circle on the red and white oilcloth of a table set against the wall. Holding her breath and without going all the way inside, Ximena looked quickly around the room. She saw Fátima curled up on an unmade bed, the ragged chenille coverlet heaped up at her feet. Next to her, on the floor, in what looked like part of a suitcase, Lourdes was sleeping. With the addition of a primus stove on one corner of the table, there were the same shabby furnishings as in all the other rooms. What made this room seem different was its total disorder. Because the light was so feeble, it took her a while to figure out who was portrayed in the clippings stuck to the wall. Then she realized that there was a mixture of religious figures and what she supposed were movie stars, some of them adorned with wreaths of dried flowers or crepe paper chains.

She would have preferred not to touch anything but she had no choice but to sit at the table. Because she was drunk, María Eugenia confused the assigned roles, and Ximena felt inhibited and unable to be rude to her. As the drunk woman struggled to bend down and select certain magazines from her big pile, Ximena thought anxiously that she might forget what she had promised and was not sure whether to stay or to slip out unnoticed.

"Ay, by the most sainted Virgin! I've never seen you make a face like that, Ximena! You look as if you've just seen ghosts! Oh, I know! I forgot that I had promised you a Coke."

"I don't like Coca-Cola," she said without thinking and before she could stop herself, she said, "You told me that you would tell me about the crazy girl."

"Yes, but first let's look at the last issue."

While she took big swallows of her beer, Ximena had to look with María Eugenia at the magazine pictures, one by one. She felt as though she would die when María Eugenia noisily kissed the lips of the man on the cover several times and then suggested that she imitate her. To deflect that, Ximena pretended enthusiasm and opened the magazine and asked her to show her her favorite actress. Maybe if the light had been better, or the pictures had been in color and on better paper, she could have felt more interested. But the men and women María Eugenia pointed to with the bitten nail of her index finger were similar to those she saw drawn or photographed in other magazines and in commercial ads. To her they all looked foreign and unreal.

"I'm going now." The air in the room suddenly seemed unbearable. She tried to stand up, but María Eugenia pushed her back down.

"Don't go," she repeated, hurting her shoulder with the pressure of her hand. "Don't go, but by the Holy Trinity, why do you want to know a story that is so sad?"

"Because I do, because she is my friend."

"How can she be your friend when not even the nuns in the hospice, with all their patience, could stand her! It's better for her to be out in the open air here than fastened into a straitjacket night and day there."

"Who takes care of her?"

"Her grandparents, because in her village, a rumor started to go around that the whole family was possessed by the devil, and it was going to make her brothers' and sisters' lives too hard to have her stay there."

"Why aren't they ever around?"

"They are around, but people hardly ever see them."

"Why does Don Serafino let them live in his back lot?"

"Ah! Just see how curious you are! Maybe you haven't heard the story about what curiosity did to the cat."

María Eugenia went over to get another bottle, and on her way back to the table she started to sing and move her hips, with the bottle and glass held high.

> "Don Serafinito killed his wife,
> he slugged her hard
> then he ran for his life"

Ximena recognized the tune right away, although try as she might, she could not remember the words of the song.

"It's like a tragedy in a movie," Mareía Eugenia paused pensively before adding, "Anthony Quinn would have played the role of Don Serafino well. Poor man! And on top of that, to have the name of an angel."

She looked for Anthony Quinn in another magazine before it occurred to Ximena to lie and say that she knew what the actor looked like. She showed her a man with a long face who reminded her of her Uncle Germán.

"He doesn't look like a gringo, does he? He is a really great artist and attractive in his way. But you're getting up again! Now I'll tell you the story." She poured herself more beer and half closed her eyes.

"What's happened is that Don Serafino has had really bad luck with women. They say that when he was young, he lost his head over a much older woman, one with more experience, and of course, a smooth tongue. He worked like a slave night and day so that woman could have luxuries she had never had before. They say that she didn't even know how to wear shoes, but she was a light skinned woman from Cajamarca, really attractive. They say that one day he came home from work early and found her in bed with a friend of his."

Without really understanding the story, Ximena could piece together enough to follow the gist.

"And so, to get even and then some, not only did he kick her out of the house, but the next week he brought home the younger sister of the Cajamarcan woman. I don't know what their mother was like, but the younger one turned out just like her sister, and he kicked her out of the house, too. The bad thing is that, like the saying goes, 'the smaller the town, the bigger the Hell' and by then everybody in town knew all about it, and his cuckold's horns were so big, no hat would fit on his head, so he decided to pack his things and go."

Ximena was less and less able to follow the story, although she didn't want to ask questions because she wanted to hear the rest of the account.

"He went way up north, and since he has a good eye for money making, he did well in smuggling and came back home to Piura, where he opened a bar. He had women at his beck and call, but he decided he wanted one just for himself, and they say he went to look for a really young one, someone who would stay close to home and was ugly enough not to fall into temptation. He went looking out as far as a poor little farm, where a family lived that was suffering from bad luck and from the misfortune of having all daughters, each one uglier and darker-skinned than the last. He picked the one that was the worst of them all."

By now, Ximena was listening so intensely that she had forgotten all about the crazy girl and started breathing naturally in the midst of the acid stench that filled the room.

"They say that for a few years everything went well for them. The girl turned out to be a good worker and he was content, and didn't take her back to her parents even though the girl kept miscarrying when she got pregnant or else the babies were born dead. Poor Don Serafino! It must have been his fate. One night he heard from a drunk in a bar that you should never leave a young woman, no matter how hideous she is, unless you put a chastity belt on her, and he thought the man was warning him. He kept an eye on her all the time, and beat her up so bad she looked worse than a Christ on the cross. One fateful Saturday night like this, he returned home unexpectedly and he found her talking to one of her cousins. He didn't even notice that his wife's father and another relative, a young boy, were there, dozing in a corner. They say he was blind with rage, and grabbing an iron frying pan, he gave her such a blow on the head that he killed her instantly. He tells how, in order not to have trouble with the police, he bought the silence of the girl's family. I think it was more just to avoid the dishonor of everyone thinking he had been cheated on again."

María Eugenia was silent for a few instants and closed her eyes. There was no beer left and Ximena was afraid she was going to fall asleep on the table.

"And the crazy girl?"

"Ah yes, the crazy girl! She is the youngest daughter of one of the ugly sisters, and since the farm could barely support them, and the scandals about the child made their life intolerable in the village, they came here with their bundles on their backs. The grandparents are not so old, and they are hard workers, which means that with Don Serafino giving them a roof and maybe even some money, they pick up jobs here and there and send what they can back to their village. So now you know why you never see them around there. They go out very early and they don't come back until late."

Laying her head on the grease-stained oilcloth, María Eugenia added, very slowly: "So there you have it. That's the end of the story."

She did not say anything more that night. Ximena touched her arm with her fingertips, but the woman did not wake up. On tiptoe she went over to the door, and closed it carefully behind her.

Confused about certain parts of the story, she would have liked to ask more questions when she crossed paths with her in the patio. But the visit and the conspiratorial revelation of the secret had created an excessively familiar manner on María Eugenia's part, and Ximena reacted with annoyance, resisting any complicity. One afternoon she refused to look at a magazine with her, and María Eugenia threatened to tell her mother on her. "I know she does not want you to be with me. With that stuck-up attitude of being a great lady that she affects when all you have to do is listen to her to know she is from the highlands. What if I tell her you came to my room and even tried my beer?"

Ximena bluffed her way through it. Without knowing exactly why, she was sure that María Eugenia would not say anything to anyone. What went on on that side of the hotel remained locked in the patio air, with its nauseating smell that hung heavily around María Eugenia and Anacleto's doors, that crept through the gate, dragged itself between the bathrooms, spread its way up the stained walls and throbbed in the cracks in the cement floor. Probably all this was felt as boding something imminent and terrible, but it was never discussed after one crossed over to the hotel side and stepped onto the wide unpolished boards that muffled the sound of footsteps in the hallway.

And now she and the crazy girl stared at each other, and Ximena thought that it would have been better not to have heard María Eugenia's story. Even with the undeniable attraction exerted on her by this human being, who was so close and yet so remote, an insidious uneasiness was convincing her that after that conversation, she could imagine her with a past which had no connection with the extraordinary. She would have preferred that she were really possessed by demons or bewitched. She would have preferred to dream that someone would arrive one day to break the enchantment, to liberate her by converting her into a swallow or an ever-flowering purple lilac bush. Nor had Don Serafino's early history managed to transform him into a criminal or terrifying person, because his story, too, portrayed him as ordinary and without mystery.

Disillusioned, she continued to watch her, prolonging and intensifying her emotion through fear of whatever gesture or movement that dusty image, so deceptively tranquil under the shadow of the ficus tree, might suddenly produce. And because her own heartbeats throbbed it out to her, she realized in that same moment that the girl's unreadable face contained the secret of the stranger, and how that secret was protected by the total absence of signs or words. The only communication they sustained was a gaze that did not connect them, and that frantic pacing to which she gave herself up, but she was not able, later, to interpret these or decipher any greater meaning.

Ximena looked up and saw a wandering cloud, transparent as a veil about to tear, that was moving across the sky with unusual velocity. She followed it until it drifted out of sight while she fretted over the idea that they just had a few more days left on the coast, and that she might have to leave without finding out the story of the most beautiful woman on earth. Observing the girl, who, indifferent to the cloud's warning, had not shifted position, she decided that since no one in either the hotel nor in the patio zone had wanted—or been able—to tell her about her, she would slip away that very evening, just after dark, and go in search of that story through the chaotic streets of the town.

Ximena takes a deep breath; the afternoon light is turning lead gray, and the wind forecasts a gentle drizzle which brings with it the smell of the sea. As so often before, she revels in the sensations of being on the coast, of absorbing in her very skin the humid, enervating sweetness that she always associates with her beach vacations, of being able to see and be seen in a way that is different than she is accustomed to elsewhere. She has gradually forgiven the village for its excessive number of trucks, taxis and busses; and right from the moment of their arrival, encouraged by her father's ebullient good cheer during these summer stays, and undeterred by her mother's reserve, Ximena has felt more intrigued than annoyed by the outgoingness of the people.

It is still quite a few days before the Carnival season begins, but some stores are already displaying colored rolls of serpentine, bags of confetti, masks, disguises, noisemakers, paper hats, and Chinese fans.

A poster with drawings of harlequins and dominos can be seen all over the place, stuck up on the outside walls of various establishments, and while she walks, trying not to bump against the people who go by her, she is caught up in the rhythm of a Carnival song blaring from the loudspeaker of a red car, filling the street with sound, while a big man with a tattoo of a ship on his bare arm tosses out handfuls of colored flyers covered with black letters and music notes. Some people catch them before they hit the ground, while others pick them up, read them and let them fall again. Ximena wishes she could grab one of the yellow ones where the letters seem to sing, but she is afraid that someone might notice, and laugh at her.

She heads for the store that is most familiar to her, and her shivering body warns her that it is not the same place she has gone to during the daytime. It is always somewhat dark, but now it is even darker, and in the far corner, several men are sitting around two little tables or are talking, leaning over the counter. The shadows on that side seem murky in the cigarette smoke and the space is full of voices and laughter. She is reassured a little by the presence of the woman shop owner, who is waiting calmly on a girl hardly any taller than Ximena. She can't be any older than ten because her dress, very short and very tight, just reveals her bones. The girl picks up the noodles wrapped in paper, and confidently hands over a bottle, asking to have it filled with vinegar. When the Asian woman tells her how much it comes to, with the same confidence as before, she takes some change out of a worn coin purse and complains that the price of either noodles or vinegar has gone up since her last visit. Then she goes out, leaving Ximena impressed and envious of such self-possession.

"And you? What can I do for you?"

Ximena looks over at the side, nervous that the man who had stuck out his tongue at her a few days ago might be there listening to her. She hesitates before she replies because her mouth is dry. She has forgotten the question that she has been rehearsing all along the way here. She speaks, trying not to stutter. "Ma'am, do you know anything about a tall girl, with very short hair and light eyes, who wears a starfish pendant on her chest?"

The store owner smiles at her. "Do you know her name?"

Ximena shakes her head.

"And where did you see her?"

"At the San Cristóbal Hotel."

"Then that's where she must be. Look for her among the guests."

"I already looked for her, and I haven't seen her again.

"Then go over and ask Doña Emperatriz, who runs the sweetshop on the corner. She knows about everybody in the town. And don't look so sad. Here, while you're looking for her, eat these candies."

Relieved to have finished her inquiries in the store, Ximena walks toward the sweetshop sucking on a lemon drop. Behind the small counter that displays purple *mazamorra*, rice pudding, *arroz zambito*, rows of flan custards, *alfajores* and other desserts, she sees the woman who has waited on them several times in the past. She does not have to lower her voice much, because the only other customers are an elderly couple Ximena thinks must be deaf, because they seem so distant. "Ma'am, might you be able to tell me where I could find a tall girl, with very short hair and light eyes, and a starfish on her chest?"

"Have you seen her here in town?"

"Yes, at the San Cristóbal Hotel."

"Well, that's where she must be, if she is anywhere around. Try knocking on all the doors."

"I already knocked on all the doors and I can't find her."

"Then go over and ask the Chinaman Basilio, who runs that little restaurant where you always have lunch. He knows everybody in the town. But don't go away so sad. Take this *alfajorcito* pastry and enjoy it while you are searching."

Ximena, cheered by the woman's wide smile, heads happily to the La Pagoda restaurant. Nearly there, her nerve fails her. She has bad memories of the restaurant. The waiter who usually waits on them, laughed because he thought it was funny that they sometimes have to tell her stories during lunch. Instead of leaving her in peace, Ximena is convinced that he stands by her parents' table longer than necessary, just to annoy her. On the other hand she knows perfectly well who the Chinaman Basilio is. He is the tall thin Chinaman who is always stationed by the cash register, whom she has never seen smile.

The restaurant is one of the biggest in town, and the tables are a distance from the door, because there is a vestibule with big decorated urns and artificial plants. Mr. Basilio is behind the cash register, as always. He has been putting bills into a big envelope and now he stares hard at her without a single change in his expression. "What do you want?"

"I am looking for a very tall girl, with short hair, who has light eyes and wears a starfish on her chest. Do you know who she is or how I can find her."

He takes a cigarette, and bends over to write something on the envelope. Then he looks at her through the smoke, and his tone is friendlier than Ximena expected. "Where did you meet her?"

"I saw her just once at the San Cristóbal Hotel."

"Ah, then there's no problem. Wait for her in the same place where you saw her that time."

"I have waited for her many times, and she has not reappeared."

"Then go over to the El Delfín restaurant. The owner, Don Manuel Reyes, spends his days talking to people in the town. He will know what to tell you."

As she walks down the street, Ximena is surprised that night is falling so quickly. Drivers are beginning to switch on their headlights, which reflect on the walls of the stores, changing people's skin color.

Even the sounds of brakes and horns and voices seem to shift into some other color. "The night is painting itself the colors of sea water," thinks Ximena while she lets herself be wrapped in the marine breezes of a green-blue dusk which is neither green nor blue. Her pleasure mixes with a fear of getting lost in these streets that are suddenly transforming themselves under her eyes. The sight of the illuminated letters of the Royal Movie Theater comfort her. Her parents are there, and she still has a while yet before the show is out. With a strawberry candy in her mouth, she runs rather than walks to the El Delfin Restaurant.

She expects to find Mr. Reyes standing there, leaning against the door frame as usual, but she has to go in, after spotting him behind the counter where, making her apprehensive, a big pig's head can be seen, crowned with vegetables and adorned with a collar of red, orange and green peppers. It is surrounded by headless grilled chickens, a little goat arranged on a bed of green herbs, and farther over, a row of whole fish with their dead eyes staring at the ceiling, laid out on wilted lettuce leaves, decorated with bright slices of lemon. Ximena concentrates on how good the strawberry candy tastes in order to distance herself from the memory of so many lunches in the past, when pieces of pork rind, chicken, goat and fish were such a struggle to swallow. Mr. Reyes is bending over, adjusting the various display plates. "Ah, the crybaby!" he says standing up straight. "Don't tell me you've come to buy a ham sandwich! What do you want?"

Ximena looks at him resentfully. Behind his fat good-natured manner, his words are trying to bite her. With her parents he is always very cordial, almost obsequious.

"I wanted to ask you if you knew where I can find a tall girl, with very short hair and light eyes, and a starfish on her chest."

"Did you meet her here in the restaurant?"

"I haven't met her. I saw her once in the San Cristóbal Hotel."

"Then Don Serafino is the one you should ask. He will help you find her. He probably has her locked up in one of those little rooms he has just built."

He guffaws, and seeing Ximena's chagrin, he hands her a little box of chewing gum. "For your nerves," he says and then he adds, lowering his voice, "Walk three blocks past the movie theater and then turn left. Cross the little plaza where the church is and at the first street, turn left again, and you'll see a small house painted several colors, with a garden full of plants and herbs. There will be two old ladies at the door. One is almost blind, but she will want you to believe that she can see. The other one will be knitting. They know everything that goes on and doesn't go on in this town."

Only a few minutes have gone by, but now the only light comes from streetlights and from cars going by. And now the air smells strongly of the sea and the leaden sky has liquid reverberations. There are more and more people on the street and Ximena looks at their dark skin that, like the sky, looks both shiny and damp, as if the heat had condensed on them in a fine green layer which gives them the appearance of both mossy rock and wet algae. She is afraid because it is getting late and she skips along faster than a walk, bumping into people, relieved that the voices she hears dissipate all doubt about whether those who move around at night are souls in purgatory of those who have drowned at sea.

She has followed Mr. Reyes' directions and soon she finds herself in a little plaza. Facing onto it, there is a church she has never entered. Even though it is late, there are still children playing, couples sitting on the benches whispering secrets, men and women moving around pacing slowly and street vendors who proffer fruit juice and ice cones. An occasional house, or store with its windows open, allows radio music to reach the edge of the plaza, and the joyous sounds of drums and guitars assuage her foreboding temporarily. If this small circle of palm trees and untended grass, and all the people walking around, seem unreal to her now, it is because she has never imagined that inhabited side streets exist here.

She finds the small multi-colored house easily. They are soft colors, like cake icing and because of the way rose, blue, yellow and green are scattered here and there, in no apparent design, on the window frames, on the door, and on various parts of the front wall, it looks more like a play house than one for people. Protected by a low wall that ends in an iron gate, between the front of the house and the sidewalk there is a garden with flowers and plants growing in a delirious disorder. As she had expected, two old ladies are in the entryway seated on tiny wooden rocking chairs. They have white hair with violet highlights, and as she looks at them, Ximena thinks she has never seen such wrinkled faces. One of them is knitting what looks like a huge scarf or maybe a baby blanket, and the other is winding balls of the wool she has in skeins in a basket at her feet. Before she comes to a complete stop in front of them, the one who is knitting asks her: "Who are you looking for, little nocturnal bird?"

"Yes, wandering night bird, what are you looking for?" repeats the other.

The two of them look at her with toothless smiles. Their expressions are sweet, but still, Ximena is startled. She can't tell which one is blind: they both seem to be looking at her.

"I would like to know if you know where I can find a tall girl, very beautiful, with short hair and light eyes, who wears a starfish on her chest."

"Mystery of mysteries," the two say simultaneously, and one of them adds, "And you saw her at the San Cristóbal Hotel, where you are staying with your parents and that withdrawn girl who gives you such a hard time?"

Ximena takes a step backward. She stops breathing for a few seconds and does not know what to answer.

"Don't be afraid," the one who is knitting reassures her, laying her work on her lap and reaching her hands out toward her. "Let's see if you are as skinny as our sparrows tell us in the mornings."

Without her being able to help it, small deformed claws feel her body. The other agrees. "Yes, you are just as skinny as we had heard. Why don't you come in for a while and eat some dessert with us. Inside, our house is carpeted with candies and chocolates. With foil wrappers, just the way you like them."

Ximena is terrified. She knows full well what happens to lost children when they enter gingerbread houses. In a faint voice, she answers that it is already night and she has to return to the hotel, but she is unable to move because her heart tells her that the old ladies know something about the stranger. "Well, if you turn us down, it doesn't matter;" the one winding the balls of wool stands up agilely and caresses her hair. "I am going to gather you some flowers to keep you company on your way back to the hotel."

She goes off, hopping along in black leather boots with gold buckles, and she sings under her breath while she pauses here and there in the garden. "She must be the blind one," thinks Ximena, while she holds out her hand to receive the bouquet. The old woman's eyes gaze over her head when she talks to her.

"Here you are. Flowers that chase away worries, flanked by lemon verbena, chamomile and mint. Go back to the hotel. The stranger has been there the whole time without leaving her room."

Ximena does not want to argue, and she thanks her for the flowers. They no longer alarm her and she would like to stay there a while longer with them, listening to them talk, but she had not expected to go to the many-colored house, and now she needs to hurry on to her last stop before her parents get out of the movies. She waves good-bye with her hand and leaves them like a painting illuminated at night by the flare of the two lamps they have next to their grilled front door.

She runs to the pharmacy, sucking a grape candy, holding the handful of flowers and herbs. She pays attention to where she is going, and she is calmer than before, even though the night is closing in completely, and the pedestrians still look a little like ghosts. She clings to the hope that the pharmacist is somehow connected to the girl she has been seeking so eagerly.

She finds him behind the counter, absorbed in the job of filling a tiny envelope with a white powder. He uses a long-handled spoon to scrape the powder out of a large glass jar that has a black skull with two crossed bones on it. On one side, he has piled filled envelopes, and on the other, he has a stack of empty ones. Ximena notices that the envelopes have the picture of the skull on them, too. The pharmacist has not seen her, or pretends not to see her. Ximena has never seen him smile, and right now he seems more distant than ever. She waits a few moments for the question customers are always asked, and she hears only her own breathing and the tinkle of the teaspoon on the counter when he puts it down to seal the end of one of the envelopes.

"Good evening, sir," she uses the polite tone of grownups. "I wonder if I might ask you a question."

The pharmacist looks down and fixes his eyes upon her, without saying anything.

"Could you tell me if you know a girl as tall as you and very beautiful, with short hair, light eyes and who wears a starfish on her chest?"

"Is that why you've come to bother me at this hour?" his voice sounds even older and more tired than he looks.

"I've been looking for her for days and Anacleto, who works at the hotel, told me that maybe she was your daughter."

The pharmacist does not answer, and Ximena is becoming mesmerized by the slow certain motions of the man's hands: translucent hands with long delicate fingers. She can't contain herself, and before she thinks, she hears her own voice asking:

"What is that powder?"

The old man looks a her without blinking and gestures toward her lips, with the full teaspoon, menacingly. "It is an ancient poison to silence little girls who tell lies."

Ximena does not even lift her eyes to make sure that the pharmacist is joking. She turns and goes out into the darkness of the street. There are more people than ever out there now, and it is hard to move along the sidewalk. Little by little, she feels a wave of anger rising from her stomach up to her mouth. If it were not so late, she would go back to the pharmacy, sweep her arm across the counter and knock all the little envelopes and the poison jar onto the floor. The glass would break into a thousand pieces and the pharmacist would have to spend the entire night cleaning it up and sweeping the sinister powder off his white tile floor. She is so caught up in her resentment, that she does not notice a group of men who are walking along the sidewalk conversing in drunken voices and gesturing expansively with their hands. She bumps into one of them and is about to fall headlong, when she feels herself lifted up in the air by two enormous arms. From up there, way up there, because the man is very tall and burly, she looks down at the face that is smiling at her, with its row of very white teeth that look even whiter in the night, and in contrast to his mahogany colored skin. "Don't be scared, Skinny! I caught you in time and saved you from dropping the flowers you're taking to the Virgin of the Fallen Souls. Hang on tight to them!" he says, laughing and tosses her even higher up in the air, as if she were a ball or a rag doll. He catches her easily under the armpits and sets her down on the sidewalk. A circle of people has gathered that applauds her unexpected flight, laughing.

In just a few minutes she has been humiliated twice. Ximena tries to swallow her tears and shoves her way through the crowd, where there is no space to move along forward. She chews the gum from the little box with the same intensity with which she chews her rancor. She does not recall, ever before, feeling as helpless and as small as she does now.

At the hotel entrance, under the round light that floods the door-way, she sees Anacleto. It has all been his fault. He should have taken on his share of the investigations, but he is so stupid he has just waited for her to go all over town, begging for answers.

"Where have you been?" he asks with concern. "I've been standing here for quite a while, waiting to see if you would come. Miss Libertad asked about you several times and finally went out looking for you."

"I went out to get an *alfajor*," replied Ximena, reacting to a com-plication that had not occurred to her. She reaches into her pocket and pulls out the battered sweet, stuck miserably to the paper wrap-per. "But I'm not hungry any longer, and you can eat it. When she comes back, tell her that right after she left, I came back and I'm in my room."

She walks on, but fury is bubbling up in her chest. She turns and faces Anacleto again.

"Just so you know," she hisses, "just so you know. I found out who the stranger with light eyes and the starfish on her chest is. She is the mermaid of the story you like so much, and because you waited too long to look for her, she is going to die here on land and will never be able to go back to her kingdom in the sea, or marry her prince who has also been looking for her. It's too late now, you've ruined it for her. And it is all your fault."

For a few instants she watches how the dwarf's expression changes. His face has the hopeless, remote look that sometimes the very old have, and at the same time, the shameless naked fear of a small child.

She expects a protest or an attempt at an excuse, but Anacleto has been left in pain and without being able to say a word. His silence makes her even more impatient. "It's your fault, Anacleto; she is going to die and it's your fault, poor little mermaid that you liked so much," she repeats with conscious cruelty as she goes off down the hallway.

As she is about to open the door to her room, she is startled to hear a howl like the crazy girl's but which is coming from the other side of the patio. Then, with fear and with pleasure, she hears Anacleto's hoarse sobs.

Don Serafino doesn't know what to do. He moves his head from side to side, he scratches his chin, and he tips his straw hat back to run his hand over his forehead, and then he jams it on straight again and sits thinking, with his arms folded, at the hotel entrance, in the patio, on one side or another of the hallway.

"I don't know what ails him," he mutters worriedly. "He's getting sick on me, he's sputtering out like a candle end, and I can't figure out what is wrong with him."

Everyone in the hotel has noticed that Anacleto has changed drastically during the last few days. He walks around with his clothes thrown on any which way, hanging lopsidedly on the small body which shrinks daily. He is very slow to complete his hotel jobs because he keeps stopping to let his head drop, first onto one shoulder and, after he gives a heartrending sigh, onto the other. His hair is not only not slicked into place but unkempt, wild as a frightened cat's fur. He does not want to eat, even though Don Serafino buys his favorite meat pies and María Eugenia fixes his favorite dishes, and Ximena's father offers him a variety of candies so he can choose, sweet-toothed and greedy as he has always been, the largest and most attractive. Even Mrs. Raimondi, who never seems to be aware of anything happening around her, follows him through the hotel, trying to get him to accept an energizing herb tea.

At first, as if they had entered into a tacit agreement, Ximena and Anacleto avoid each other, and if they have no choice but to cross paths in the patio or hallway, they exchange looks with eyes equally full of guilt. Ximena had not expected such an extreme reaction. She thought he would follow her around, full of urgent questions, and she had even taken pleasure in imagining the answers she would have ready that would dismay him more and more. Anacleto's silence, his evident depression, dumfounded her for the first two days, but curiosity to see what it would lead to, and what form the dwarf's extreme desolation would take, kept her waiting to see what would happen next. It was later, when Anacleto stopped showing up at the hotel both during the day and at night, and when Don Serafino would go out worriedly to look for him in town and bring him back, each time weaker and more shrunken, that she thought about talking to him. And now, probably because her mother had been questioning her severely about Anacleto, or because she thought she saw María Eugenia and Libertad Calderón giving her accusing looks, despite her fear and her desire, she could not find any words of comfort. She, too, was submerged in a mute melancholy, which exasperated her mother, who wanted to take maximum advantage of their last days of vacation. If she could spend an hour by her magic pool, perhaps she could figure out a way to straighten out what she had twisted out of shape so violently and thoughtlessly. However, the time for departure to Lima was drawing near, and her parents wanted to spend more time at the beach.

Tossing in her bed, unable to sleep, Ximena prays and asks her *ama* for a dream of clear and decipherable images that will help her to find an escape from her indecision. She is awakened by Libertad Calderón's hard voice telling her that it is time to get up, her tense hands shaking her by the shoulders when she turns her face to the other side and refuses to get out of bed. Before she can take in the warm light of the room, and with the light, the mental and daily routine of mornings on the coast, the image of Anacleto's emaciated figure goads her. Her body, lethargic with the tiredness that the sharp and fleeting bits of her various nightmares have inflicted, would like to go back to sleep and wake up refreshed by other, happier dreams, to begin the day all over again.

One afternoon, she leaves her parents' room with a message for Libertad Calderón, and without thinking about it or being able to foresee it, she heads for Anacleto's room. She pays no attention to the smells of the patio, intensified in the sun's heat, without a whisper of breeze to dissipate them. The door is closed and when she tries to push it open, it does not move. She whispers his name because she doesn't want to attract the attention of María Eugenia, who is taking a nap at this hour, and after a few minutes of persevering, she returns to the passageway. Her intention is to deliver her parents' message, but her feet take her all the way to Don Serafino's room, where Anacleto has been spending more time because the owner can take care of him more easily there.

She enters the room without knocking, hurried by her own impatience and disconcerted by the unplannedness of this visit. The blinds of the enormous window with antique cornices are open, and the whole room can be seen clearly. Don Serafino's meticulous order and characteristic tidiness dominate the space. The small sofa against the wall has been converted into a child's bed big enough for Anacleto. The smell of his cheap cologne and the semi-naked women of the calendar pin-ups create dissonant notes in the spartan atmosphere of the room. Ximena has never looked at them close up, perhaps because the few times she has entered, the blinds have been closed. Like everything else she has done in the last few minutes, without thinking ahead, without really even wanting to, she goes over to them.

And then, appalled, she recognizes her: there she is, the stranger, right there. She is there, with her short wet hair, her big light calm eyes, her pleasant smile, naked to the waist, with a speckled towel in shades of green wrapped around what seem to be unnaturally long legs. The pin-up is one of the ones highest on the wall, and trembling, Ximena pulls over a chair and climbs up on it to see if the medallion that hangs on her chest is a starfish. But from where she stands, all she can see is that the pendant is not oval or round like most medallions. She thinks she can count five points, but she no longer knows whether it is a a starfish or a celestial star, because without noticing, she has started to weep in shame and can no longer see well enough to count.

In vain, she assures him that it was just one of her stories, that she invented it, that the stranger does not exist, that the images on paper got mixed up, and that while it is true that, at first, she thought she had actually seen her and therefore had searched for her, now she knows that she was mistaken. She tells him, her words tumbling out in a hurry, that afterward it occurred to her to tell him, she doesn't know why, she just burst out with it, that it was about the little mermaid.

Ximena is sitting on the edge of the small sofa in Don Serafino's room. Since night before last, Anacleto has not been able to get up, his legs are too weak, and he can barely make his voice audible when he asks them to take him to the bathroom. He stares at Ximena and it is as though he either cannot hear her well or cannot understand her words. Ximena confesses her crime over and over again. Lifting the book up right in front of him, she shows him the illustrations of Andersen's stories; she forces Anacleto's hands, almost the same size as her own, to touch the bright pages of pictures.

"They are stories," she insists, while she turns the pages. "They are just stories for children."

Equally to no avail, she has tried to explain her terrible error, and gently has tried to force him to look at the pin-ups of women on the wall. Anacleto moans and stiffens up, and if she manages to turn his face in that direction, he closes his eyes and makes a face of disgust and pain. Then he opens his eyes and looks at her without seeing her, as Ximena continues with her story, getting confused about what happened that night in town, which now seems very remote to her, as she keeps repeating over and over again that it has all been her fault and that of the pharmacist.

Her mother comes looking for her. She hasn't even heard her enter the room, and now she feels her pulling on her sleeve, and, toning down the anger in her voice, she orders her to come outside with her immediately. Anacleto is left alone with the weight of the book on his chest. "This is the last straw," her mother says, stopping in the middle of the hall to feel her forehead. "Tomorrow we have to go back to Lima, and we have to pack and make a thousand arrangements and you pick today to come down with a fever."

They make her lie down and they leave her with Libertad Calderón, who with poorly disguised relief has begun to put her books into her suitcase. In a little while, Ximena thinks maybe she can say she has to go to the bathroom, and thus get back to Don Serafino's room and return to the delirium of her explanations so that somehow Anacleto will understand her and forgive her. But a sudden fatigue robs her of all her remaining breath, and thinking that it is all hopeless, she falls asleep, huddled into a ball.

They postpone their trip because Ximena is ill. They are afraid she has food poisoning because she has been vomiting every little while, but they do not understand what could have made her sick when they have all eaten the same things and the others are fine. The town doctor prescribes medication and concentrated broth, the smell of which nauseates her even more and which she refuses stubbornly. All they can get her to drink is herb tea, and when Libertad Calderón is the one lifting the cup to her mouth, she tells Ximena in a low voice that she really deserves to feel bad. Ximena does not know what she is referring to with those words, so she decides not to answer back. She asks her father and Mrs. Raimondi about Anacleto. She finds out that he has gotten better these last few days, and that he can be seen walking around the hotel again. Ximena sighs, calmed, and submerges herself again in the drowsy haze of her own weakness. She is unable to quench her thirst and she asks for water so often that it does not seem normal to her mother and she asks the doctor about it. "Let her drink," says the old man wisely. "She is washing the poisons out of her body."

And so she, too, recovers her strength little by little, and three days later she is able to walk around the hotel and go out to sit in the sun in the patio at noon. She crosses paths with Anacleto several times, but he refuses to meet her eyes, even when she greets him or smiles at him. He walks very stiffly and awkwardly like before, carrying his pails and his scrub rags on his back and without looking at anyone. Everyone is happy he got better, and only Ximena seems to notice that he looks worn out, and that his expression has become dour and resentful. It is no longer possible, as it was before, to discern a child-like innocence on his wrinkled face.

Ximena cringes inside and then she, too, lowers her eyes or fixes them on a distant point when Anacleto goes past her. She has understood that she will have to live with this memory that burns her chest when she thinks about it, and she knows that they will never speak to each other again.

The night before their return to Lima, she opens the forbidden door. She had awakened, feeling uneasy, from a dream full of hummingbirds and statues. The birds, like frenetic butterflies, flew in circles around the statues, and when they tried to rest on the naked shoulders or extended arms of the stone women, the unexpectedly agile hands of the statues grabbed them, and let them fall, before going back to their feigned immobility. The flights and the sporadic captures went on and on, without Ximena being able to change their terrifying rhythm.

She awoke and tried to dream of the sea, tried to imagine herself beside her magic pool in order to say good-bye to its transparent depths, to the enchantment of its colors, to the child reflected in its surface. And each time she began to drift back to sleep, she found herself surrounded again by hummingbirds and statues. Then again she would be calmed by her bed and by the barely discernible dimensions of the room lulled by Libertad Calderón's regular breathing. Unable to go back to sleep without slipping back into the same dream, the temptation of the forbidden door became more and more alluring.

There was a full moon that night. It was so bright that Ximena thought it must be nearly daybreak. The sky was an electric blue color, and contentedly, she breathed in the fragrance of the sea which canceled out the mixture of contrasting odors in the patio. It was almost totally silent. The only sound, far in a distance, muffled by her desire to banish it, was the noise of a motor in the street. She opened the gate without worrying that the sound would give her away, now that she was liberated from the hope of finding the stranger by the washtub. She thought that probably the crazy girl would be asleep tied up somewhere in the hut, and she consoled herself by thinking that at least she could say good-bye to the big ficus tree, and would be outdoors, in the serenity of the night, and far from the uneasiness of her dream. But she was not really surprised to find the girl awake, and upon seeing her in the same position as the first time, her whole body told her that the crazy girl was also looking forward to this last good-bye.

Ximena walked over until she was only a few steps from the girl, without worrying about the danger of that daring proximity. Nothing moved in the lot; the branches of the ficus tree barely stirred with the breeze and the sound of its leaves was a murmur that suspended the two of them, protecting them from all fear. They gazed intently at each other for a long time. Breaking the pattern of their earlier encounters, for the first time, it was Ximena who initiated the wordless dialogue. She tipped her head to one side. The girl, a few steps away from her, did the same thing. Ximena tipped it over to the other side, and like a mirror which reflected back her image, the demented girl imitated her. Their next movements reflected each other in parallel. They both lifted their arms, their right feet, then their left, at the same time. They smiled and it was exactly the same smile. They began to spin around like they had before, only now they were both dancing under the moon around the tree. They jumped up in high leaps, and waving their arms up and down, they moved around in a flight in which one was the shadow of the other. Exhausted, breathing heavily, they paused in their nocturnal dance. They rested, stretched out flat on the ground, absorbing its odor, caressing it with the palms of their hands.

They did not embrace when they said good-bye. Ximena was afraid that in an embrace, her body would merge with that of the crazy girl, and the girl made no attempt to initiate it either, probably because she did not know how to, or because she was afraid of the same thing, and the world beyond the gate was incomprehensible to her. They drew close to each other until they were facing one another, their bodies almost touching, both staring deep into each other's identically dark irises, and they barely brushed the tips of their earth-covered fingers together, in the gesture of children playing a clapping game with a partner. They pulled back from each other at the same time, but their gaze held until one had reached her place by the ficus tree and the other her destination at the gate.

Ximena looked back over her shoulder when she was about to cross the patio and saw her hunched down again, the rope swirled around behind her and her eyes fixed on hers. She would always remember her connected to the memories of this vacation, of the divided zones of the San Cristóbal Hotel, of María Eugenia and her daughters, of the Raimondis, of Don Serafino, and in a confusion flooded with remorse, of Anacleto, of the pharmacist and of the stranger of her disillusionment. Above and beyond her nostalgia for the sea, which would be a constant in Ximena, she would remember her, mixed with the emotion and the turbulence that the thought of the coast would always arouse in her, mixed with the nights of full moons, and, without her being able to understand it, mixed also with the image of the other girl she had seen, unreachable and mirrored in her magic pool.

VI / THE FAIR

"You can stay out here for a while until it gets cold, but no playing in the dirt, and don't you even think about opening the gate," Ama Grande tells her, drying her veined, reddened hands on her apron and going back in a hurry to what she was doing in the kitchen.

Ximena sits on the top step (there are five steps that lead up to the back door of the house) and pulls her dress down under her legs because even though it is an early afternoon in June, the cement is still cold. A few feet away from her is the wooden fence, painted white, and to the right is the section that opens and closes, fastened with a crude iron latch. By climbing up on the cross board that runs along the bottom of the gate, Ximena can just reach the latch and dislodge it, so that suddenly the whole gate springs open, and she is left swinging back and forth for a few seconds, clinging to the latch until the rusty hinges stop squeaking.

Don Sebastián's son, who comes with his father to deliver the firewood, is not very tall—he is only a few years older than she is— but he can climb easily over any part of the fence and drop down inside with a triumphant smile. Then Ximena smiles back at him, accepting his feat as a gift, but her chest feels tight whenever this happens because it becomes clearer and clearer to her that the fence and the latch do not serve to protect her family from outsiders but only to lock her into that arid patch of land called, for lack of a better word, the patio. It cannot be called a garden since grass or flowers do not grow there because of the smoke and the altitude, and it is not a corral, for they keep no animals.

Sitting on the step, Ximena gazes out beyond the fence with intense interest. Through daily repetition, her scrutiny of the countryside has acquired the fervor of a ritual. Beyond the wide stretch of bare ground where nothing grows, no trees or bushes, not even green weeds, sometimes she catches a glimpse of the train that comes through twice a day and disappears quickly, much too quickly, to the left or to the right. The rhythmic clatter of the train is usually the last sound she hears before falling asleep at night. She listens to it, matching up its sounds to whatever melody she can remember from the radio; she lets herself be carried away, far away, with the rhythmic beat until she can no longer hear it, and the melody loses its enchantment, and silence returns her to her pillow and to the walls of her bedroom.

Beyond the railroad tracks, which she cannot see but can imagine, she can barely make out the outlines of the camp where the smelter workers live, a place of which she has only a blurry image. She has only glimpsed it a few times when going past it in a fast-moving car. She closes her eyes and concentrates on the place, as though it were a dim photograph where time had faded the sharp outlines of the objects it pictured. She sees a long gray mass, a monotonous hulk stretching out in an endless number of small doors and windows, evenly spaced dark patches, openings through which nothing, not even air, seems to move in and out. Nevertheless there are a lot of people over there, so many, Ama Grande has told her grumpily, that the Company will have to build a new camp sometime soon. Ximena has stopped asking questions about this alien strip of earth in the distance, because the answers she gets are evasive, and she senses that the grownups are uncomfortable talking about it. When she gazes beyond the fence for a long time, when the train reminds her of that other side, and confused questions rise up in her throat, she represses them, and instead asks them for stories, or goes off, obediently, to look at the colored illustrations in her father's encyclopedia or at the photograph album that her mother keeps in her bedroom.

Today, in any case, she is absorbed in contemplating the reflection of the sunlight, only pale sunlight, hardly enough to warm the corrugated iron roofs. Then she sees an orangish or bright pink glow that rises up from the farthest stretch of land along the horizon and that finally transforms the bleak photograph her memory has evoked. She breathes in deeply, closes her eyes tight and opens them again to see if the colors are really still there in the distance, or if they are like the others she manages to see, even though she knows they are not really there, on the walls of her room when she is bored but cannot fall asleep. She shivers as she makes out a city of vaulted arches, domes, tall towers, luminous shining castles, and, most of all, balloons, hundreds of balloons that are being set free by an invisible hand and are rising joyfully like giant coral beads over this celebrating city which undulates, shimmering in every shade of orange. She runs to the kitchen door and calls to Ama Grande to come out and look. "Come, Ama!" she tugs her, pulling at her skirt. "Come see how pretty the camp looks; they must be having a fair!"

Ama Grande cannot get out there as quickly as she would like because she is old and moves slowly and drags her feet, but even as she protests, she takes Ximena's hand and goes out with her to have a look. "There is nothing there," she says angrily to her, pulling her back into the house. "And it is getting cold. Come in now."

Over her shoulder, almost in tears, insisting on the existence of what she has just seen, Ximena manages to peer over the top of the fenceposts at the bare field and beyond it, at the place where she had seen the fair, but she sees nothing there now.

A few days ago, they brought Ama Chica from the ranch in the valley. One night after they had said the Our Father and the Hail Mary together, her mother tells her that she is about to have another *ama*, a new nanny. "But I already have one who has been here for ages!"

"That's why," says her mother as she pulls up the covers. "Because it has been such a long time, and now she is getting old and gets tired. And she can't see very well; haven't you noticed?"

She speaks in a whisper as though Ama Grande, who at this hour of night is in her room at the other end of the house, could be listening. It is true that she does not see well any more. She has very fine spider webs in her eyes that used to be black but lately have been changing to lead gray. It is also true that she gets tired, that it is difficult and painful for her to walk when she has to get somewhere quickly, and that she scolds her more often than before.

"But she won't go back to the valley, will she?" She tries to keep her voice from wavering. Several times lately she has heard her mother affectionately urging the old woman to think about returning to the ranch. "We don't want you to leave, Mama Cristina, but you do too much here and it will be more restful for you there," she has suggested. She has to raise her voice so that Ama Grande can hear her because she is also getting a little deaf. Even when she is almost yelling, her mother's voice is full of the respect and the affection she has always felt for the old woman.

"If I leave, *niña*," she always answers, "your house will be topsy turvey. You can't possibly handle it. You still have no idea how to manage."

Her mother does not insist. They continue to talk, telling each other things, making arrangements, deciding things together. Ama Grande must have felt really tired to have agreed to let another servant come. In the past she has been impossible whenever they have brought a girl from the valley to help her out, so difficult that after a few days they always end up sending the girl back to the ranch. Her father complains, "We know who is the boss in this house!" But her mother argues that she likes to do housework and that it is not a bad idea to save a little money. This time, however, Ama Grande has not protested the arrival of a helper. One morning Ximena wakes up and, beside her mother, she sees a young woman in a black skirt, with a green shawl, a *lliclla*, knotted on her chest. She tries not to stare at her wide bare feet with their hardened black toenails. The girl smiles in open curiosity. Vaguely, Ximena remembers having played with her at the ranch.

"Ximena," her mother tells her, "María Ester will be your new *ama*."

Because the other one has always been called Ama Grande, Ximena immediately thinks of María Ester as Ama Chica, Little Nanny, and pretty soon, this is what the others call her, too.

At first Ximena resents her and gives her a hard time. She pretends not to understand her awkward Spanish that ties knots in her voice, and she makes fun of her, imitating her mistakes. She purposely mixes up and confuses the usual routines of household chores that the girl is learning with such difficulty, not because she is slow but because there is so much to be learned. She refuses to obey her, and to emphasize her rejection, she takes refuge more often than usual in Ama Grande's skirts. The old woman gives her a hug, then shakes her loose, pleading with her in a low voice: "You should be ashamed of yourself! Behaving like this, when she hasn't done a thing to you!"

Ama Chica is not easily discouraged. She is good looking and cheerful, and sings while she works. Ximena begins to accept her little by little because she is seduced by the stories she tells about her hometown in the valley. It does not take María Ester long to catch on to Ximena's weak points and she bribes her, talks her over to her side, buys her good behavior with fantastic stories that include descriptions of sowing and harvest rituals, Easter and Christmas celebrations, the poisonous or curative magic of certain plants and of certain empowered hands, of condemned souls that ceaselessly wander around in search of peace or vengeance, of miracles brought about by dark-skinned saints who carry staffs made of silver rings when they loom proudly into view upon sacred mountains. She has already heard some of these things from Ama Grande, but Ama Grande's versions seem more distant and less intense, seem to want to fade away just as soon as they are conjured up. Ama Chica speaks from the heart, with sounds and gestures, making horrible faces. Ximena is terrified but keeps wanting more. She follows Ama Chica around the house, holding a little yellow rag in her hand so she can help her to dust the moldings, urging her, "And then?"

"And then what?" Ama Chica replies in Spanish, jokingly tipping her head to one side, swinging her heavy black braids over her shoulder, teasing her, "I'll tell you later." The stories are swathed in the pleasure and temptation of the forbidden because both her mother and Ama Grande have asked her not to let her talk in Quechua until she is really fluent in the new language.

"But she *is* talking in Spanish!" she protests whimpering.

"No, Ximena, you aren't even noticing. She starts off in Spanish and ends in Quechua. Besides, you are walking around looking startled all the time as though you were seeing ghosts on the walls. Any little thing makes you jump, and you look as though you're about to run and hide any minute."

It is true that sometimes she walks around with her heart in her throat and that sometimes she speaks Quechua and understands almost all of it. Her mother and Ama Grande habitually mix up the two languages, sometimes on purpose when they don't want her father to understand. If Ximena cannot figure out the meaning of an unfamiliar word in a story, she runs and finds Ama Grande to ask her what this or that means. At first the old woman gives her the answers, as a matter of course, without thinking about it, but after a few days, she begins to scold the new girl, who half admonished and half smiling, bites her lips and mumbles, "All right, *mamita*, don't yell at me, it's all right."

Ximena has learned to not ask any more. Once in a while, if it has rained the night before, she and Ama Chica go out into the patio in the morning to make dishes for her dolls out of the damp earth. Squatting down she listens to her, mesmerized, and it does not bother her to realize that by the next day, the little pots they have shaped with such care, irritating the skin on their hands, will dry out and look lumpy and ugly and will break the minute they are touched. Because Ximena wants to give something in exchange, and cannot think what else, one morning she points with her hand, caked with clay which is quickly drying out in the cold air, in the direction of the camp. "One afternoon," she tells her very confidentially, "I saw a really pretty fair, all orange colored, and with lots of balloons, way over there where the camp is."

Ama Chica turns her head to the right and half closes her eyes in order to be able to peer. "Really?" she answers her without much conviction.

Her indifferent reaction annoys Ximena so much that she reaches over and squashes the little flower vase that Ama Chica is shaping with her fingers. She runs back to the house leaving behind her a trail of bits of clay which dry out as they hit the ground near the back door.

Her mother is making arrangements for them to go down to the ranch in a few days. Ximena watches her hurrying around, bustling from here to there, turning the house upside down, bumping into things as though she had forgotten the placement of the furniture and even the location of the walls. Now and then she sighs deeply or lets her head tilt toward one shoulder in that gesture that always strikes Ximena as immensely desolate. In the midst of preparations for the trip to the valley, which are always frenetic but joyful, Ximena suspects that something is going wrong. "Is Grandaddy sick?" she asks while her mother is combing her hair.

"No," she answers, fastening her barrette. Irritated she asks sharply, "Where did you get that idea? That's all we need. Thank God everything is fine there."

Ximena would like to ask what, then, is going wrong here, but her mother's tone of voice silences her words. She notices that sometimes the telephone rings very late at night, too late, after even her father is asleep. From her bed she can hear him go into the dining room to answer it and although she is afraid, she tries to listen and find out what is happening, but he speaks in a very low voice, almost a whisper, or else he talks, more clearly and slowly, in English. She has seen her mother, who is also standing by the telephone, wipe her eyes with her little perfumed handkerchief and she has heard her say that she is very, very upset by the situation. During the last few days Ximena has noticed the absence of their usual visitors. Her mother's friends, the Peruvian ones and the North American ones, are not coming by at teatime the way they had before. Only Mr. Estévez comes to visit, more often than he had before, always when it is starting to get dark, leaning on his silver handled cane, dragging his wooden leg and puffing out smoke rings for her when he catches her looking at him. They converse in the dining room, drinking coffee, and they continue talking for a long time, but they do not let her bring her dolls in and play beside the table they way they used to.

"María Ester," her mother calls, "Take Ximena into the kitchen so she can play there."

She could complain, kick her feet a little, start to cry, but her mother's air of distress and Mr. Estévez' serious eyes, without their usual friendly twinkle, bewilder her. They close the door leading into the pantry as well as the kitchen door, and she can no longer hear anything except when her father raises his voice and yells that he is fed up and they can all go to hell.

The telephone keeps ringing almost continuously. That is something new, like the fact that Miss Murphy's kindergarten has closed. She misses those mornings in the big room full of toys and all the widow's books with bright pictures. They would cut out shapes that they glue to big pieces of cardboard and when nobody was looking, Ximena breathed in the smell of the white glue they were using. She also liked the smell of the fat wax crayons and of the jam on the soda crackers the teacher served them at ten o'clock. She played with Debbie and Diana, who defended her against the rowdier boys, not only because she was the smallest but because she was only then beginning to understand a little bit of the English. She cannot explain it, and she does not want to ask why, but when she is hunting for a word in English, the Quechua syllables pop into her mouth. Debbie and Diana live a few houses down the road and sometimes they come over and spend the afternoon with Ximena or else she goes over to play at their house, but she has not seen them for days now. It is as if the North American families had vanished into thin air.

When Don Sebastián comes by to drop off the firewood, he parks his truck alongside the gate as usual. He dumps the fireplace logs down over the fence every which way. Ximena goes out when she hears the sound of the logs knocking against one another. No one has seen her slip out and as she goes over toward the gate she thinks of the rides don Sebastián usually gives her in the wheelbarrow he uses to move the logs so he can stack them up in a symmetrical pile against the side of the house, under the eaves. Those are wild rides; Don Sebastián's son climbs into the wheelbarrow with her or else he pushes her himself, pretending that he is going to tip her over, that he is going to make her fall, and then straightening out the wheelbarrow with a skillful twisting movement, and the two of them laugh and laugh. This time the boy remains on the other side of the gate with his hands in his pockets, staring stubbornly at his shoes or only looking in his father's direction. Ximena asks him to come in and play. The boy does not move a muscle, he does not budge, he just stands there as though he had not heard her. Don Sebastián barely acknowledges her greeting, nodding his head. They both go off somberly, leaving the pile of jumbled logs by the gate so that later she and Ama Chica have to carry them one by one and stack them under the eaves. Ximena asks Ama Grande why the two of them acted like that, and she answers testily that maybe they are sick. Ximena lifts the white curtain with yellow dots in the pantry window, and gazes at the gray sky which is almost always that same shade of leaden gray. The smelter spews up smoke that hangs like a dirty awning over the town all year long. People get sick because the air is full of little particles that you cannot see but which make you cough and make your eyes water. Ximena's, too, although she is lucky, as they have told her over and over because she should learn to be grateful, that she can be whisked right down to the valley by car when the congestion in her chest begins to be a problem.

Her favorite outings, to the market and to the shops, have also come to an end. For days now, Ama Chica has gone alone to do the shopping. Ximena yelled so much, inside the closet they close her into as punishment for talking back, that when she remembers it, her throat still feels scratchy and her chest feels heavy. She has listened through the bathroom door and heard her mother trying to intercede on her behalf, saying that that was just why they had brought María Ester from the ranch, because she is young and strong, but her father, unyielding, has said that it is better to be safe than sorry, that an ounce of prevention is better than a pound of cure. From the living room window on one side of the front door, Ximena stares out at the forbidden outdoor spaces, the steps on which they have never allowed her to sit by herself because right across the road is the rail fence she could easily climb through, and on the other side of the fence is the cliff, with the Mantaro River running swiftly just below it. Before Ama Grande's feet started to hurt, when she still did the shopping, she took Ximena to the market with her, going by way of the other side, in order to stay well away from the river. They went out the patio door and walked through the empty field, past the neighbors' houses, all Company houses, all identical to their own, with white gates and some with imported swing sets. With Ama Chica it was different, with her they went out the door on the river side and despite the strict orders from her mother, they went close to the iron rail fence in order to look down. "How ugly!" said Ama Chica, the first time.

It looks beautiful to Ximena. The current carries the water along rapidly and when they have walked to the bridge, the river stretches out in both directions as far as she can see. The sound of the water, its continuous movement, and its infinite extension, make her think of the train. Ximena is used to its smell, but Ama Chica says that it stinks; she holds her nose and points her finger at the greasy yellow foam that clumps into islands that keep breaking up and reforming again a little farther downstream. In the valley, she says, the river is clean and you can reach out and touch the tiny silvery fish that know how to hide under the moss on the rocks. There, they can drink the water; there, they wash their hair with a soapy lotion that comes from little bright colored frogs; there, the girls play in the valley while they wash clothes; there, they get soaking wet just like when they play water games at Carnival time. The blue sky of the valley jogs Ximena's memory and then she interrupts Ama Chica to tell her that all that is a lie, that it is just a story and nothing more. Ximena does not know why, but she feels that she has to defend that river which she hears rumbling way down there on those rare occasions when they have the windows open in the house.

For a second time, they have postponed their trip to the valley. Her mother has opened the door of the pantry, where they have now put the telephone, probably so that Ximena cannot pester them so much when they talk. Her mother's face is very pale. She sits down at the dining room table and barely has the energy to call Ama Grande. Ximena runs to look for her in the patio where she is out hanging up laundry with Ama Chica, and the old woman comes in muttering a Hail Mary under her breath. They find her mother with her head down on her folded arms, on the linen tablecloth, sobbing away. Ama Grande tells the girl to get a glass of water and her mother puts her arms around her waist while the old woman caresses her hair soothingly. She comforts her in Quechua but Ximena tries to not understand; she concentrates on the patterns that the crocheted roses have imprinted on the inner side of her mother's arm. When she can't stand it any longer, she goes to the bathroom and closes herself in until her legs stop feeling so weak and she can cope with the shame or the embarrassment that burn her cheeks and whistle in her chest.

A little later, while she is having a snack in the kitchen, in the midst of a silence in which she can hear herself chew even though she is trying to do it quietly, she looks closely at Ama Grande. She has become even older that afternoon. As though it were the first time she were really seeing her, Ximena looks closely at her thin gray braids hanging against her blue sweater, at her neck which is almost purple, covered with loose folds, at her high smooth cheekbones from which the bags of her cheeks hang, cheeks that she has always thought of as firm but which now inflate and deflate with the rhythm of her breathing. She does not want to see her like that. She yearns to seek refuge pressed against her apron, and breathe in her tenuous but persistent smell of the valley, of woods, of eucalyptus. But she is held back by the big tears she sees for the first time on Ama Grande's face which drip like rain from those clouds in her eyes that are gradually making her blind.

She is awake, although she pretended not to be a few minutes ago, when her mother came into her room to pull up her covers. She had been wakened by some sharp cracking sounds over on the bridge side of the house. During the last few nights, her mother has come into her room frequently and hovered over her as though she were sick. Then she tiptoes back to her bed, and since now they are leaving both the connecting doors into the bathroom open, Ximena can hear fragments of their conversation. She hears *Lima, reinforcements, threats, fire, camp, the ranch, highway, I don't want to leave you, you have to, horror, even with children.* She does not want to hear more. She covers her head with the blankets; she puts her hands over her ears. For days the train has been going by off its usual schedule, at odd times, and she has almost forgotten about waiting for it so that its rhythm can rock her to sleep. Nor can she make the shapes appear on the walls the way she does when she plays in the dark with her eyes, because she would have to pull her head out from under the blankets and look out. She tries to recall the photographs in the album, one by one, and in the order in which the images are arranged on the black pages. She can conjure up clear images of certain places, some of the people from the valley, Ama Grande and herself in different rooms of this house, friends of hers and of her parents whom she recognizes despite all the changes over time, festive family occasions or Company get-togethers.

Most of all, she is consoled by the way they smiled then, her father's eyes which rarely look at the camera but usually contemplate her mother serenely. Tonight she finds the images painful and then, taking comfort in the warmth of her body, she tries to fall asleep and think about the orange colored fair over there beyond the bare field.

In the morning, she behaves very badly to Ama Chica. She does not want to listen to her stories. She does not want to sit with her and look at the encyclopedia illustrations. She does not want to do her spelling lesson with her. She does not want to help her dust the moldings. She does not want her to think that she prefers her to Ama Grande who is shrinking hour by hour and turning into a grotesque wooden doll. María Ester, who now insists on using her own name, takes all the rejections without saying a word. She no longer laughs about everything, and she sings nostalgic tunes in such a low voice that she can hardly be heard even a few feet away. When she wipes up the juice Ximena has spilled on her dress, however, she says, with barely contained rancor, "Just to let you know. They are kidnapping the bosses' children."

Ximena is startled but hides it. She goes off giving her a shove and yells at her from the haven of Ama Grande's skirts: "Liar! Those are just stories, just your stories!"

Her mother has had to go out to make some last-minute arrangements for their trip. Ximena gets bored and is overwhelmed by the chaos of boxes, packages and wrapping paper for the move. They will go to the ranch and then to Lima. María Ester is standing on a chair pulling out clothing, hangers, hats, artificial flowers, bundles of letters tied with blue ribbons smelling faintly of gardenia: the entire contents of her parents' bedroom closet. Ama Grande does not have the strength to carry anything, but it is she who decides where things should go.

Ximena wants to poke around and help at the same time, but she does not really insist: the two are so grumpy and they are not paying any attention to her, mostly they treat her like an irritating fly. They order her to go to the kitchen and eat some bread with honey. They have rolled up the rugs and the cracks between the boards of the wooden floor remind her of railroad tracks. Maybe it is time for the train to come past. In any case she prefers not to ask because she thinks they will just scold her again. She pushes the yellow dotted curtains aside so she can see out and gets impatient because the angle is not right for her to see what she wants. Carefully, she closes the door that leads to the dining room and opens the back door, the one that faces onto the empty field.

It has been a long time since they let her sit on the steps and now the two of them are so busy they will not notice her absence. She arranges her dress under her legs so she will not feel the cold of the cement so much. It is almost totally silent; only a metallic sound is heard, like the lowering of the warning barriers beside the railroad track on the bridge side. At first she thinks it is her own desire that makes her see, off in a distance, farther away than the imagined railway tracks, the fair, the orange city that flares up before her eyes. She turns her head to make sure that they are not watching her and goes over to the fence. She cannot see as well from there as from the top step, but she can make out the castle towers, and drifting balloons are floating up all over the place. For an instant she wonders whether she should call the *amas* and prove to them that she was not lying, but the memory of the first experience, of how the fair disappeared when she tried to enlist a witness, makes her change her mind. Besides, there is a hot smell in the air, like that of their fireplace on a winter night, and that smell hypnotizes her, makes her completely forget the possibility of calling them so that they will see it, too.

She goes toward the gate in the fence, she climbs up to reach the latch and opens it, managing not to make a sound. She stays there, swinging back and forth, damping the sound of the creaking hinges which could give her away. Before she climbs completely down, with the toe of her shiny patent leather shoe touching the ground, she turns around again to see if they are watching her. There are no sounds coming from the house, and it is not too hard to half close the gate and take a few steps into the open field. The farther she gets from the fence, the more she feels the heat, and the colors are so bright that they hurt her eyes like when in the valley she tries to look at the sun and cannot do it. At first she is afraid they will call her, that they will drag her back inside the white fence. Then, fearlessly, feverish with balloons and towers, dizzied by the space, by anticipation, by the orange color that now has flecks of blue in it, she starts to run toward the fair without turning around to look back one single time.

VII / FAREWELL

Seated at the dining room table, her whole body concentrating so hard that she bites her lip, Ximena is holding back tears as she struggles to write out the letters of her first word clearly. She positions the pencil carefully, leaning over her work attentively, then she straightens up to see if her A has two equal sides and if the little cross stick in the middle has come out straight this time. Unsatisfied, she erases it again, and blows away the crumbs of red eraser that have covered the dark varnish of the table with tiny dots. She starts all over again without getting discouraged, and when she is drawing the two upside-down Vs that make the M, she lifts her eyes and, amidst the jumble of suitcases and packing boxes set out for the imminent move, she sees a woman watching her from the rocking chair. She is troubled by this, because she has not heard her at the door, nor has she seen her enter, and because she is alone in the house. Her parents have gone out and have left her with a Company employee who is out on the back porch right now, arranging the things they have asked him to box up. Ama Grande left for the valley at dawn yesterday, and María Ester has gone, too, several days ago.

Ximena does not recognize her and yet the woman is not entirely unfamiliar to her. She cannot quite place her among the photos in the album nor among the people she has seen from a distance in town or in the valley. She is anxious, because she cannot associate her with a particular place, this woman with eyes so much like her father's, and dressed simply in blue denim pants and a garnet sweater. She has a thick pad of yellow paper propped on her lap. Ximena notices that she has the pad open to a blank page, and that she has used up almost all the paper. From where she sits, she can see that there are lots of pages filled with writing, and that right now she is holding a pen in her hand, as though she were about to continue.

"What are you writing, Ximena?" her voice has the same cadences as her mother's.

"A letter to my *ama*."

"Even though your *ama* does not know how to read?" the woman smiles.

"It doesn't matter. I want to tell her that I'm going to miss her a lot, and that I am sad that she doesn't want to come to Lima with us," answers Ximena. She intends to write to her every single day, so that Ama Grande won't forget her. Optimistically, she trusts that someone will read her the letters and that maybe, when they go to the valley, she will realize how much Ximena misses her and decide to come back with them.

"You will see her in the valley, but your *ama* will never go to Lima," states the woman. Softening her tone, she continues: "You know full well that she is very old and wants to spend her last years with her family."

Ximena thinks, "We are her family, too."

As if she had divined her thought, the woman says firmly, "No," and noting her disappointment, changes the subject and asks her, "Do you know how to read yet?"

"A little, but only in capital letters like Miss Murphy showed me in kindergarten. The little letters that my father wants to teach me are really hard for me, and syllables, too, because in kindergarten we memorize whole words, with cardboard flashcards." Proudly, she adds, "I can already read most of the first *Dick and Jane* book."

"The world in reverse!" exclaims the woman. "You are learning to read in the Company's language and not in your own. You're going to have problems when you get to school in Lima."

"That's what my mother says, but my father has told me that I will go to an American school. I am going to be ahead of the other girls," the defiance in her voice is a result of the sudden fear the woman arouses in her.

"No," the woman repeats. "You are going to have tremendous problems in adapting to school, especially the first year." She sounds nostalgic, and again she modifies her tone of voice. "Do you know why you are going to Lima all of a sudden?"

Ximena feels nervous. She does not want to think about the tumult of the last few days. Her chest tightens up, and she has to hold in the tears that come to her so readily these days. "I don't know," she answers.

She evades the woman's probing eyes and turns her face toward the window. Everything seems quiet, as though nothing were happening. The strike and the workers' revolt have ended, but her father has asked the Company to transfer him to Lima. With a pessimism which is unusual for him, he says that it is just a matter of time, and then the problems will begin again. They will go directly to Lima, so as to get comfortably settled there with plenty of time.

The silence between the two seems long.

"What are you writing?" Ximena asks, peering at the woman's pad curiously.

"I am trying to finish a collection of imagined memoirs, and, you know, there is one part that is very hard for me to write. It's like your struggle with cursive letters. That's why I've come looking for you here. I need you to help me finish my stories."

Ximena does not answer. With a shudder, she has remembered the photos of her mother as a girl and the illustration of the arteries in the encyclopedia. She gazes at the woman and feels both attracted and repelled by her simultaneously.

"Don't be afraid of me, Ximena. Instead, why don't you tell me what happened to you in the workers' camp."

Ximena is startled. "How do you know that something happened to me?"

"Because even though there are things that I cannot remember of my imagined world, or which, perhaps without being aware of it, I have wanted to erase from my invented memoirs, I know a lot about you. Come on, tell me your version of what happened to you, and I will write it down as well as best I can."

A terrible anxiety makes a lump in her throat. During the last few days, she has tried with all her might to blot out the images of those hours, and although she does not want to go to Lima, especially because of her *ama*, she thinks that she will be safer there from the terrible vengeance which they predicted for her in the camp, and she also thinks that in Lima, which is so far from the highlands, she will stop having nightmares and can find consolation in forgetfulness.

"You will never forget completely, Ximena, because even when you bury the details of that day in the past, as the years go by, you will feel that right behind your back, those memories are slipping into your footsteps. If you will help me to remember, perhaps we can begin a new page together."

Ximena closes her eyes, and all she is able to murmur is what her body has kept repeating to her every time the fragments of that adventure, which she has already had to retell so many times, surge up in her thoughts. "I want to be with my *ama*," she manages to say.

"Because you think that she will protect you? Your *ama* is where she wants to be. What you have to do now, is get used to living without her and leave her in peace. Tell me what happened to you when you reached the burning camp."

"The smoke and the heat made me feel sick," sighs Ximena. She rests her head on her arms, which she has crossed on the table. "I couldn't find any trace of the fair or the balloons that I saw from the steps of my house that lead to the field. There were women and children running around like crazy people, carrying their bundles and their pots. Everyone was yelling and I thought I was in a bad dream because of all the things María Ester had told me."

"But it was not a nightmare, right? There you were, feeling lost and without being able to find the path that would take you back to the field by your house."

"The camp turned out to have more than the single row of houses I thought it had."

"No, it wasn't just a single row. Behind it, there were other similar houses, lots and lots of them, blazing or scorched, and the smoke made you cough and your eyes run and you found yourself going around in circles and more circles without being able to find an exit. But here you are, so how did you get out?"

Ximena covers her face with her hands. That way, she can clearly hear the sound the woman's pen makes, in the intervals when she stops talking. "Tell me, Ximena," she asks implacably. "Where did you end up?"

"When I thought I was about to pass out, because I was suffocating, I saw an open door way in a back corner, and I went in. It was very hot in the room, but the smoke wasn't so thick."

She searches for the words that correspond to the images that hover around her, haunting her mercilessly whenever her defenses drop. She longs to be silent, just as she yearns to forget all about this, but the presence of the woman threatens to return her to that past. By fits and starts, she tries to explain that, despite the fact that the camp was burning, right where she was, among houses that were blackened by soot, there were some that were still standing intact.

She falls silent. She wishes that what happened would erase itself, and she presses her eyes tight closed so as not to see what her heart-beats resurrect in such detail.

"The room was not empty," says the woman, writing and speaking at the same time. "Tell me, who did you see?"

Ximena pauses for a few seconds before continuing. Then her voice recalls, step by step and falteringly, the first part of her adventure. She speaks of a woman and a child hardly any bigger than Ximena. The woman wore layers of skirts and a *lliclla* around her shoulders, and the child was dressed like Indian children. Only when her eyes had adapted to the darkness of the room, did she see that in a corner, on some animal skins, a little baby was sleeping. The woman was frightened to see her and spoke to her in Quechua, but she talked too fast and moaned, while she pushed her toward the door, so Ximena was not been able to understand what she was telling her so frantically. With equal urgency, Ximena had told her that she was lost, that she could not breathe, and had asked her to help her get back to her house, but the woman had either not wanted to listen to her or didn't understand her. The boy had stepped in, and in Spanish he explained to her that she had to leave because she would bring them bad luck, and when Ximena explained her plight again, he had translated it easily for his mother. She kept on yelling angrily and shoving her so she would leave. Between the two of them, they pulled her out of the room, and then Ximena had started screaming and banging on the door, because she had felt safer inside there. Outside, she was not only horrified by people screaming and by the gunshots that rang out every little while, but the smoke and heat were even worse now. Ximena could not tell whether the woman took pity on her, or what it was she thought. She let her come in and then she went off crying, with the baby in her arms, after telling the boy to watch the bundles. Ximena's eyes had stopped running, and while she tried to get her cough under control, she started looking around her. The room was very small; it just had one little window that looked out on an identical house, and even without the smoke, it could never have gotten much light. There were no beds or other furniture, just the skins on the floor, some bundles, two pots, and a few metal bowls. She remembered, as in a dream, that once her mother and Ama Grande had been talking about the poverty in which the smelter workers lived, and her mother had said that often the huts in the highlands were just as poor. Her *ama* had replied angrily that it was not the same thing, because however poor it was, it was their hut, and when they stepped out, the air they breathed was clean, and they could look at the blue sky and the fields spread out all around them.

The memory of the old woman feels like an invisible weight on her shoulders, penetrates her skin and her bones, until it reaches her chest and turns into a sob that halts her words. While Ximena tries to get her grief under control, and looks blindly at the two letters written on her piece of paper, the woman continues to scribble rapidly on her pad. Without lifting her eyes from her page, she asks, "What did the boy say to you? Tell me about the boy, Ximena."

"He told me that his mother had gone to look for her husband so they could get away soon, and if I didn't go and the guards came to look for me, it would be easier for them if they found me alone with him. And she also wanted the boy to watch the few things they owned." Ximena stops, and then adds, "I don't want to remember any more."

"Because you are thinking that at that moment you were saddened to realize that those few odds and ends were all they had, that they were all their possessions on this earth, and in that instant you realized that you had much more, and that losing your things would never would have mattered so much to you, because you could easily replace almost all of them."

"I thought that God punishes those who have too much."

"Don't lie, Ximena; not for a minute did you think about God."

Ximena covers her eyes again with her hands. No. She hadn't thought about God, but she had thought about how her *ama* was always sorry for those who lived in the camp, and that one time Uncle Jorge had told her that to the poor of the earth should it be given that their last lamb would be taken from them. "But it did make me feel very sad."

"And what did you do with your sadness?"

At first she had not done anything, because she had come with her hands empty and had nothing to give him. Since they were alone in the room and Ximena did not want to go, and they were just standing around, looking at each other furtively, she started to ask him questions. He was neither ashamed nor afraid, and he asked her questions right back. "He told me his name was Pablo. After a long while, he told me his name in Quechua but that one is a secret and I can't tell anyone. And I don't know how old he is, because even though I kept trying to show him numbers with my fingers, he didn't understand."

"Then you asked him where he was from, and he told you that before, his family had had a big farm and several animals, and that one day the authorities had come to make them leave, and told them that the owner of a nearby farm had legally bought all of the peasants' land in that area. At first, the landowner called them together and offered them beer and work. The boy's father and others like him had gone to make a claim for their rights; some of them went as far as

Lima, but no one paid attention to them, and they were threatened with all going to jail. Days went by and the new owner said he didn't want anything to do with seditious Indians, and then many of them had to sell their animals for a pittance, and they moved farther up, higher in the mountains, to look for work in the mines, but Pablo's father began to get sick, and since they had seen others die spitting up blackness, they came to work in the smelter. Ah! It is such an old and often repeated story that it irritated me to hear it and even more to read it."

Ximena listens to her intently. She doesn't know why, but at that moment, it no longer amazes her that the woman should know so much about that day. Facing her, the expression in her eyes holding steady and her lips compressed in a gesture very much like her mother's, the woman gets up and goes over to the window that is beside the rocking chair. She is slight in stature and very fine boned. She is not wearing leather shoes, but rather, ordinary tennis shoes with thick soles reinforced with rubber at the toes and heels. Ximena can see that they have letters running along the outer sides and she thinks that she has never seen such ugly tennis shoes, or any quite like that. She also notices the canvas backpack, instead of a purse, that the woman has leaned up against the rocking chair. "Oh, my Mantaro River!" she exclaims in a low voice, and even though she is still facing away from Ximena, still looking out the curtainless window, Ximena can hear her clearly.

"Not long after they arrived in this town, the problems with the strike began. You asked if they were happier here, and the boy looked at you angrily and said that at first they were, although what they paid his father was never enough to live on, and his mother had to go work at several houses washing clothes. Around that time, some university students had been meeting with the workers at night, and had convinced them that they did not have to put up with abuse because the

Company, with the permission of the authorities, had appropriated land that used to belong to various Indian communities. The boy told you how the gringos had come and how with their jeeps and their armed guards to protect them, they went around deciding where they wanted to build their fences. Quick as a flash, the communities were left without water for their herds, and both the people and the animals were dying of hunger. Some of them left, although many of them had no choice but to stay and work for the Company. Uncle Jorge was right, don't you think, Ximena?"

Ximena does not answer her and the woman, without turning around yet, keeps talking softly.

"And although by temperament you are a fighter and you like being contrary, you didn't want to argue about any of this, because you remembered with anguish that your *ama* and your mother used to talk about the camp people every once in a while, and it made them very sad. Once your mother had said that the clothes and the cakes that the bosses' wives took them at Christmas time were just an insult, because after all, they had taken everything that was theirs away from them. Your father didn't say anything, and sometimes he defended the Company, saying that although the gringos treated them badly, Peruvians would treat them worse, and he added that your mother's great grandfather had taken possession of land by putting up his fence across what had been others' fields."

Ximena hides her head in her arms again. She thinks she hears the Company man entering the kitchen and turning on a faucet. The pantry and dining room doors are closed and although he cannot hear them, it might occur to him to come in and look for something. The woman does not seem to be worried by this possible interruption. She has sat down again and is writing. From time to time she raises her eyes and looks around the room breathing in deeply.

"And what did you tell the boy about yourself?"

"I told him the first thing that occurred to me, because I didn't want him to know that my father was one of the bosses. I told him that we were visiting an uncle and aunt in town, and I talked a lot about my *ama* and about the house in the valley. He wanted to know if I had a tricycle and I said no, but that I had a very pretty red wagon and that someday maybe I would give it to him."

"And you weren't lying to him about that, because if you could have, you would have given it to him, but he did not believe you and he said you were a liar."

"Yes, he did call me that," replies Ximena without being able to hide the remains of her accumulated frustration. And then, her face brightening, she adds: "And because I had nothing with me to give him, I asked if he liked stories, and since he said yes, I started to tell him 'Sleeping Beauty.'"

Ximena chews the end of her pencil while she thinks for a few seconds. The woman smiles at her and asks her what the boy's reaction had been.

"I think he liked it, although he didn't say anything. I wanted to know if he knew any other stories and he said yes, but I had to ask him several times before he told me the first one. We sat down together on the skins, and he told me about a huge mountain that had a lake at its foot that looked like a black mirror."

Ximena chooses her words with care. When she tells stories, she does not like to leave out any details, and because this time she knows that her words are not evaporating into thin air, but being fixed onto the yellow paper that she can see from her chair, she knows the exact wording is important, and she pauses to think before speaking, without taking her eyes off the hand that writes.

"Since way before the white people came, nobody had dared to go near that lake, because it brought them the image of death, and in any case, no one could have gotten close because in the bottom, hidden, there was an enormous lion who protected its still waters. The grin-gos, who do not respect the beliefs or the lands of the local people, and who also tend to be very daring, came hunting in this region and immediately proposed to trap the lion. Then the mountain allied itself with the clouds, the morning turned dark, and although they did not see any lightning flashes, it began to thunder as though the sky were going to come crashing down. Right at the edge of the lake where the hunters were, heavy snows fell, and whichever way they tried to escape, the snow galloped after them, pursuing them. The gringos could not find the path that had brought them to this place. They could hardly see each other because of the snow. So some of them died of hunger and others of cold, and the survivors never came back to this place. The lion still rests at the bottom of the black lake, and when he comes out to render tribute to the sun, the mountain warns him if its snowy peaks see any daring gringos in a distance who are approaching with guns."

The woman has not finished writing, when, smiling, she is already asking, "And then? What else did you tell each other?"

"I told him 'Cinderella' and 'Snow White.' And he especially liked the dwarves who live in the forest and work in the mines, but he laughed about how every story had a prince who arrived on a white horse to free the maiden. He also enjoyed the story about the little red hen who found a grain of wheat, the one about the ugly duckling who becomes a swan, and the one about the tortoise and the hare, but he liked the labors of Hercules best of all."

"You had to tell the stories several times, didn't you? Because since you are never quite sure what goes where, even though on this occa-sion you were trying to tell the stories carefully, you mixed up or pur-posely spliced in episodes from other tales. And in the fairy tales, you probably changed a detail here and there without his seeming to notice."

"That is true, but he hadn't heard them before, so what did it matter?" Ximena asks defensively. She looks straight at the woman and notices that there are no traces of accusation in her expression.

"No, it doesn't really matter, because nothing in the world ever stays the same," she assures her.

Ximena thinks about how irritated she gets when her father jumps over entire sections of the stories he reads. She gets impatient, because she wants to hear the whole, complete story. She has noticed that her father does not always use the same words when he is telling her Greek myths, but he never mixes his stories up the way she does. She observes the woman carefully, and now it is she who guesses what her next question will be. "He loved the myth of Persephone who returns to our world each spring, and the one about Orpheus when he goes down into the depths of Hades to rescue Eurydice."

"And did you like all the stories that Pablo told you?"

Ximena's expression becomes animated as she speaks.

"Yes," she answers, "although I had already heard some of them from my *ama*, and others from the servants in the valley. And Pablo also changed them around, the same way I change them," she added again, defiantly. Because the woman does not dispute anything, and just smiles over her pad of paper, Ximena continues:

"Have you heard about the boy who discovered one night that it was golden princesses who had been descending from the sky to rob the beautiful potatoes from his parents' farm and who trapped one of them, and closed her in their hut, so she wouldn't be able to escape? I had heard it a little differently. Remember that the condor asked him for two llamas to eat on the long journey to the sky, where they would search for the golden princess, who was really a star? Pablo told me that the boy, out of fear of his father, had tried to outwit the condor by leaving him just one llama rather than two, and since he had done that, while they traveled across the firmament, he had to cut off slices of his own flesh in order to feed the condor. In Pablo's story, at the end, the boy goes back to his parents' farm after having lived in the Kingdom of the Sun and Moon, but when he got back, he realized that the weeks he had spent away there were years and years here on earth. Nobody recognized him because they were all so old, and he died alone and sad. My *ama* had told me that the star felt so sorry for him, that the Sun and the Moon let her assume human form, and when he was about to die, she descended, luminous and beautiful, to live with him forever. Do you want me to tell you another?"

The woman flips to a new page, while she settles in to write a few more lines. "Yes, tell me as many as you wish, since that is also why I have come." Her voice has the eager tone of a child pleading for something.

Proud that she has been asked, and relieved because this distracts her from what tortures her so, when she thinks about the hours she spent in the camp, Ximena absorbs herself in her storytelling. She makes her voice high or low depending on the degree of emotion she wants to confer on certain parts; and she is silent for a few seconds before she dramatically introduces the suspenseful moments. Because she has heard these stories several times, and in turn has told them to anyone who will listen, she recites some sections from memory, blending the words of others with her own. The pleasure she feels makes her speak faster than before, and every little while, the woman gestures with her free hand, letting her know that she should pause until she catches up.

"He told me the one about the rich couple that could not have children, who pestered God so, pleading for just one little one, that the woman, who was old, became pregnant. She gave birth not to a baby but to a monster, a horrible lizard with a human head. And they loved it as though it were really a child and the lizard grew and wanted to get married, but on his wedding night, he kept eating his brides. Until one of them, a poor girl whose parents had made her marry the monster, asked a witch for help, and the witch told her what she should do to survive. The bride did everything right, everything, but just like Orpheus, who couldn't resist the temptation to look at Eurydice, the girl looked at the lizard. The lizard had turned into a handsome prince with blond hair, but in the end, because she had looked at him when she shouldn't have, the prince turned into wind, and that is the sad wind that howls and complains at night on the high mountain plains."

Ximena thought for a while before she continued. "In the valley, Paulina told me the story of the bad daughter who rejected her brother and sisters and parents, and Pablo told it to me again. Paulina had told me that the daughter went to serve her *mita* service, helping in the priest's house, and that it was the priest who fell wildly in love with her. In Pablo's story it wasn't a priest but rather the *curaca*, the mayor of the Indian community. The rest of the story was pretty much the same, except that Paulina never told me that the priest had wanted to kiss the girl's dead body; she just told me that the girl had died suddenly, because she had been so ungrateful to her father and brothers and sisters, and that the priest, out of grief, stopped eating and died too. In Pablo's story, the *curaca* went to the cemetery, dug her up out of her grave, and since her body was full of worms, he went mad and wandered around the mountainsides playing the flute he had made from one of his beloved's bones."

"And which story did you like best?"

"The one about the condor and the shepherdess, because there are always lots of condors in my *ama*'s stories. Hardly anyone knows that a long time ago, parrots were large and powerful, and that was why one of those parrots flew up to the high snowy peaks, where the love-besotted condor was keeping a shepherdess captive. In punishment for his daring, the condor tore the big parrot to shreds, and those shreds were transformed into little parrots. That is why we see them today in the mountains, green and raucous, flying in groups singing their hearts out, and their song tells us that they want to unite again in order to be large and powerful like before. The tears of the solitary condor are the nocturnal butterflies that fly into houses and flutter all over the place looking for the shepherdess, driven by grief and hope."

"I had forgotten that people mutter that you are like an old crone because of the stories you tell. You seem incredible even to me," says the woman in a low voice, her pen continuing to move rapidly over the paper.

Ximena falls silent and stares at her while the woman, busy with her page, writes on. She looks a lot like someone else, but Ximena still isn't sure who. When she feels on the verge of figuring it out, the image slips out of her memory, leaving her baffled and intrigued. Then Casilda's face appears clearly in her thoughts. It is not a physical similarity. It is the identical way they seem to absent themselves when they are absorbed totally in writing; that's how they are alike. Just like Casilda, this woman, leaning forward over her pad, during long periods of silence, both is and is not in front of her. Then she lifts her face and her eyes, squinting into the depths of the room as though she had just come inside after being in bright sunlight, meet and question the other eyes that observe her curiously.

"And he didn't tell you anything more?"

A sudden chill paralyzes Ximena's body. She wants to stand up and run away, but her legs do not obey her. "I don't remember any more," she says finally.

"You need to remember for yourself and for me: otherwise, all these pages I have written will remain unfinished. Come on, tell me the story that frightened you so. If you tell it to me, when you hear your own voice saying it, and see my hand writing it, that story will probably stop terrifying you at night, and I, too, will feel relieved of some of the sorrow and guilt," and in an almost inaudible but intense murmur, she adds, "Remember it always: we never can and never should forget it completely."

And now Ximena has no other option and is forced to confront the story she has tried so hard to erase from her mind. Even though she has forgotten the sound of Pablo's voice by now, his words resonate sharply and clearly within her, tormenting her. How many times during those last days, her arms wrapped around her *ama*'s skirts, she had felt the need to confide in her so that the old woman might find words of comfort for her and relieve her sorrow. But each time, the story had seemed to get stuck in her throat, and Ximena had only managed to plead with her not to leave her alone, and to come with them to Lima. Convinced that the woman would keep on insisting, Ximena begins to tell the story of her misadventure. Tongue-tied again, stammering fragments of unconnected phrases mixed with complete sentences, she speaks of a remote monarch, the last King of the Indians, who was punished for having thought he was God. Nobody had ever been able to convince him of the existence of any power superior to his, since he had command over the waters, the rocks, the mountains, and all other things, large or small, encompassed within his sight. His total arrogance led him to mock the word of Jesus Christ, and it was this same arrogance that made him lose the great empire he possessed. The Spanish, who preached a doctrine of forgiveness without understanding its meaning, and who were just as arrogant as the Inca, beheaded him. However, some Indians were faithful subjects of their king, and in complicity with the pumas and with the night, which covered the mountains in deepest darkness, they managed to hide his head and bury it. Among the Indians, there were wise men whose spirits were enabled by special ceremonies to soar through space to reach a mysterious place where they could hear the voice of the great Wiracocha, and Wiracocha prophesied that a humble peasant couple, a weaver and a shepherd, would be chosen to fulfill a great mission several centuries after the death of the Inca. When the hour came for the prophesy to be fulfilled, this woman and the shepherd would dig up the decapitated head and with the aid of the air, of the waters, of the mountains, and of the earth itself, while she cradled it in her arms and moistened it with her tears, the body would grow, just as a plant grows, until it recovered its original shape. Thus would the Inca King be resurrected, Pablo had affirmed, making his small hand into a brown fist raised to the level of Ximena's eyes; thus will he be resurrected, he had repeated, and Indians from everywhere, from the coast, the high mountain valleys, and the farthest reaches of the jungles, will join together then to form invincible armies, and will defeat all those who have ever humiliated them. They will kill their oppressors without mercy and will thus recover all that had been theirs since the beginning of time.

"And you thought that this story was true?"

Ximena lets her shoulders sag in defeat. "I have never been good at telling the difference between what is true and what is false. I know that my *ama*'s stories and the ones I've heard in the valley are not like the tales in my books with colored pictures. The condors, the butterflies, the wind, and the little parrots exist. Besides," she adds, biting her lip nervously, "Pablo told it to me just as my *ama* had told it to me before that, and just as María Ester and Paulina in the valley tell it. He told it with his whole body, and the anger in his voice was not pretend."

"And you thought that you could intuit, without being able to understand it completely, what was going on under your Uncle Jorge's strange ways, under your mother's surprising contradictions, and under your father's silent frustration. And more than anything, you thought that not only they, but you, too, were lost and condemned, that your ancestors also made you into an unforgivable accomplice, and you started to cry. And then you were even more afraid, because you thought that the strike and the revolt of the smelter workers were the beginning of a new reign, and that Pablo had not wanted to reveal the secret that the Inca King had already been resurrected. You cried so much, now I remember how your whole body shook with woe, that he offered you some of the *maschka* he had in a little bag, and he pleaded with you not to cry any more."

"Yes, and afterwards, he told me that my *ama* was like my mother, and that she would save me, and he that he would help me, too, when the hour of final judgment came."

Ximena pauses so that the woman can keep writing. Her face has lost the enthusiasm it held a little while ago. Her lips have thinned into a familiar grimace and her still, lowered eyelids remind her of her father's on the few occasions when she has seen him sad. She is gazing at her this way, when the woman's voice interrupts her distraction.

"And what happened next?"

"I don't remember," she answers, covering her ears and closing her eyes. "I don't want to remember."

The woman offers no respite. Her look of sorrow changes into one of impatience, and then the silence seems unbearable to Ximena. The Company man must be over on the patio side, because nobody is moving around within the walls of the dismantled house.

"Right at that moment we heard an explosion..."

"...such a violent and close-by explosion that it shook the room, breaking the glass in the little window."

"We ran out through the door, and the smoke was awful, you couldn't see a thing."

"Suddenly you realized that Pablo had sprinted off in another direction, and everything else happened quick as a flash."

"It was terrible," she adds, almost losing her voice, "so terrible that I don't want to think about what happened."

The woman waits for a few moments. Her face looks very tired now, and Ximena is calmed. Maybe she will feel sorry for her, and stop asking her questions. But, after bending her head to write a few lines, the woman continues, and this time, her tone of voice is firm.

"As you ran through the thick clouds of smoke, you bumped into a young man. You recognized him as one of the workers by his denim overalls, and smelling his breath, you realized that he was drunk. A second later, you heard the siren of a patrol car, and before you and the man could move, several soldiers had blocked you in. One of them picked you up and told you not to cry, that there was no danger, and that they would take you back to your parents. The young man, who was struggling against the blows aimed at him, was handcuffed and kicked into the patrol car. You were still crying and they set you down on the front seat. The soldier who sat on your right tried to comfort you along the way. Remember? Now you tell me where they took you."

"To the police station," says Ximena, trying desperately to calm the congestion churning in her chest. "They telephoned my father, and they started asking the young man questions. He did not answer."

"His eyes were glazed and he was gritting his teeth. They slugged him in the stomach and a fat policeman grabbed him by the collar, yelling at him about did he know how the law punishes kidnappers. As they kept asking him the same question over and over, the young man looked at you, but still did not speak."

"I was dying of fear."

"And then the door opened, and first your father came in. You had never seen him like that. His face was ashen and distraught. Your mother pushed him aside to get to you, and kneeled down to hug you.

She was wearing her gray dress with blue flowers that you like so much, and you smelled the perfume on her neck as though it were a fragrance from another life. Suddenly she threw herself at the young man and hit him over and over, until your father restrained her by holding her arms behind her back."

"They sat me on a chair and one of the policemen squatted down in front of me. I could see that the paper he was holding on his knees on a big notebook was already partly filled in on a typewriter. My father came over and stroked my hair and told me I shouldn't be afraid of the officer. All they wanted to know was whether the young man had been alone when he came into the house to kidnap me."

"And you said no, but then they thought you were saying that he had been with others. They asked you to try to remember how many there had been, and whether you could describe them. The young man looked at you with hate and remained silent."

"I started coughing hard and my mother told them that was enough, that if they couldn't take into account that I was too young and that I was terrified, that all she wanted was to take me home, and they could carry on with their investigation. The officer looked at her from head to toe and very severely answered that the law was the law, and they were only fulfilling their duty as Peruvians."

After a pause in which Ximena rubs away some poorly restrained tears with the back of her hand, the woman flips to a new page, writes a few more lines, and turns to her again. "And why didn't you tell them the truth?"

Ximena has hidden her head in her arms again. To no one, not even her *ama*, has she been able to confess the remorse that has tormented her since that day. Asleep or awake, when she least expects it, the accusing face of the young man pursues and haunts her.

"Ximena, why didn't you tell them that no one kidnapped you, that you had gone over to the camp all by yourself, thinking you would find the orange fair? Is it because no one would have believed you if you'd said you'd seen a fair, and because your parents had reminded your *ama* a thousand times that she shouldn't let you out of her sight while they were out of the house?"

"Not just that," answers Ximena. Her voice keeps faltering, but she knows she has to go on, that as long as the woman keeps on writing, whether it is now or later, in this house or in another, she will appear to her and ask her the same question.

"If I had told them that I had run off to go look at the fair, and that I hid in the camp, they would have wanted to know where in the camp. And then they would have figured out that I had been in Pablo's family's room. Don't you see, they found me nearby, and it was one of the only ones that hadn't been destroyed. How were they to blame? Don't you see that, after all, they had helped me?"

"And what fault was it of the young man's?"

"None," confesses Ximena. "But I didn't know the young worker; we had not told each other stories. And I asked them several times to leave him in peace. I kept saying it over and over; I begged my father to believe me; I asked everyone to let him go because he hadn't done anything to hurt me. And they didn't believe me."

"No, no one believed you. They just told you that compassion has its time and place. They yelled at you that you were protecting him because maybe he had threatened to kill you if you turned him in, and that rebellious Indians like him didn't deserve any pity."

The woman turns to a new page. From where Ximena is, she can see that there is only a page or two left of the pad of paper.

"There is something else you have not wanted to tell me, something else that made you keep quiet about your time with Pablo. What are you hiding, Ximena?"

Cornered by the woman's tenacity, and by the hope that the tablet is running out, she decides to be open about her cowardice.

"I thought," she says lowering her burning face, "that my *ama* was very old, and that if she died, and the reign of the Inca King came, no one would protect me in the New Peru. Pablo talked and talked about a new order, a community or a nation where everything would change, where there would be no chiefs or bosses. I didn't understand much of anything of what he was saying..."

"...but you thought that you would probably be in danger in that society, and that when that order was established, you would look for Pablo. You would say that he was your friend and it would be easy to prove it, because you remembered and could tell the stories that he had told you. Also, you knew his secret name and that would be like an irrefutable password in your favor."

"Yes, I would look for him day and night, and he would help me. In case that new kingdom really came about, and in case I were able to find Pablo, I could not say his name or show them his room. Don't you see that I couldn't?" Ximena confronts the woman. "What is going to happen to me?" she adds, without thinking, and she realizes that now she has relieved herself of the weight that was oppressing her, she yearns for an answer, and does not want the woman, who has closed her pad and tucked her pen into a pocket of the backpack, to leave yet.

"I don't know; you will find out with time."

Ximena is bewildered by the hardness of her voice. The two stare at each other for a few moments, as if they had just met.

"But however far away you may go," she adds changing her tone, "and you will go far, far away, you will never be able to forget your early years, and the stories that you heard in your childhood will remain at your side always, just as the shadow of your *ama* will always accompany you, and the furniture in this room. Without being able to avoid it, you will live for a long time anchored in this era of your life, tangled in weavers, in a cousin's blond hair, in the amazing letters written by an adolescent, in the image of a crazed grandmother, in the columns and illustrations of the encyclopedia, in the inexplicable tracks worn around an old ficus tree in a forbidden patio, and in a pool of seawater. One day you will have to pull yourself away from those years, in order to forge ahead on the trail of other stories."

The woman contemplates the living room walls, the bundles and the packed suitcases. She remains absorbed for a few instants, with the air of those who know they have to leave, but haven't quite made up their minds to go. From where they are, they can hear the Company man, who is rattling around just on the other side of the pantry door. In the dim light of the living room, Ximena watches her close the backpack carefully and look around her one last time. A kind of vertigo keeps Ximena from stopping her, and even more, from asking her who she is, or what her name is, because she is afraid that the answer might be incomprehensible or that it might sweep by her, fleeting and intangible, like a bird flying through a dream.

"I'm leaving now, Ximena; I've finished my task here," says the woman, standing up and running her hand over the back of the rocking chair that moves back and forth soundlessly. "Keep writing your letter, even though your *ama* can't read it."

Unexpectedly, the Company man knocks softly a few times, and opens the door a crack to stick his head through. Ximena gives a startled jump, annoyed by the interruption.

"I wanted to know if you need anything before I go back to the patio," he says, sizing up the disorder of the living room. Evidently he has not noticed the presence of the woman. Ximena waves her hand to signal to him that no, she does not need anything, and before he leaves the room, she turns her eyes toward the rocking chair. The woman is no longer there. She has entered and departed from her life in the same way, silently and without warning. Ximena is not even aware that the young man has closed the door behind him, and gone back to his work.

Then Ximena grasps the pencil between her fingers, and gazes at the white sheet of paper that stands out against the dark wood of the table, immobile and waiting. The light blue lines reclaim her, and she understands that she cannot escape, that she has to continue, and she concentrates on the imperturbable shape of the next letter. She bends down close, and distances herself from all that surrounds her; she immerses herself in the pencil marks that the difficult representations of the syllables dictate to her; she erases and starts over again. And while Ximena absents herself, the words, in the ebb and flow of life to death, and of death to life, become fixed in place and fill her first page.

THE AUTHOR

Laura Riesco was born in the Andean region of Perú. After high school, she came to the United States where she completed her university studies. She resides in Maine where she taught until very recently at the University of Maine. In 1978, Laura Riesco published *El Truco de los Ojos*, an experimental novel. *Ximena at the Crossroads* was selected as both the Best Novel of the Year and as the Best Prose Written by a Woman in Peru in 1994. The book also won the 1995 Latino Prize in Literature in the fiction category. It is now in its third printing in Perú.

THE TRANSLATOR

Mary Guyer Berg is well-known as both translator and critic. She spent her childhood in Colombia and Peru and has lived in Spain and France.She holds M.A. and Ph.D. degrees from Harvard University, where she presently lectures in the history and literature program. Her work has appeared in numerous anthologies and magazines. Her translation of *Latin America In Its Literature* was published by Holmes & Meier, New York, in 1980 and her translation of *Starry Night*, poems by Marjorie Agosín, was published by White Pine Press in 1996.